1622-1673 Molière

The works of Moliere ; a new translation

Vol. II

1622-1673 Molière

The works of Moliere ; a new translation
Vol. II

ISBN/EAN: 9783743383760

Manufactured in Europe, USA, Canada, Australia, Japa

Cover: Foto ©Andreas Hilbeck / pixelio.de

Manufactured and distributed by brebook publishing software (www.brebook.com)

1622-1673 Molière

The works of Moliere ; a new translation

THE WORKS OF MOLIERE.

IN SIX VOLUMES.

VOL. II.

A NEW TRANSLATION.

BERWICK:

PRINTED FOR R. TAYLOR.

MDCCLXXI.

THE
ROMANTIC LADIES.

A

COMEDY.

VOL. II.   A

The ROMANTIC LADIES, *a Comedy of One Act,
acted at Paris, at the Theatre of the Little Bour-
bon, the* 18*th of November,* 1659.

THE comedy of the ROMANTIC LADIES deserves to be ranked among the best of Moliere's performances, although it is not one of the
best with regard to the plot. He ventured, in this
piece, to forsake the common path of complicated
intrigues, to lead us in a comic road, first known
by him. The main end of a good comedy appeared to him to be, to criticise the follies and manners
which were peculiar to his time.

THE passion for wit, or rather the abuse they
made of it, was a kind of contagious malady then
in fashion. The forced bombast style in romances,
which the women admired for the very reasons
which have since discredited those works, had got
into conversation: In a word, both the quality and
common people were affected; and at this con-
juncture did the comedy of the ROMANTIC LA-
DIES make its appearance; never was greater success known; the prodigious number of spectators
made the company demand double prices at the
second reprefentation of it, and the piece run for
four months together: It produced a general re-
formation, people saw themselves in it, laughed,
and gave the truest applause to it by forsaking their
folly. Mr. Menage, who assisted at the first representation, said to Chapelaine, " You and I both
" approved of all these follies which have been now
" so excellently and so sensibly criticized; believe
" me, we must burn what we have admired, and
" admire what we have burnt." This acknowledg-

ment was only the reflection of a man of sense
who found himself undeceived; but the saying of
an old man, who in the middle of the pit cried
out through instinct, " Take courage, Moliere,
" this is a good comedy," is the pure expression of
nature, which shews how much the human mind
is swayed by truth.

ACTORS.

LA GRANGE.
DU CROISY.
GORGIBUS, a rich Citizen.
MAGDALEN, Daughter of Gorgibus. } The Romantic Ladies.
CATHOS, Niece of Gorgibus.
MAROT, Maid to the Romantic Ladies.
ALMANZOR, Valet to the Romantic Ladies.
MARQUIS DE MASCARILLE, La Grange's Valet.
VISCOUNT JODELET, Du Croisy's Footman.
LUCILIA.
CELIMENE. } Neighbours to Gorgibus.
TWO CHAIRMEN.
FIDLERS.

SCENE Paris, in Gorgibus's house.

T H E

ROMANTIC LADIES.

SCENE I.

LA GRANGE, DU CROISY.

DU CROISY.

MR. La Grange.

La Grange. What?

Du Croify. Look at me a little without laughing.

La Grange. Well, I do look at you.

Du Croify. What think you of our vifit? ——
are you pleafed with it?

La Grange. Why, do you think we have any
reafon to be fo?

Du Croify. Indeed, I think we have not much.

La Grange. For my part, I own to you, that I
am quite fhocked at it.——Pray now, did ever a-
ny body behold a couple of foolifh gypfies give
themfelves fuch airs as thefe, or two men treated
fo infolently as we have been?—They could hardly condefcend to order chairs for us.—— I never
faw fuch whifpering as there was between them;
fuch yawning, fuch rubbing of eyes, and en-
quiring fo often what o'clock it was. Befides, we
could get them to fay nothing but yes or no to all

we could fay to them.   In fhort, it muft be confeffed, that if we had been the greateft fcoundrels
in the world, they could not ufe us worfe than they
have done.

Du Croify. I think you feem to take it much to
heart.

La Grange. I do, and am determined to revenge myfelf for this impertinence.——I know well
enough the reafon of their flighting us. The conceited air has not infected Paris only, but has
extended its influence to the country towns, and
our ridiculous nymphs have fucked in their fhare
of it. In a word, they are a ftrange medley of co-
quetry and affectation.   I plainly fee what fort of
perfons are likely to meet with a favourable reception from them, and if you will truft me, we will
play them a trick fhall make them fee their folly,
and teach them to diftinguifh people a little better.

Du Croify. How can this be done?

La Grange. I have an arch dog of a footman,
named Mafcarille, who paffes for a fort of a wit, in
the opinion of many people; for nothing now-a-days
is cheaper than wit.   This fellow has taken it into
his head, forfooth, to fet up for a perfon of quality.
He ufually values himfelf for intrigues and poetry,
and defpifes other valets fo much as to call them
brutes.

Du Croify. Well; what mean you to do with
him?

La Grange. I will tell you.   He fhall——But
let us retire; I will difclofe my fcheme to you as
we go along.

SCENE II.

GORGIBUS, DU CROISY, LA GRANGE.

GORGIBUS.

WELL, gentlemen, you have seen my daughter and niece; how stand matters between you and them? What succefs have you had from your vifit?

La Grange. That is a thing you may better learn from them than us. All we can fay to you, is, that we return you thanks for the favour you intended us, and remain your moft humble fervants.

Gorgibus alone.] Hey-day! methinks they feem diffatisfied! what can be the meaning of this? I muft enquire. Soho there!

SCENE III.

GORGIGUS, MAROT.

MAROT.

DID you call, Sir?

Gorgibus. Yes, where are your miftreffes?

Marot. In their clofet, Sir.

Gorgibus. What are they doing?

Morat. They are making lip-falve.

Gorgibus. Bid them come down.——[Alone.] Thefe huffies, with their lip-falve, have, I think, a mind to ruin me. The houfe is filled with nothing but whites of eggs, nun's cream, and a thoufand other fooleries. They have ufed, fince we came hither, the lard of a dozen hogs at leaft; and four fervants might be daily fed with the legs of mutton they deftroy.

SCENE IV.

MAGDALEN, CATHOS, GORGIBUS.

GORGIBUS.

THERE is great need, indeed, of all this time and expence to greafe your muzzles.——Inform me, pray, how you have behaved to thefe gentlemen, that I faw them go away with fo much coldnefs. Did not I charge you to receive them as perfons that I intended for your hufbands?

Magdalen. Dear father, what regard would you have us pay to the irregular proceedings of thefe people?

Cathos. Dear uncle, can a woman of any tafte or fafhion be able to reconcile herfelf to men of their figure?

Gorgibus. What fee you in them to find fault with?

Magdalen. Fine galantry of theirs, indeed!—— Would you believe it, Sir? they began with propofing marriage to us.

Gorgibus. With what would you have them begin? with whoring?—Is not this a way of acting which both of you have reafon to approve of as well as I? Can any thing be a greater fign of their good intentions? And that holy tie they defire, is it not a proof of the fairnefs of their defigns?

Magdalen. O father! what you fay is extremely like a citizen. I really blufh to hear you deliver yourfelf in fuch uncouth terms. Indeed, papa,

you should learn to speak with a more courtly
air.

Gorgibus. I've nothing to do with your airs.—
I tell you, that matrimony is an holy and a sacred
thing, and to begin with that is to act like honest
people.

Magdalen. Lard! were the whole world like
you, a romance would soon draw to a conclusion!
what a fine thing it would have been if Cyrus had
immediately married Mandana, and if Aronce had
been espoused in all haste to Clelia!

Gorgibus. What is this she talks of?

Magdalen. Sir, my cousin will tell you as well
as me, that matrimony ought never to be brought
about till after other adventures.——A lover who
would make himself agreeable, should begin his declaration with fine sentiments, short and passionate
speeches; and make his addresses in the necessary
forms.——In the first place, he should behold, either at church, or in the park, or at some public ceremony, the person of whom he becomes enamoured:
or, else, he should be fatally introduced to her by a
relation or a friend, and go from her melancholy
and pensive. He should conceal his flame, for
some time, from the beloved object, but, however,
make her frequent visits, at which some discourse
about galantry never fails to be brought upon the
carpet to exercise the wits of the company——
When the time comes to make his declaration,
which should always be contrived to happen in
some shady walk or arbour, while the company is
at some distance in the garden; it should be accom-
panied with a pressing earnestness, and sudden
starts of passion, which gives occasion for the fair
one to exercise her rigour, and banish the too pre-

fumptuous lover, for fome time, from her prefence. He finds afterwards the way to pacify us, to accuftom us infenfibly to hear his paffion, and to draw from us that confeffion which caufes fo much trouble.——Then follow the adventures; the rivals that thwart an eftablifhed inclination, the perfecutions of fathers, the jealoufies arifing from falfe appearances, the complainings, the running off with, and its confequences. This is the manner in which things are to be conducted according to the modes of tafte; and thefe are the rules which no lover can difpenfe with obferving in a polite courtfhip——But to come point blank to the conjugal union! to make no love but by making the marriage contract, and take a romance juft by the tail! in fhort, dear father, nothing can be more mechanic than fuch a proceeding, and I am ready to faint at the very thoughts of it.

Gorgibus. What the devil of nonfenfe is this I hear? Where the pox did you learn this lofty ftile?

Cathos. In fhort, uncle, my coufin tells you the truth of the matter. How is it poffible to fhew countenance to perfons who are the very antipodes of all politenefs? I will lay a wager they have never feen the map of tendernefs, and that fond epiftles, little difquietudes, polite letters, and fprightly verfes are regions to them unknown. Do not you obferve their whole perfon fhews it, and that they have nothing of the air which gives one at firft fight a good opinion of people?——And then to make a love-vifit without a fnuff-box! in a plain hat! a head with the locks irregular! and a habit indigent of embroidery!——heavens! what lovers are thefe! what a ftinginefs in drefs! what a bar-

renness of converfation! it is over with them prefently, they keep it not up at all.   I took notice
likewife of the clumfinefs of their neckcloths, and
the cut of their cloaths, which looked as if they
were of the laft age.

Gorgibus. Zounds! I believe the girls are both
mad! I do not know one word in ten they fpeak.
Heark'e, Magdalen, and you, Cathos.

Magdalen. Ah! pray, father, leave off thefe
ftrange names, they found fo horribly unfafhion-
able!

Gorgibus. Strange names! are they not your
chriftian names?

Magdalen. Lard! how vulgar you are!——for
my part, one thing I wonder at, is how you could
be the father of a girl of my tafte and fpirit. Did
you ever hear Cathos or Magdalen mentioned in
genteel ftile? Why, one of thefe names is alone
fufficient to fpoil the beft romance in the world.

Cathos. Really, uncle, an ear that is a little delicate fuffers extremely at hearing thefe words pro-
nounced; and the name of Polixena, which my
coufin has chofen, and that of Amintha which I
give myfelf, have fomething fo inexprefsibly grace-
ful, that—

Gorgibus. Heark'e,—there needs but one word.
I do not know that you have other names than what
were given you by your godfathers and godmo-
thers; and as to the gentlemen in queftion, I am
acquainted both with their families and their for-
tunes, and pofitively refolve that they fhall be your
hufbands.   I am tired of keeping you upon my
hands, and the care of two fuch flirts as you are, is
enough to make any fober man mad.

Cathos. For my part, uncle, all I can fay is, that

I think matrimony a mighty ſhocking thing. How can one endure the thought of lying by the ſide of a naked man? I am ready to faint at the thoughts of it?

Magdalen. Give us leave to take breath a little amongſt the beau monde of Paris, where we are but juſt arrived. Permit us to form the contexture of our romance at leiſure, and do not hurry on the concluſion in ſuch a manner.

Gorgibus aſide.] There is not the leaſt doubt of it; they are quite diſtracted. [Aloud.] Once more, I tell you, I comprehend nothing of all this non-ſenſe, but I am reſolved to be obeyed. And, to cut ſhort all further diſputes, you muſt either determine to marry in a very ſhort time, or be ſhut up in a nunnery for life. So now you know my reſolution.

SCENE V.

CATHOS, MAGDALEN.

CATHOS.

LARD! my dear, how is thy father immerſed in matter! how groſs is his underſtand-ing! and how unenlightened his mental faculties.

Magdalen. What would you have, my dear? I am in confuſion for him.—I can hardly perſuade myſelf that I am indeed his daughter, but believe ſome adventure one time or other will happen to diſcover a more illuſtrious deſcent.

Cathos. Nothing ſo probable. And, for my part, I declare to you, couſin, when I conſider my-ſelf, I—

SCENE VI.

CATHOS, MAGDALEN, MAROT.

MAROT.

HERE is a footman afks if you are at home, and fays, his mafter would come to fee you.

Magdalen. Learn, creature, to exprefs thyfelf with more delicacy. You fhould fay, Ladies, an e-miffary attends below, to know if it is convenient for you to become vifible.

Marot. Lord blefs me! I do not underftand your Latin, and hard words, not I,—I never ftudied floflophy, as you have done in Sirrus the Great.

Magdalen. Impertinent creature! how can this be endured!—Canft thou tell who is the mafter of this footman?

Marot. He told me it was the marquis de Maf-carille.

Magdalen. Ah! my dear! a marquis, a marquis!—Well, go tell him we are vifible.—This muft certainly be a wit, who has heard of our arrival.

Cathos. Undoubtedly, my dear.

Magdalen. He muft be received below in the palour rather than in our chamber; let us adjuft our hair a little, and maintain our character.——Come in hither quickly, and hold to us the coun-fellor of the graces.

Marot. O' my faith, I cannot tell what creature that is; you muft talk to me like a Chriftian if you would have me underftand you.

Cathos. Bring us the looking-glafs, you igno-rant wretch! and take care not to contaminate its purity with the reflection of your grofs image.

[Exeunt.

SCENE VII.

MASCARILLE and two CHAIRMEN.

MASCARILLE.

HOLD, chairmen, hold.   La, la, la, la, la, la—I think thofe varlets have a mind to fhake me to a jelly, by jumbling me againft the walls and pavement.

1. Chairman. Ay, marry: becaufe the gate is narrow, and you would make us come quite in with you.

Mafcarille. I think fo truly—Would you have me expofe the delicacy of my features to the inclemency of the rainy feafon, you rafcals, and let the dirt receive the impreffion of my fhoes?— begone : take away your chair.

2. Chairman. Then, pleafe to pay us, Sir.

Mafcarille. Hem!

2. Chairman. Pleafe to give us our money, Sir.

Mafcarille, giving him a blow.] Infolent rafcal! to afk a man of quality for money.

2. Chairman. Are poor people to be paid thus? and will your quality get a dinner for us?

Mafcarille. Ha, ha, ha, I fhall teach you better manners than to ftand parlying with a gentleman.

1. Chairman, taking one of the poles of his chair.] Come, pay us quickly.

Mafcarille. What!

1. Chairman. I fay, I will have the money this moment.

Mafcarille. Oh! this man talks reafon.

1. Chairman. Make hafte then.

Mafcarille. Ay, you fpeak properly, for your part: but the other is a rogue that knows not what he fays.—There: are you contented?

1. Chairman. No, I am not contented, you ftruck my companion; and—   [Holding up his pole.

Mafcarille. Hold, there, that is for the blow.—People may get any thing of me, when they afk for it in a proper manner.—Well, vanifh now, and call for me again to carry me to court.

SCENE VIII.

MAROT, MASCARILLE.

MAROT.

SIR, my miftreffes will come prefently.

Mafcarille. Pray do not let the ladies hurry themfelves, I am perfectly well fituated to attend their leifure.

Marot. They are here.

SCENE IX.

MAGDALEN, CATHOS, MASCARILLE, AL-MANZOR.

MASCARILLE, after having faluted them.

LADIES, you will undoubtedly be furprifed at the boldnefs of my vifit: but your reputation brings this unlucky affair upon you, and merit has for me fuch potent charms, that I run every where after it.

Magdalen. If you are in queft of merit, Sir, I am afraid you have miftaken the fpot.

Cathos. To find merit at our houfe, you muſt have brought it hither yourſelf.

Maſcarille. Ah! I engage to prove the contrary.——Fame has done juſtice to your deſerts, and you abſolutely *pique*, *repique*, and *capot* all that is polite in Paris.

Magdalen. Your complaiſance, Sir, makes you too liberal in your praiſes; my couſin and I ſhall endeavour not to give too much credit to your polite adulation.

Cathos. My dear, we ſhould call for chairs.

Magdalen. Here, Almanzor.

Almanzor. Madam.

Magdalen. Quick, quick, convey us hither the conveniencies of converſation.

Maſcarille. But hold, am I ſafe here?

Exit Almanzor.

Cathos. What do you mean?

Maſcarille. I fear ſome deſign againſt my heart, ſome attempt upon my freedom. Theſe eyes ſeem to me as if they took delight in triumphing over the ſufferings of an helpleſs heart.——What the duce! do they put themſelves upon their murdering guard as ſoon as one comes near them? Ah! by my faith, I am ſuſpicious of them, and muſt either ſcamper away, or expect city-ſecurity that they ſhall not do me miſchief.

Magdalen. My dear, how infinitely ſprightly he is!

Cathos. The very quinteſſence of wit and politeneſs.

Magdalen. Fear nothing, our eyes have no ill deſigns, and your heart may be well aſſured of their good behaviour.

Cathos. But, good Sir, be not inexorable to that

elbow-chair, which has so long extended its arms
to embrace you.

Mascarille, adjusting himself at a glass.] Well,
ladies, how do you like Paris?

Magdalen. Alas! what can we say of it? we
must be the very antipodes to all taste and knowledge, not to confess that Paris is the grand cabinet
of wonders, the center of good taste, wit, and galantry.

Mascarille. I think, for my part, that out of Paris there is no living for people of fashion.

Cathos. That is an indisputable truth.

Mascarille. 'Tis a little dirty; but then one has
so many convenient chairs.

Magdalen. True; and a chair, I think, is a most
sovereign protection against the insults of dirt and
bad weather.

Mascarille. I presume you have abundance of
visitors, ladies: What wits have you of your
party?

Magdalen. Why really, my lord, we are scarce-
ly known as yet, but I hope we shall be soon. A
lady of our acquaintance has promised to bring se-
veral gentlemen, who write in the reviews, to visit us.

Cathos. And they, you know, are the sovereign
arbitrators of all good things.

Mascarille. I will do your business better than
any body; they all visit me, and I can say that I
never rise without half a dozen wits about me.

Magdalen. Good heavens! we shall be obliged
to you to the last degree if you will do us that
kindness; for, in short, one must have the acquaintance of all these gentlemen, if one would be of
the *beau monde*. It is these that influence repu-

tation at Paris; and in such a manner, you know, that only to keep them company is enough to occasion the report of one's being a critic, though there should be no other reason for it.   But what I consider principally in such a connexion is, that by means of these ingenious visits, one is taught an hundred things which there is a necessity of knowing, and which are the quintessence of fine wit. One learns by it every day the little new galantries, the pretty correspondencies in prose or verse. One knows for certain, that such a person has composed the finest piece in the world upon such a subject; such a lady has made words to such a tune; this person has formed a madrigal upon enjoyment; that has composed stanzas on infidelity; Mr. Such-a-one wrote an ode of six lines yesterday evening to Mrs. Such-a-one, to which she sent him an answer this morning at eight o'clock; such an author engaged in such a subject; this writer is about the third part of his romance; that other is putting his works into the press.——In a word, this is what constitutes one a person fit to appear in the world.

Cathos. In short, I think it is excessively ridiculous, for a person to pretend to wit and not know even the least stanza that is made every day; and, for my part, I should be ashamed to shew my face, if any one should ask my opinion of a new piece, and I have not seen it.

Mascarille. It is a shame, indeed, not to have the first of whatever is composed; but do not be uneasy, I will establish an academy of wits at your house, and give you my word, not a rhime shall be made at Paris, which you shall not have by heart before any body else.——As for myself, such as you see me, I amuse myself in that way sometimes;

and you may fee things of mine in all the witty female affemblies at Paris. Let me fee;—aye, I have compofed above two hundred fongs, as many fonnets, four hundred epigrams, and more than a thoufand madrigals, without reckoning riddles and lampoons.

Magdalen. I muft acknowlege that I am furioufly for lampoons; I think nothing is fo gallant.

Mafcarille. They are fo, but they are very difficult to hit off, and call for a prodigious fund of wit; you fhall fee fome of mine, that perhaps may not difpleafe you.

Cathos. For my part, I am terribly fond of riddles.

Mafcarille. They exercife the wit, and I have made four of them already this morning, which I will give you to guefs the meaning of.

Magdalen. Madrigals are agreeable, when they are well turned.

Mafcarille. That is my particular talent. Have you heard, ladies, that I am turning the whole Roman hiftory into madrigals?

Magdalen. Ah! certainly, that muft be incomparably fine; I befpeak one book at leaft, if you print it.

Mafcarille. I promife each of you one, bound in the beft manner. It was below my quality; but I do it only for the benefit of the bookfellers, who are perpetually teazing me.

Magdalen. I fancy it is a great pleafure to fee one's felf in print.

Mafcarille. Without doubt; but a-propos, I muft tell you an extempore that I made yefterday at a duchefs's, a friend of mine, whom I was vifiting; for I am immoderately fond of an extempore.

Cathos. An extempore is certainly the touch-stone of wit.

Mascarille. Will you honour me with your attention?

Magdalen. We do, with all our ears.

Mascarille.

Oh! oh! quite off my guard was I;
Whilst no harm thinking,
    You
    I view;
  Slily your eyes
  My heart surprize;
Stop thief, stop thief, stop thief, I cry.

Cathos. Ah! my stars! how excessively gallant!

Mascarille. All I do is easy and genteel, I have nothing of the pedant in me.

Magdalen. Two thousand leagues removed from any thing of that!

Mascarille. Did you mind this beginning, " oh ! oh !" this is extraordinary, " oh ! oh !"—like a man that bethinks himself all at once, " oh ! oh !"—The surprize, " oh ! oh !"

Magdalen. Ay, I think that, " oh ! oh !" is inimitable.

Mascarille. And yet at first it seems nothing.

Cathos. Oh! my stars! what is that you say? Nothing! why it is inestimable; inexpressibly fine.

Magdalen. No doubt of it, and I should like better to have made that " oh ! oh !" than an epic poem.

Mascarille. Egad, you have a good taste.

Magdalen. Eh! I have not an exceeding bad one.

Mafcarille. But do not you admire alfo, "quite off my guard was I;—quite off my guard was I," I minded nothing of the matter: a natural way of fpeaking, "quite off my guard was I."——"Whilft no harm thinking;" whilft innocently, without malice, like a poor fheep, "you I view;" that is to fay, I amufe myfelf with confidering, with obferving, with contemplating you. "Slily your eyes" —What think you of the word "flily"? Is not it well chofen?

Cathos. Extremely fo.

Mafcarille. "Slily," cunningly, it feems as it were a cat coming to catch a moufe, "flily."

Magdalen. Nothing can be better.

Mafcarille. "My heart furprize," fnatch it away, force it from me; "Stop thief, ftop thief, ftop thief, ftop thief." Would not you imagine a man were crying out and running after a thief to feize him? "ftop thief, ftop thief, ftop thief, ftop thief."

Magdalen. It muft be acknowledged that there is an amazing deal of wit and fprightlinefs in this turn.

Mafcarille. I will fing you the tune I have made to it.

Cathos. You have learned mufic?

Mafcarille. I?—not at all.

Cathos. Is it poffible?

Mafcarille. People of quality know every thing, without ever learning any thing.

Magdalen. His lordfhip is quite in the right, my dear.

Mafcarille. Hear if the tune be to your tafte: hem, hem, la, la, la, la, la. The brutality of the feafon has furioufly injured the delicacy of my voice:——but no matter, it is quite ungenteel to fing well. [He fings.] "Oh! oh! quite off my guard was I."—

Cathos. How tender and fine is the mufic! every one who have heard it, muft certainly have expired.

Magdalen. It is fomething in the cromatic tafte.

Mafcarille. Do not you find the thought well expreffed in the tune, " ftop thief, ftop thief?" And then as if a body cried out violently, " ftop, ftop, ftop, ftop, ftop, ftop thief." Then all at once like a perfon out of breath,—" ftop thief."

Magdalen. This it is to know the effence of things, the grand nicety, the nicety of niceties. I declare it is altogether an incomparable performance; I am quite enchanted with both air and words.

Cathos. I never yet met with any thing fo ftrong as this.

Mafcarille. All I do comes naturally to me, it is without ftudy.

Magdalen. You are the darling of nature, I muft fay that for you.

Mafcarille. Well, ladies, how is your time engaged?

Cathos. We have nothing to do.

Magdalen. We have been here under a hideous abftinence from diverfions.

Mafcarille. Will you permit me to wait on you to the play? a new comedy is to make its appearance to-night, and I fhould be extremely happy to attend you to the firft reprefentation.

Magdalen. There is no refufing you any thing.

Mafcarille. But I befeech you to applaud it well, when we fhall be at it; for I am engaged to cry up the performance; the author vifited me this morning to beg me fo to do.—It is the cuftom here for authors to come and read their new perform-ances to us perfons of quality, in order to engage us to approve of them, and give them a reputation; and I leave you to imagine, whether, when we fay any thing, the pit dares contradict us.—For my part, I am, to the laft degree, punctual in thofe things, and when I have made a promife to the poet, I am always fure to clap, and cry, bravo! be-fore the candles are lighted.

Magdalen. Say no more of it, Paris is a won-derful place; an hundred things happen in it every day, which one knows not in the country, howe-ver witty one may be.

Cathos. It is enough; now we are told, we will do our part in crying out as we ought at every word that is faid.

Mafcarille. I cannot tell whether or not I am deceived; but methinks, by your looks, ladies, you fhould have written at leaft one play a-piece.

Magdalen. Eh! there may be fomething in what you fay.

Mafcarille. Ah! faith, we muft fee it.—Between ourfelves, I have compofed one which I will have acted.

Cathos. Ay! which company of actors will you give it to?

Mafcarille. A fine queftion truly!—to the ac-tors of the theatre-royal;—none but they are ca-pable of gaining things a reputation; the reft know nothing, but fpeak their parts juft as one talks: they do not underftand to make the verfes roar, or paufe at a beautiful paffage; how can it be known where the fine lines are, if the actor does not stop at them, and apprize you thereby to clap?

Cathos. Really, there is a way of making an audience sensible of the beauties of a performance, and things are well esteemed but according as they are well set off.

Mascarille. How do you like this embroidery? is it well adapted to the cloaths?

Cathos. Perfectly.

Mascarille. The ribbon is well-chosen.

Magdalen. Furiously well. It is an excellent plum colour.

Mascarille. What say you of my rollers?

Magdalen. They have an excellent air.

Mascarille. I may boast, however, that they are a quarter of a yard wider than any that have been made.

Magdalen. I must confess I never saw the elegance of dress carried to such a height.

Mascarille. These gloves too! tolerably well scented, ha? please to honour them with the reflexion of your smelling faculties.

Magdalen. They smell terribly fine.

Cathos. I never breathed an odour more agreeable.

Mascarille. And this here. [He gives them his powdered wig to smell too.]

Magdalen. It has the true quality odour; the sublime is most admirably blended with the soft.

Mascarille. You say nothing of my feathers: how do you like them?

Cathos. They are extravagantly handsome.

Mascarille. It cost me near ten guineas. It is my passion, you must know, to have all things a-la-mode, cost what they will.

Magdalen. You and I fympathize, I affure you; I am immoderately nice with regard to every thing I wear; and even to my very focks, I cannot endure any thing which is not made by the beft hands.

Mafcarille crying out fuddenly.] O! o! o! gently, gently;——damme, ladies, this is very ill ufage; I have reafon to complain of your behaviour: this is not fair.

Cathos. For heaven's fake, what is the matter with you?

Mafcarille. What! two at once upon my heart! to attack me thus right and left! Oh! it is againft all law of nations! the combat is too unequal, and I muft be obliged to call out for aid.

Cathos. It muft be owned he fays things in a particular manner.

Magdalen. He is a confummate wit.

Cathos. You are more afraid than hurt, and your heart complains before it is wounded.

Mafcarille. The devil it does! I am certain I feel it pierced through and through! good God! how it bleeds!

SCENE X.

CATHOS, MAGDALEN, MASCARILLE, MAROT.

MAROT.

MADAM, there is one defires to fpeak with you.

Magdalen. Who is it?

Marot. The vifcount Jodelet.

Mafcarille. The vifcount Jodelet?

Marot. Yes, Sir.

Cathos. Are you acquainted with him?

Mafcarille. He is my beft friend.

Magdalen. Conduct him in immediately.

Mafcarille. It is fome time fince we have feen one another, and I am overjoyed at this lucky meeting.

Cathos. Here he is.

SCENE XI.

CATHOS, MAGDALEN, JODELET, MAS-CARILLE, MAROT, ALMANZOR.

MASCARILLE.

AH, vifcount!

Jodelet. [Embracing one another.] Ah, marquis!

Mafcarille. How happy am I to fee you fo un-expectedly!

Jodelet. How delighted am I to fee you here!

Mafcarille. Prithee, let me embrace thee once more.

Magdalen to Cathos.] We begin to be known, my deareft, fee the beau monde find the way to our houfe.

Mafcarille. Ladies, give me leave to prefent this gentleman to you, as a perfon worthy the honour of your acquaintance.

Jodelet. Ladies, juftice forces me to offer that i cenfe which is fo defervedly due to your merits, and thofe unparalleled charms call for adoration f in every fenfible being.

Magdalen. This is to drive your civilities even to the borders of flattery.

Cathos. This day ought to be marked with a red letter in our almanack.

Magdalen to Almanzor.] Come, boy, muſt things be always told you over and over? do not you perceive that a chair is deficient?

Maſcarille. Do not wonder to behold the viſcount a little pale, he is but juſt recoved from a fit of illneſs.

Jodelet. It is the fruit of court attendance, and the fatigue of war.

Maſcarille. Let me tell you, ladies, that in the viſcount you behold one of the braveſt men of the age;——he is a perfect hero.

Jodelet. Nay, marquis, you are not ſecond to any man in that reſpect; every one knows you have done ſomething.

Maſcarille. It is true, we have ſeen one another upon occaſion.

Jodelet. And in places where it was very warm.

Maſcarille looking at Cathos and Magdalen.] Ay, but not ſo warm as it is here. Ha! ha! ha!

Jodelet. Our acquaintance began in the army, and the firſt time we ſaw each other, he commanded a regiment of horſe aboard the gallies of Malta.

Maſcarille. True, but you was in ſervice before me, and I remember I was only a cadet when you headed a company.

Jodelet. War is a fine thing; but, faith, the court now-a-days rewards people that are of ſervice like us very ill.

Maſcarille. And therefore my ſword ſhall reſt in its ſcabbard.

Cathos. For my part, I have a furious tenderneſs for men of the ſword.

Magdalen. I love them too: but I would have wit to temper bravery.

Mafcarille. Do you remember, vifcount, our ftorming the half-moon at the fiege of Arras?

Jodelet. What do ye mean by an half-moon? it was a whole moon, indeed.

Mafcarille. I believe you are right.

Jodelet. I ought, faith, to remember it very well; I was wounded in the right leg by a hand-grenade, of which I ftill carry the mark. Pray feel, ladies, what a cavity is here.

Cathos putting her hand to the place.] The fcar is large indeed.

Mafcarille. Your hand, if you pleafe, madam. What do you think of this fcar in the back part of my head? Do you feel it?

Magdalen. Ay, I feel fomething very hard.

Mafcarille. It is a mufket-fhot which I received the laft campaign I made.

Jodelet opening his bofom.] Here is a wound which went quite through me at the attack of Gravelin.

Mafcarille putting his hand upon the button of his breeches.] I am going to fhew you a terrible wound.

Magdalen. There is no occafion for it, we believe you without feeling it.

Mafcarille. They are honourable marks, that fhew what a man is made of.

Cathos. We do not in the laft doubt the valour of either.

Mafcarille. Vifcount, have you your coach in waiting?

Jodelet. Why?

Mafcarille. We will give the ladies an airing, and carry them to the jelly-fhop.

Magdalen. We cannot go abroad to-day.

Mafcarille. Let us have mufic then and dance.

Jodelet. Faith, that is well thought of.

Magdalen. With all our hearts. But we fhall want more company.

Mafcarille. Who is there?——Champagne, Picard, Bourgcgnon, Cafquarat, Bafque, la Verdure, Lorrain, Provencal, Violette.——What is become of all my fellows?—I do not think there is a gentleman in France worfe ferved than I. Thefe rafcals are always out of the way.

Magdalen. Almanzor, tell the fervants of my lord marquis to go look for mufic, and run with our compliments to fome of the neighbours, and tell them to people the defert of our ball with their prefence. [Exit Almanzor.

Mafcarille. Vifcount, what fay you of thefe eyes?

Jodelet. Why, marquis, what do you think of them yourfelf?

Mafcarille. I? I fay, that our liberty is furioufly in danger; at leaft mine has fuffered moft violent attacks; and my heart hangs by a fingle thread.

Magdalen. How natural is all he fays! he has fuch a pleafing manner of turning things!

Cathos. Really, he is moft fuperabundantly lavifh with his wit.

Mafcarille. To fhew you I am in earneft, I will make an extempore upon it. [He mufes.

Cathos. O! I conjure you by all my foul holds facred, let us have fomething made upon us.

Jodelet. I fhould be glad to do as much for you;

but the prodigious lofs of blood I have fuftained, has greatly exhaufted my poetic vein.

Mafcarille. Deuce take it! I always make the firft verfe well, but I am perplexed about the reft. Faith, this is a little too hafty, I will make you an extempore at my leifure, which you will find to be the fineft in the world.

Jodelet. How devilifh witty he is!

Magdalen. His wit is gallant and finely turn-ed.

Mafcarille. Vifcount, when did you fee the countefs?

Jodelet. It is above three weeks fince I vifited her.

Mafcarille. Do you know that the duke came to fee me this morning, and would have taken me into the country a ftag-hunting with him?

Magdalen. Here come our friends.

SCENE XII.

LUCILIA, CELIMENA, CATHOS, MAG-
DALEN, MASCARILLE, JODELET, MA-
ROT, ALMANZOR, and FIDLERS.

MAGDALEN.

LARD! my dears! we beg your pardon for the freedom we have taken in fending for you in fo abrupt a manner; but thefe gentlemen having propofed to give us a dance, we fent for you to fill up the vacuum of our affembly.

Lucilia. You have obliged us certainly.

Mafcarille. This is a kind of extempore ball; but one of thefe days we will give you one in form. Is the mufic come?

Almanzor. Yes, Sir, they are here.

Cathos. Come then, my dears, take your places.

Mafcarille dancing alone by way of prelude.]
Tol lol derol derol lol.

Magdalen. How excellent a fhape!

Cathos. Certainly he muft dance nobly.

Mafcarille, having taken out Magdalen to dance.]
Faith, ladies, I believe my freedom will prefently
keep time with my feet. Play in time, fidlers, in
time. O what ignorant wretches! there is no
dancing with them. The devil take ye, cannot
ye play in meafure? Tol lol derol derol lol. Silence, ye country fcrapers!

Jodelet, dancing afterwards.] Hold, do not play
fo faft, I am but juft recovered of a fit of fick-
nefs.

S C E N E XIII.

DU CROISY, LA GRANGE, CATHOS, MAG-
DALEN, LUCILIA, CELIMENA, JODE-
LET, MASCARILLE, MAROT, and FID-
LERS.

LA GRANGE, with a ftick in his hand.

SO, fcoundrels! what do you here? we have
been feeking you thefe three hours.

Mafcarille, feeling himfelf beaten] O! o! o!
you did not tell me the blows fhould be thus.

Jodelet. O! o! o!

La Grange. What! you fet up for perfons of
quality, do you?

Du Croify. This will teach you to know yourfelves.

SCENE XIV.

CATHOS, MAGDALEN, LUCILIA, CELI-
MENA, MASCARILLE, JODELET, MA-
ROT and FIDLERS.

MAGDALEN.

PRAY, gentlemen, what is the meaning of this?

Jodelet. It is a joke, a wager.

Cathos. What, let yourfelves be beaten in this manner!

Mafcarille. Lard, I would not be feen to take any notice of it; becaufe I am violent, and fliould have been guilty of fome extravagance.

Magdalen. To fuffer an affront like this in our prefence!

Mafcarille. It is nothing, I tell you.—Come, let us proceed. We have known one another a long time. They are two comical dogs. Why, if friends were to quarrel for a frolic, there would be no living.

SCENE XV.

DU CROISY, LA GRANGE, MAGDALEN,
CATHOS, LUCILIA, CELIMENA, MAS-
CARILLE, JODELET, MAROT, and FID-
LERS.

LA GRANGE.

WE will let you know, rafcals, what it is to make a jeft of us.

[Three or four bullies enter.

Magdalen. What means this impudence, to come and difturb us thus in our own houfe?

Du Croify. What, madam, do you think we can tamely look on, and fee our footmen better received by our miftreffes than ourfelves? and have the impudence to give them a ball at our expence?

Magdalen. Your footmen?

La Grange. Ay, our footmen; it is neither decent nor honeft to encourage other people's fervants to fuch infolence and extravagance.

Magdalen. O heavens! what impudence!

La Grange. But they fhall not have the advantage of our clothes to dazzle your eyes; if you will love them, it fhall be, faith, for their handfome looks. Quick, ftrip immediately.

Jodelet. Farewel finery.

Mafcarille. The marquifate and vifcountfhip are at an end.

Du Croify. You impudent rafcals! how dared you to fet up for the rivals of your mafters?

La Grange. It is too much to fupplant us in our own cloaths.

Mafcarille. O fortune! how fickle thou art!

Du Croify. Quick, take every thing away from them.

La Grange. Carry away thefe clothes, begone with them. Now, ladies, you are extremely welcome to your new gallants in their prefent condition. As for this gentleman and myfelf, we promife you we fhall not be jealous; and fo leave you to finifh your dance.

B 5.

SCENE XVI.

MAGDALEN, CATHOS, JODELET,
MASCARILLE, and FIDLERS.

CATHOS.

AH! what confusion!

Magdalen. I burst with vexation.

1. Fidler to Mascarille.] What it he meaning of this? who is to pay us?

Mascarille. Ask the viscount.

1. Fidler to Jodelet.] Who is to give us the money?

Jodelet. Ask the marquis.

SCENE XVII.

GORGIBUS, MAGDALEN, CATHOS,
JODELET, MASCARILLE, and
FIDLERS.

GORGIBUS.

WELL, flirts! you have made fine laughing-stocks of yourselves. The gentlemen have told me a curious trick of you.

Magdalen. Ah, father! we have been cruelly used.

Gorgibus. A trick with a vengeance! you may thank your own insolence for it, you jades! I think your lovers have punished you very properly for your treatment this morning—And here I must be laughed at for your folly and impertinence.

Magdalen. Ah! I swear we will be revenged, or I shall die with the vexation of it. And you,

rafcals, dare you continue here after your infolence?

Mafcarille. Do you ufe a marquis thus? This
is the way of the world, the leaft difgrace makes us
be flighted by thofe that before careffed us. Come,
let us go and feek our fortune elfewhere: I fee nothing but outfide takes with this world; and now-
a-days naked virtue goes unrewarded.

SCENE THE LAST.

GORGIBUS, MAGDALEN, CATHOS,
and FIDLERS.

I. FIDLER.

SIR, we expect that you fhould pay us, fince
they do not, for it was here we played.

Gorgibus beating them.] Ay, ay, villains, I will
pay you! but it fhall be in this coin. And as for
you, ye gipfies, I know not what prevents me
from ufing you in the fame manner. You have
made both yourfelves and me the jeft of the town.
Begone out of my fight for ever! [They go out.]
And as for romances, verfes, fongs, fonnets, and
fonatas, which have been the occafion of all this,
may the devil fly away with them all.

THE END.

DON GARCIA

OF

NAVARRE:

OR, THE

JEALOUS PRINCE.

AN HEROIC COMEDY.

DON GARCIA

OF

NAVARRE;

or, the

JEALOUS PRINCE.

AN HEROIC COMEDY.

DON GARCIA *of* NAVARRE, *or the* JEALOUS PRINCE, *an Heroic Comedy of five Acts, acted at Paris, at the Theatre of the Palace-Royal, February 4th,* 1661.

THE choice of the subject, in imitation of the Spanish, in which the incidents are more suitable to comedy, than to any thing heroic; the original of which is vicious, and might be a means of the small success of this work. Moliere succeeded no better as an actor, when he played the part of Don Garcia. He did not appeal from the judgment of the publick, nor did he print his piece, though there were some passages in it, which he afterwards thought deserved to be inserted in other comedies, particularly in the MAN HATER; see the third scene of the fourth act of the MAN-HATER, and the eighth scene of the fourth act of DON GARCIA.

A C T O R S.

DON GARCIA, Prince of Navarre, in love with
Elvira.

ELVIRA, Princeſs of Leon.

DON ALPHONSO, Prince of Leon, thought to be
the prince of Caſtile, under the name of Don
Silvio.

AGNESA, a counteſs, in love with Silvio, beloved
by Moorgat, the uſurper of the ſtate of Leon.

ELIZA, confident to Elvira.

DON ALVAREZ, confident of Garcia, in love with
Eliza.

DON LOPEZ, another confident of Don Garcia,
in love with Eliza.

DON PEDRO, gentleman-uſher to Agneſa.

A PAGE to Elvira.

SCENE lies in Aſtorga, a city of Spain, in
the kingdom of Leon.

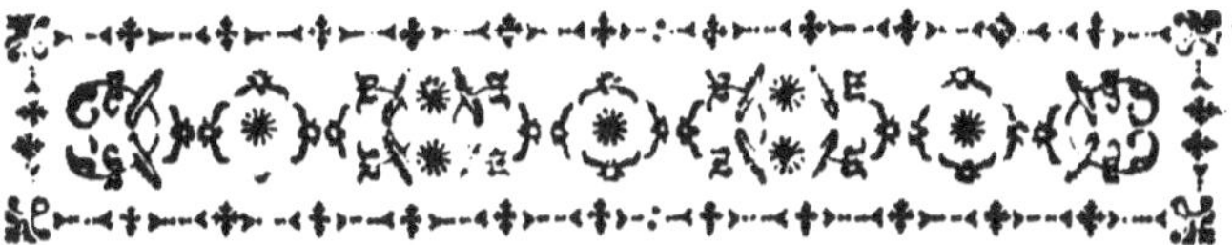

DON GARCIA

OF

NAVARRE.

ACT I. SCENE I.

ELVIRA, ELIZA.

ELVIRA.

IN short, I have no choice to determine the sentiments of my mind concerning these two lovers; I can find nothing in the prince to induce me to prefer his love. Don Silvio possesses all the good qualities of a glorious hero as well as him. The equal birth of both, added to their noble virtues, often induces me to speak in both their favours: and if merit alone were to plead a right to my heart, the conqueror would be yet unnamed—But heaven intends it otherwise, and weighs down the scale in Don Garcia's favour.

Eliza. Indeed, madam, as you have been so long in determining between the two rivals, I am afraid the love your stars have inspired you with for him, has but a small possession of your soul.

Elvira. The love of these worthy rivals has gi-

ven me very great uneafinefs. When I looked on
the one, I found no reafon to reftrain my tender
regard for him: but when the facrifice of the o-
ther prefented itfelf to me, I chid the former
movement of my foul as an act of injuftice, and
thought Don Silvio deferving of a happier fate. I
confidered the obligations which the late king Leon's daughter was under to the blood of Caftile,
and the ftrong friendfhip which had long united
the interefts of his father and mine; and as the one
gained my affection, the bad fuccefs of the other
gave me pain. When his melting fighs demand-
ed my pity, his defires were amufed with a favourable appearance, with which fmall advantage
he was willing to make amends for the fecret difficulties he met with in my heart.

Eliza. You fhould make yourfelf eafy, fince you
have been made acquainted with his firft paffion.
Donna Agnefa received the homage of his heart
before he felt a paffion for you; and as fhe is your
intimate friend, and has intrufted you with the fecret, you have a good opportunity of freeing yourfelf, and may refufe him under a pretence of friendfhip for her.

Elvira. Really the account of Don Silvio's infidelity may give me pleafure, as it gives my weak
heart liberty to determine againft him, and I may
with propriety refufe his offers, and beftow the feel-
ings of my heart on another. But if the feverity of another fort of conftraint ftill gives me pain,
this fatisfaction will not equal my uneafinefs, when
the continual weaknefs of a jealous prince unwor-
thily receives my tender regards, and will certainly make me be obliged to drop all correfpondence
with him.

Eliza. Can you blame him not to believe his happiness compleat, when he is not yet assured of it from your own mouth? And is it not natural for that which gives hopes to his rival to make him suspect your tenderness for him?

Elvira. No, there is no excuse for the extravagance of his jealousy; and he must see too plainly by my actions, that he has my secret good wishes. A person's thoughts may be interpreted by other ways than speaking. A look, a blush, a sigh, or even silence, is sufficient to discover the sentiments of one's heart. Every thing in love speaks, and every ray is a sun; as the delicacy of our sex will not allow us to discover what we feel, I own I have endeavoured to divide my favours with an equal hand between them, and to look impartially upon the merits of both; but it is in vain to strive against our wishes, and it is very easy to discern between favours which proceed from the sincere inclination of the heart, and those bestowed out of policy. The one always appears forced, but the other natural; like pure and limpid streams which flow from their native sources calmly. In vain did my pity towards Don Silvio strive to move me; the insufficiency of it discovered itself, whilst the prince must observe in my eye, more than I chose he should.

Eliza. If there is no foundation for the suspicions of that illustrious lover, they are the signs of a well affected soul; and what makes you uneasy would give others pleasure. Jealousy in a person who is disagreeable to us, may give pain; but in an agreeable object who loves us, it should give joy. He only expresses his passion in that manner, and the more his jealousy appears, it should increase our love.   Therefore since in your soul a brave prince————

Elvira. Ah! do not advance such a strange maxim ; at all times and on all occasions, Jealousy is odious; nothing can soften its hurtful attacks, and we feel the affront more sensibly the dearer the object. To see a passionate prince laying aside that respect with which love inspires him, and in his jealousies chiding my pleasures and disgusts, construing every thing I do or say in favour of a rival ! No, no, these suspicious tempers are too offensive ; I will give you my opinion without deceit. I confess I love Don Garcia, and his bravery in the midst of Leon has given me a proof of his flame, by defying the greatest dangers, delivering me from the designs of wicked tyrants, and securing me from the horrors of an unworthy match. I own, I would not wish to owe my deliverance to any other person. Indeed, Eliza, it gives great pleasure to an enamoured heart to be under obligations to what it loves; and its fearful flame gains more strength, and shines out stronger, when it imagines it satisfies its obligations by the means of favours. Yes, I am pleased that his venturing his life for me appears to give his love a right of conquest : it gives me pleasure that my danger put me under his protection; and if reports are true, and my brother return, my sincere wishes are, that he may assist my brother in the recovery of his throne, and that he may by lucky successes of a noble valour deserve all manner of thanks from me. Yet if his jealousy does not cease, and he do not subject himself to my laws, but continue to incite my anger, he will hope for the possession of Donna Elvira in vain. I hate the appearance of certain mifery to both, and in that cafe Hymen can never join us.

Eliza. Madam, he is a prince that I dare fay will conform himfelf to your defires, which you have explained fo well in this letter, that when he reads it——

Elvira. Now, when I have thought better upon it, I will not have it delivered, Eliza; it will be better to inform him of my thoughts by word of mouth; to favour a lover with writing, leaves in his hands too clear proofs of our inclination.

Eliza. I fhould make a law of your inclination, but I am furprized that heaven fhould throw fuch diverfity into people's minds. What fome look upon as an hardfhip, others defire as a happinefs. For my part, I fhould be glad to have a jealous lover; his mifery would be joy to me, and what difappoints me is to fee Don Alvarez fo eafy.

Elvira. Here he comes; we did not think he was fo near.

SCENE II.

ELVIRA, DON ALVAREZ, ELIZA.

ELVIRA.

I Am amazed at your fudden return: are we to expect Don Alphonfo? what is the news? is he coming?

D. Alvarez. Madam, the time is now come, when that brother brought up in Caftile will enter into the poffeffion of his own again. Don Louis, to whofe care his infancy was committed by the late king, has concealed his quality from the whole ftate, to fave him from the rage of that

traitor Mcorgat; and notwithftanding the tyrant
has often made enquiry for him, under the pretence of giving up his place to him, yet he would
never truft the dangerous bait of his fham-juftice.
But as the people are enraged at that violence
which would have been offered to you by an unjuft power, that generous old man thought it high
time to try the fuccefs of twenty years expectation. He has founded Leon, and his faithful agents
have praactifed upon the minds of both great and
fmall. When Caftile was preparing ten thoufand
men to reftore that prince to the wifhes of his people, he fpreads his fame abroad, and fhews him only at the head of an army, ready to launch the a-
venging thunder on the bafe ufurper's head. Leon
is befieged and Don Silvio commands in perfon the
fuccour you have from his father.

Elvira. A fuccour fo powerful may readily flatter our hopes; but I am afraid my brother will be
under too great obligations to him.

D. Alvarez. Is it not furprizing, madam, that,
notwithftanding the ftorm that threatens the ufurper, all reports from Leon confirm, that he is going to marry the countefs Agnefa?

Elvira. I have heard nothing from that illuftri-
ous maid lately, which makes me uneafy; fhe always detefted that tyrant. He endeavours to
ftrengthen his intereft by an alliance with her.

Eliza. She is under other engagements of honour and affection, too powerful to—

D. Alvarez. The prince is coming.

S C E N E   III.

D. G A R C I A, D O N N A E L V I R A, D. AL-
VAREZ, E L I Z A.

D. GARCIA.

MADAM, I am come to rejoice with you at the good news you have received. That brother who threatens the infamous tyrant with death, at the fame time gives hopes to my love, and offers me a welcome occafion of expofing myfelf to new dangers for your fake. If heaven proves kind to me, this right hand fhall lay the infidel dead at your feet, and reftore your family to its former grandeur. And what gives me more plea-fure ftill, is, that the ftars have reftored your bro-ther to the throne; for fo my love may fhine out, without imputation, as if by means of your perfon, I only fought to gain myfelf a crown. Yes, my heart would fhew the world that my regards were for you alone; and I have a thoufand times wifh-ed you in a humble ftation, that the facrifice of my heart might repair heaven's injuftice to you; and that you might be indebted to my love for all you owe to your birth. But as heaven has depriv-ed me of that fatisfaction, be fo obliging as to let my love have fome hope from his death whom I am preparing to meet, and allow me by my faith-ful fervices to difpofe the minds of a brother, and a whole nation to be favourable to me.

Elvira. The favour of a brother, and of a nation are not enough to crown your hopes: I am fenfible, that by efpoufing our caufe, you can make an hun-died glorious exploits fpeak in favour of your love.

Elvira is not the prize of that attempt, there is still a greater difficulty to surmount.

D. Garcia. I know what you mean, madam, and am sensible that my heart sighs in vain for you; and am not unacquainted with the mighty difficulty, though you do not mention it.

Elvira. People often take ill what is well meant. We may be led into mistakes by too much heat: but since I must, I will speak. Shall I tell you when you may expect to please me, and when you may have some hope?

D. Garcia. I would look upon that, madam, as a very great favour.

Elvira. When you know how to love as you ought.

D. Garcia. Alas, madam, can any thing equal the passion you have inspired me with?

Elvira. When your passion does not displease me.

D. Garcia. That is my only study.

Elvira. When you shall cease to entertain unworthy thoughts of me.

D. Garcia. I love you to madness.

Elvira. When you have made amends for your offences, and laid aside that jealous humour which hurts the addresses you offer to me, and prejudices me against them with just anger.

D. Garcia. Indeed, madam, still some remains of jealousy cleave to my heart, in spite of my best endeavours to prevent it; a rival, though at some distance from your charming person, does disturb me. Whether through reason or fancy, I always imagine you are unhappy in his absence, and that, notwithstanding my assiduous behaviour to please you, you continually sigh for that too happy man.

But if you are difpleafed at my fufpicions, it is in your power to eafe me of them: Yes, you can drive jealoufy from my mind, and diffipate all the horrors with which that monfter fills my foul. Submit therefore to refolve the doubt that afflicts me, and with a kind confeffion from your charming mouth, make me certain of what my greateft diligence could not find out.

Elvira. The tyranny of your fufpicions is very great, prince. A heart fhould be underftood at the leaft intimation, and does not love the importunity of thofe flames which require fuch particular explanations. The firft movement which our fouls difcover fhould fatisfy a difcreet lover. Were I to chufe for myfelf, I do not know in whofe favour I fhould determine, whether your's or Don Silvio's: but the very defiring to conftrain you not to be jealous, might have given fome information to any one but you; I thought that rule might have given light enough, without faying more; but your love is not fatisfied, and requires an open declaration: I muft fay plainly, I love you, nay, perhaps fwear to it.

D. Garcia. Indeed, madam, I confefs I am too forward: I fhould be fatisfied with what you pleafe, and require no other information; I flatter myfelf you have fome fmall compaffion for me, and that I am happier than I deferve. My jealous fufpicions are all over; my fentence is very agreeable, and I receive the law thereby prefcribed to fet my heart free from this unjuft empire.

Elvira. You promife a great deal, prince, and I very much doubt whether you can put that force upon yourfelf.

D. Garcia. Ah! madam, to render me credible,

it is enough that what is promifed to you ought to
be inviolable; becaufe the happinefs of obeying you
renders every thing eafy. May heaven declare e-
ternal war againft me, may it lay me breathlefs at
your feet, or which is worfe, may your wrath be
poured on me, if ever my love defcends to fuch
weaknefs as to fail in the duties of that promife;
if ever the leaft jealous tranfport in my foul—

S C E N E IV.

ELVIRA, D. GARCIA, D. ALVAREZ, ELIZA.
[Footman prefenting a letter to Elvira.]

E L V I R A.

I WAS uneafy, and you greatly oblige me: let
the meffenger ftay.

S C E N E V.

ELVIRA, D. GARCIA, D. ALVAREZ, ELIZA.

ELVIRA low and afide.

I Plainly fee by his looks how much this letter
difturbs him. Prodigious effect of his jealous mind! Prince, what ftops you in the middle
of your oath? [Aloud.

D. Garcia. I was afraid of interrupting you,
as I thought you might have fome fecret together.

Elvira. I think the tone of your voice is much
changed, and your eyes look wild; I am amazed
at this fudden alteration; pray tell me from what
it proceeds.

D. Garcia. I am fick at heart fuddenly.

Elvira. Are you often thus affected? Some imme-

diate remedy is needful; thofe illneffes are very
frequent.

D. Garcia. Sometimes.

Elvira. Alas, frail prince! here let this writing
cure your diftemper, it is no where but in the
mind.

D. Garcia. That writing, madam! no, my hand
refufes it: I know your thoughts, and what you accufe me of, if—

Elvira. Read it, I tell you, and fatisfy yourfelf.

D. Garcia. That you may afterwards call me
weak, jealous; no, no, I will convince you that
this letter has not in the leaft difturbed me, and to
juftify myfelf, I will not read it, though you are
pleafed to allow me.

Elvira. If you perfift in your refufal, I fhould
be in the wrong to force you; it is fufficient I let
you fee whofe hand it is.

D. Garcia. My will ought always to fubmit to
yours; if it is your pleafure I fhould read it for
you, I fhall do it very willingly.

Elvira. Yes, yes, prince, take it; you fhall read
it for me.

D. Garcia. To obey you, madam; and I may
fay——

Elvira. What you pleafe; pray difpatch.

D. Garcia. It comes from Donna Agnefa, I
perceive.

Elvira. It does fo; and I am glad of it, as well
for your fake as my own.

D. Garcia reads.] " Notwithftanding all con-
" tempt, the tyrant perfifts in his love to me; and
" more effectually to compafs his ends, has, fince
" your abfence, turned on me all that violence
" with which he purfued the match between your-

" self and his son. Thofe who can claim any pow-
" er over me do all approve this unworthy pro-
" pofal, being infpired by the villainous motives
" of falfe honour. I do not know as yet where
" my perfecution will end. But I will die foon-
" er than confent. May you, fair Elvira enjoy a
" happier fate."

D. AGNESA.

Her foul is endued with a furprifing virtue.

Elvira. I will go and write an anfwer to this il-
luftrious friend. In the mean time, prince, learn
to arm yourfelf better againft fuch accidents. I
have calmed your tempeft this time, and the thing
has paft mildly off: but, perhaps, I may not be in
a humour to do fo again.

D. Garcia. What? you think then———

Elvira. I think what I ought: farewel, do not
forget my advice; and if your love of me be really fo great as you pretend, let me fee fuch proofs
of it as I expect.

D. Garcia. Be affured, that I intend nothing
more than to obey you; and I would fooner die than
fail in it.

ACT II. SCENE I.

ELIZA, D. LOPEZ.

ELIZA.

TO be plain with you, I am not furprized at
what the prince does; as a foul fired with
a noble paffion cannot avoid being tranfported with
jealoufy fometimes; it is very natural that its wifh-

es be often crossed by doubts, and I must think well of it; but what I am amazed at, Don Lopez, is to be acquainted that you prepare suspicions for him, that you contrive them, and he is only jealous with your eyes, and disturbed by your cares. Really I must tell you again, that I am not surprized at the anxieties and suspicions of a sincere lover, but to see a person who is not in love have all the jealousies of a real admirer, is a very particular case, which belongs only to you.

D. Lopez. Let every body talk upon that subject as they please: every man must rule his conduct by what he proposes to himself; and as you reject my love, I must endeavour to make my best court to the prince.

Eliza. But if you still encourage this temper in him, he will make his court very ill.

Don Lopez. My charming Eliza, was it ever known that people about great men ever studied any thing but their own interest? Was there ever a compleat courtier increased his prince's retinue by censuring the faults he saw in them, or give himself concern for their real interest, in case he could enlarge his fortune by them? All such people aim at is to get the easiest way to their favour, which they may easily do by flattering their infirmities, and blindly commending what they chuse to do, and never encouraging any thing that may give them offence; that is the whole secret of getting into their favour. If a man give them good advice he is looked upon as a troublesome fellow, and will be thrown out of that confidence which he got into by an artful compliance. Really, we see that the art of courtiers is to make their advantage of the follies of the great, not to reprove, but encourage them in their errors.

Eliza. For a time thofe maxims may anfwer, but there are fuch things as reverfes of fortune. If the miftaken great ones fee into their error, they will be revenged on all fuch fawners for the injury done their honour; and I muft tell you, that you are too free in explaining your politics. If a juft account of your reafons were laid before the prince, I am afraid your fortune would not be made by it.

D. Lopez. I know very well Eliza's difcretion will prevent her from making this converfation public; and I can deny all I have faid: befides, every body knows what I have faid to be true, and why fhould I keep my proceedings private? When we make ufe of tricking or treafon, we may be afraid of a fall; but I can be accufed of nothing but a little complaifance, and need fear nothing. I only follow the prince's inclination to jealoufy: his foul is fed by fufpicions, and I ftudy to find occafions to give him uneafinefs, and look fharp out on all fides for matter to make up our private converfation. And when I have it in my power to difturb his quiet by a piece of news, then he regards me moft, and I can obferve him fwallow the poifon eagerly, and be as thankful for it as for the account of a victory, that crowned him with honour and happinefs. But I fee my rival coming, and I will leave you together; and notwithftanding I give up all hopes of ever poffeffing you, yet your giving him the preference, in my prefence, would give me pain; therefore I will avoid that mortification as much as I poffibly can.

Eliza. All fenfible lovers will do the fame.

S C E N E   II.

D. A L V A R E Z, E L I Z A.

D. A L V A R E Z.

WE are at laſt informed that the king of Navarre has declared himſelf this day in favour of the prince's love, and that a freſh re-inforcement of troops is ready to be employed in the ſervice of her to whom he wiſhes to aſpire.   I am ſurprized at the quick advances they have made. But—

S C E N E   III.

D. G A R C I A, E L I Z A, D. A L V A R E Z.

D. G A R C I A.

WHAT is the princeſs doing?
Eliza. I ſuppoſe ſhe is writing letters, my lord; but I will acquaint her that you are here.
D. Garcia. I will wait till ſhe is at liberty.

S C E N E   IV.

D. G A R C I A alone.

WHEN the proſpect of ſeeing her is ſo near, I feel my mind uncommonly diſturbed; reſentment and fear makes me tremble all over. Take care, D. Garcia, that a blind caprice do not lead thee to ſome precipice, and the ſtrong diſorders of thy mind betray thee into too aſſured a belief of thy ſenſes.   Take thy reaſon for thy guide, and ob-ſerve whether the appearance of thy ſuſpicions are well grounded; do not refuse their voice, but take care they do not impose upon thee to put too much confidence in them, that they may not give too much into thy first transports: read again sedately this half letter.   Ha! I would give any thing for the other half! But this is more than sufficient to shew me that I am unfortunate.

> If your rival——
> you should however——
> and you may destroy——
> the greatest obstacle——
> I gratefully remember——
> in delivering me from——
> his love, his devoirs——
> but he is despicable to me with——
> purge therefore your flame from——
> merit the regards that are——
> and when you are promised——
> do not absolutely refuse——

Yes, in these characters, my fate is very plain; by this she shews her heart as well as hand; and the imperfect meanings of these fatal words do not require the other half to discover it.   We must at first, however, carry it fair, and not discover our resentment to the faithless woman: we will puzzle her with the same arts she uses. I see her approaching; reason, contain my transports, and guard my outward appearance for a short time.

S C E N E V.

E L V I R A, D. G A R C I A.

E L V I R A.

FORGIVE me for detaining you.

D. Garcia low and aside.] How eafily fhe can diffemble!

Elvira. We have been informed juft now, that the king your father approves of your intentions, and has confented that his fon fhould reftore us to our fubjects.　It gives me great pleafure.

D. Garcia. Yes, madam, I am alfo very glad of it: but——

Elvira. Undoubtedly the tyrant will not eafily fcreen himfelf from the thunder that threatens him from all parts; and I pleafe myfelf with hoping that the fame bravery with which I was delivered from his brutal fury, and placed fafe within the walls of Aftorga, will, by the conqueft of Leon, finifh that horrid monfter's feverity.

D. Garcia. The fuccefs will foon fhew it: but I beg we may have fome other converfation: may I be fo free as to beg to know who you have written to fince fate brought us here?

Elvira. From whence does your concern arife? Why do you afk this queftion?

D. Garcia. Only out of pure curiofity, madam.

Elvira. Curiofity is fuppofed to be the daughter of jealoufy.

D. Garcia. Not the leaft of what you fuppofe. Your commands deter me from that vice.

Elvira. Without making further enquiry into the reafon for your afking, I have wrote two letters

to the countess of Leon, and to the marquis Don
Louis at Burgos two: does this satisfy you?

D. Garcia. To no other person, madam?

Elvira. Really no. I am surprised at this conversation.

D. Garcia. Pray recollect before you deny it.
People often perjure themselves by not considering well.

Elvira. In this my mouth cannot be perjured.

D. Garcia. It is guilty of a very great falshood,
however.

Elvira. Prince!

D. Garcia. Madam!

Elvira. Heavens! what means this extravagance!
tell me, have you lost your senses?

D. Garcia. Yes, indeed, I lost them, when I
had the misfortune to suck in the poison of your
love, and when I expected to meet with sincerity
in those faithless charms that bewitched me.

Elvira. What treachery do you complain of?

D. Garcia. Ah! deceitful heart! how well she
understands the art of feigning! But every door is
shut against her; no hole left to creep out at: here,
look on this, and confess your own writing. The
style of this part of a letter shews plainly who you
intended it for.

Elvira. And does this disturb you?

D. Garcia. Do not be ashamed of this writing.

Elvira. It is not usual for innocence to blush.

D. Garcia. Here indeed we see it oppressed,
you will deny the letter, because it wants a name.

Elvira. I do not deny it: it is my own hand
writing—

D. Garcia. I am amazed you own with it; but
I suppose you will say it was wrote to some indif-

ferent perfon, or that the kind expreffions in it were intended for fome relation, or female friend.

Elvira. No; I intended it for a lover, and a lover I efteem.

D. Garcia. And may I, perfidious—

Elvira. Unworthy prince, ftop the violence of your fury: though I do not need to obey any perfon here, and am only accountable to myfelf, yet I will clear myfelf of the offence you fo bafely charge me with, to punifh you. Do not doubt but you fhall be undeceived. I want not a defence to fhew my innocence; you fhall judge in your own caufe, and fhall be obliged to pronounce your own fentence.

D. Garcia. This myftery I cannot underftand.

Elvira. To your misfortune you fhall foon underftand it. Eliza, come here.

S C E N E VI.

D. G A R C I A, E L V I R A, E L I Z A.

ELIZA.

Madam.

Elvira to D. Garcia.] Take good notice whether I ufe any art to deceive you, whether by any movement of the body, or motion of the eye, I endeavour to ward off this fudden ftroke. [To Eliza.] Tell me immediately, where did you leave the letter I wrote juft now?

Eliza. I confefs I am to blame, madam; I am ignorant how it happened, I left it upon my table, and have juft now been told, that Don Lopez, with his ufual freedom, came into my room, and obferving every thing that was lying about, found this letter. When he was opening it, Eleonor, endeavouring to catch it from him, before he could read it, it was torn in two pieces, one of which Don Lopez run off with, notwithstanding all her efforts to the contrary.

Elvira. Have you the other half?

Eliza. Yes, madam, here it is.

Elvira. Give it me, [to D. Garcia.] and we will see who is to blame; here, join this to that you have, and read it; I will hear you.

D. Garcia. To the prince Don Garcia. Hah!

Elvira. Read on; are you thunderstruck at the direction?

D. Garcia reads.] " If your rival, prince, a-
" larms you, you should, however, fear yourself
" more than him, and you may destroy, whenever
" you please, the greatest obstacle your passion
" meets with. I gratefully remember what Don
" Garcia did in delivering me from our haughty
" ravishers; his love, his devoirs are agreeable to
" me, but he is despicable to me with his jealou-
" sy. Purge, therefore, your flame from that foul
" blemish; merit the regards that are bestowed
" upon you; and when you are promised by peo-
" ple to be made happy, do not absolutely refuse
" to do so yourself."　　　　　ELVIRA.

Elvira. Well, what think you of this?

D. Garcia. Ah! madam, I am quite distract-ed. Too great a punishment cannot be inflicted upon me.

Elvira. Enough; know that I desired the letter should be read to you now, for no other reason but to falsify your assertions, and that I might have an opportunity to unsay all that I find there in your favour. Farewel.

D. Garcia. Whither do you fly, madam?

Elvira. Where you, too jealous man, never fhall come.

D. Garcia. Forgive, madam, a wretched lover, who has made himfelf hated by you, by a wondrous turn of fate, and who, if he had remained quiet and unconcerned, had deferved to be more blamed. For, can a foul, which mixes not fear with its hope, be truly enamoured? And could you believe I had loved you, if I had been unalarmed at this letter? If I had not trembled at the thunderbolt which I fancied had deftroyed all my happinefs? I leave it to your own judgment; fay, would not fuch an accident have thrown any other lover into my error? Alas! how could I withhold my affent to fo clear a proof?

Elvira. Yes, you might have done it: my fentiments fo clearly explained to you, might have fecured your doubts: you had not the leaft to be afraid of, and if fome others had had fuch a pledge, they would never have paid the leaft regard to what people faid.

D. Garcia. The lefs deferving we are of an expected benefit, with more difficulty we depend upon it; a deftiny too replete with glory feems flippery, and leaves to our fufpicions an eafy declivity. As for me, who fo little deferve your goodnefs, I doubted of my happy fortune: I thought that being in a place of my jurifdiction, you forced yourfelf to be a little complaifant; that difguifing to me your feverity——

Elvira. And was I capable of condefcending to fuch a mean fhift! to make ufe of fhameful fiction! to act upon motives of a fhameful fear, to betray my fentiments, and becaufe I was in your power, to cover my hatred with a mask of favour! Could my heart be so little swayed by glory! can you think so, and dare to tell me it? Know that this heart cannot debase itself; that nothing under heaven can force it to do it: and if, by this odd mistake, you have seen marks of a goodness of which you are not worthy, know, that notwithstanding your power, I can shew the contempt I resolve to have for you, defy your fury, and convince you that I was not guilty of any baseness, nor ever will be so.

D. Garcia. Well, I am guilty, I do not deny it; but I beg pardon of your divine charms, I beg it for the sake of the most lively flame that ever two fair eyes kindled in a mortal's breast. But if your wrath cannot be appeased, if my crime is too great to be forgiven; if you do not look upon the love that caused it, nor the speedy repentance which my heart manifests to you; I must then, by putting a period to my days, free myself from these horrid pains. You must not imagine that I can live a minute under your displeasure; the cruel length of that minute already makes my heart sink under its cutting remorse; the terrible wounds of a thousand vultures are not to be compared to its mortal pangs. Tell me, madam, if I am to expect pardon, else this sword, by a favouroble stroke, shall, in your presence, pierce the heart of a wretched man; this treacherous heart, whose anxieties have offended your excessive goodness so much. I shall be too happy in death, if this last stroke cancels in your mind the image of my fault, and leaves no part of your hatred in the weak remembrance of my love: this is the only kindness my affection requires from you.

Elvira. Ah! too cruel prince.

D. Garcia. Say, madam, speak.

Elvira. Should I still be kind to you, and allow myself to be affronted so frequently?

D. Garcia. A mind that is in love can never give an affront, and that love excuses its faults.

Elvira. Love cannot excuse such fury.

D. Garcia. All its ardour arises from its movements, and the stronger it is the more difficulty it finds—

Elvira. Speak to me no more of it; you deserve my hatred.

D. Garcia. Do you hate me then?

Elvira. I will try to do it at least; but I fear my endeavours will be to no purpose, and that all the displeasure your behaviour has excited will not be sufficient to make me carry my revenge far enough.

D. Garcia. Do not try the effects of so heavy a punishment, as I offer you my life for your revenge; pronounce my sentence, and I will obey you immediately.

Elvira. A person who cannot hate, must be ill qualified to kill.

D. Garcia. Determine either to forgive or punish me; I cannot live except your goodness grant a pardon to my rash mistakes.

Elvira. Alas! my resolutions are too plainly seen; I think it is forgiving a criminal, when one tells him they cannot hate him.

D. Garcia. Ah! it is too much. Allow me, adorable princess—

Elvira. Hold, I hate myself for my weakness.

D. Garcia alone.] At last I am—

S C E N E VII.

D. G A R C I A, D. L O P E Z.

D. L O P E Z.

I AM come to inform you of a secret, that may juftly alarm your love.

D. Garcia. Do not, while I am in this charming tranfport, come to tell me of fecrets or alarms; after what I have juft heard and feen, I will encourage no fufpicions; the unequalled goodnefs of fo dear an object fhould fhut my ears againft all vain reports; fo let me hear no more of them.

D. Lopez. My lord, your intereft is all I confider, fo let it be juft as you pleafe: I thought what I had difcovered fhould be immediately communicated to you; but as you do not chufe to hear it, I am ready to change the difcourfe, and tell you, that every family in Leon has already thrown afide the mafk, upon the report of the troops of Caftile; and efpecially the populace have fhewn fuch refpect to their new king, that it, to all appearance, makes the tyrant tremble for fear.

D. Garcia. However, Caftile fhall not have the victory without our attempting to fhare the honour of it; our troops may be able to imprint fear in the mind of Moorgat. But let me hear that fecret you have to tell me.

D. Lopez. I have nothing to fay, my lord.

D. Garcia. Come, come, I give you free liberty to fpeak.

D. Lopez. I am too well informed by what you faid, my lord, for that, and as my intelligence may give you uneafinefs, I will be filent for the future.

D. Garcia. I am determined to know it, without any more to do.

D. Lopez. I muft obey you, my lord; but it would be imprudent to explain it in this public place. Let us go from hence, and you fhall know it, and judge of it.

ACT III. SCENE I.

ELVIRA, ELIZA.

ELVIRA.

WHAT do you think of this ftrange weaknefs in the heart of a princefs, Eliza? to lay afide my refentment fo foon, and forgive fo bafe an affront?

Eliza. I am not furprized, madam, at your anger being abated; notwithftanding the provocation you had to be difobliged. I know it is very difficult to put up with an affront from the man we love; but as there is nothing more provoking, fo nothing we fooner forgive. If a beloved offender throw himfelf at our feet, he foon gets the better of our anger, and the more eafily, if the offence proceeds from fincere love.

Elvira. But this is the laft time I fhall blufh for my weaknefs, whatever power love may have over me: and if he ever give me reafon again to be angry, he muft not expect forgivenefs; if my tendernefs for him foftens my refentment, I will guard myfelf againft him by an oath: for really a mind inspired by pride, let it be ever so small a share, is ashamed to break its word; and frequently at the expence of a painful struggle makes a bold attempt upon its own wishes, stands upon its honour, and sacrifices every thing to the noble pride of maintaining its word; therefore by my having now pardoned him, no judgment can be made of what yet may happen; and whatever fortune may seem to prepare, I do not think I can be the prince of Navarre's, till he has manifested an entire cure of those melancholy fits by which he is disturbed, and give me sufficient reason to think that he will never relapse into the like affront again.

Eliza. But pray, madam, what affront is the jealousy of a lover to us?

Elvira. Nothing deserves a greater resentment, and since we undergo so much when we are forced to own we love, since the rigid honour of our sex opposes a mighty obstacle to such acknowledgments, ought a lover, when he sees us surmount that obstacle in his favour; ought he, I say, with impunity to doubt that testimony? And is he not very much to blame to disbelieve that which is never said without the greatest reluctance.

Eliza. For my part, I think that we should not be offended when they are a little diffident upon such occasions; and that it is a dangerous thing, madam, for a lover to be absolutely perfuaded that he is beloved.

Elvira. Let us argue no more about this; every one thinks for themselves; and in short, my soul is offended with this scruple, and notwithstanding my wishes, I feel something which forbodes an eclaircisement between the prince and me, which,

·in spite of his great virtue—But who comes here?
Heavens! it is Don Silvio of Castile!

SCENE II.

ELVIRA, D. ALPHONSO, thought to be
D. Silvio, ELIZA.

BY what surprizing turn of fortune, my lord,
have you come hither?

D. Alphonso. My arrival, madam, must needs surprize you, and my entering this town without noise, whose access is rendered difficult by order of a rival, to escape being seen by the soldiers, is an accident you did not expect to meet with; but if in this I have surmounted some obstacles, the desire of seeing you is able to affect much greater wonders. My heart has felt inexpressible torments in being absent from you, and I was not able to deny myself any longer the sight of your amiable person. I come, therefore, to tell you that I return thanks to heaven, that you are rescued from the hands of an execrable tyrant; but in the midst of this happiness, it is the greatest torture to me to see that my rigorous fate envied me the honour of this glorious deed, and too unjustly offered to my rival the agreeable dangers of that piece of service. Yes, madam, my resolutions to break your chains would undoubtedly have been equal to his; and I should have gained this victory for you, if heaven had not deprived me of that honour.

Elvira. That you have an heart capable of overcoming the greatest dangers, I very well know, my lord, and I make not the least doubt but that generous zeal which animates you to revenge my quar-

rel, would have been able to have done for me all
that another hand has performed; but without this
action which you was capable of I am sufficiently
obliged to the house of Castile. Every one knows
what the count your father has done for the late
king. After having aided him to the last hour,
he made his kingdom a safe asylum for my brother; full twenty years he concealed him from the
cruel rage of his enemies, and now to restore to
his forehead the splendor of a crown, you are march-
ing in person against our usurpers. Are you not
content? Do not these brave efforts sufficiently o-
blige me to you? Would you, my lord, obstinate-
ly expect to captivate my whole fate to you? And
must I never receive so much as the shadow of one
sole benefit, but what comes from you? Ah! suffer me in these misfortunes I am exposed to by my
destiny, to owe something to the cares of another
likewise, and do not complain that the glory has
been acquired by another person where it was impossible for you to be.

D. Alphonso. Yes, madam, I ought not any
longer to complain; you are pleased with too much
reason to constrain me to it; and we unjustly complain of one misfortune, when a much greater afflicts us. This succour from a rival greatly mor-
tifies me; but, alas! this is not the greatest of my
miseries. The blow, the severe blow, which wounds
me to the heart, is to see that rival preferred to me.
Yes, I but too plainly see that his happy pretensions prevailed above mine; and that opportunity
of serving you, that advantage which offered of
signalizing his bravery, that glorious exploit in sav-
ing you was nothing but the pure effect of the good
fortune of pleasing you; the secret power of a

wondrous ſtar which made the glory fall where
your wiſhes were fixed. Thus all my endeavours
will be nothing but air; I am leading an army a-
gainſt your cruel tyrants, but I march with trem-
bling when I conſider that your wiſhes will not be
for me, and that if they are obtained, fortune pre-
pares the happineſs of more noble ſucceſſes for my
rival. Ah! madam, muſt I ſee myſelf precipi-
tated from the glorious expeſtations I flattered myſelf with? And may I not be informed what I
have done that deſerves this terrible fall?

Elvira. Aſk me nothing before you conſider what
you ought to aſk of my ſentiments: and as for this in-
difference of mine which ſeems to diſturb you, I
leave it to you, my lord, to anſwer for me; for, in
ſhort, you cannot be ignorant that I knew ſome of
the ſecrets of your ſoul, and I believe that ſoul to
be too noble and generous to deſire me to do what
is not juſt. Speak; I make you the judge whether it is equitable to ſuffer myſelf to be crowned
by an aſt of infidelity, whether you can, without
the utmoſt injuſtice, offer me an heart which another has already gained; whether you have reaſon
to complain and blame my refuſal, which would
prevent you from committing a crime. Yes, my
lord, it is a crime, for the firſt flames have ſuch
ſacred rights over a generous ſoul, that it ſhould
rather chuſe to renounce grandeur, and even life
itſelf, than incline to a ſecond love. I have that
ardour for you, which eſteem may ſuggeſt for an exalted courage, for a magnanimous heart; require
no more from me than what I owe you; but maintain the honour of your firſt choice. Notwithſtanding your new flames, conſider what tenderneſs the lovely Agneſa retains for you; who for

an ungrateful man, for fuch you are, my lord, has rejected the greateft offers. How generoufly fhe difdained the fplendour of a diadem; remember what dangers fhe has defied for your fake, and render to her heart what you owe it.

D. Alphonfo. Ah! madam, prefent not her merit to my view; it is but too confpicuous to the ungrateful man who forfakes her; and if my heart fhould tell you what it feels for her, I fear it would not feem innocent with regard to you. Yes, that heart dares deplore her, and does not, without difficulty, follow the imperious violence of the love that drags it. No expectation ever flattered my defires towards you, but at the fame time it extorted fighs for her, and in the midft of it's pleafing thoughts employed on you, ftill my foul caft a melancholy look towards my firft love, reproached itfelf with the effect of your heavenly charms, and mixed remorfe with my beft wifhes. I have done more, fince I muft tell you all, I have endeavoured to free myfelf from your empire, to break your chains, and again fubject my heart under the innocent yoke of it's firft conqueror. But after all my endeavours, my conftancy being overcome, is ftill forced to fubmit to the evil that kills me, and were I to be for ever wretched, I cannot renounce my defires, or bear the melancholy idea of feeing you poffeffed by another; and the Father of all, who difcovers your charms to me, before he lends his light to that marriage, muft lend it to me by death. I know I betray a charming princefs, but after all, madam, is my heart guilty? Does the powerful afcendant of your beauty leave the mind any liberty? Alas! I am much more to be pitied than fhe; fhe, by lofing me, lofes only a faith-

lefs man; and fuch a forrow is eafy to be comfort-
ed; but I have that unparalleled misfortune to a-
bandon an amiable perfon, and of enduring alfo all
the torments of a rejected love.

Elvira. You have no torments but what you yourfelf run into, for our heart is always in our own
power; it may indeed fometimes fhew a little weaknefs, but, in fhort, of all our paffions reafon is the
chief.

S C E N E III.

D. GARCIA, ELVIRA, D. ALPHONSO.

D. GARCIA.

MY coming is not, madam, I obferve, very feafonable, as it difturbs your converfation. I muft needs fay I did not expect to meet with fuch good company here.

Elvira. This fight indeed furprized me extremely, and I no more expected it than you did.

D. Garcia. Yes, madam, fince you fay fo, I do
not believe you were forewarned of this vifit; but
you, Sir, ought at leaft to have done us the honour
to have advifed us of this happinefs, that we might
have been prepared without furprize, to have performed thofe honours which are due to you.

D. Alphonfo. My lord, you are fo taken up
with heroic cares, that I had been much to blame
to have interrupted you; the fublime thoughts of
victorious princes cannot eafily ftoop to compliments.

D. Garcia. But victorious princes, whofe heroic cares are fo commended, inftead of loving
fecrecy, choofe to have witneffes of what they
do; their fouls bred up to glory from their in-

fancy, makes them, in their undertakings, go bare-faced, and being always fupported by high fentiments, never defcend to mean difguifes. Do you not, therefore, injure your heroic virtues in paffing fo fecretly through thefe places; are you not afraid of people's looking upon this action as below your character?

D. Alphonfo. Whether any body will condemn my conduct in this fecret vifit, I know not, but I can faithfully fay I never courted obfcurity in fuch undertakings as required the light. And were I to undertake an enterprize upon you, you fhould have no reafon to think I furprized you, for I would take care to tell you of it beforehand. In the mean time let us continue upon the ordinary terms, and poftpone our debates to other affairs. Let us fupprefs the boiling of our too warm blood, and not forget before whom we are both fpeaking.

Elvira to D. Garcia.] My lord, you are in the wrong, and his vifit is fuch, that you——

D. Garcia. Ah! madam, it is too much to efpoufe his quarrel, you ought to diffemble a little better, when you pretend that you were ignorant of his coming. Your warmth and quicknefs to defend it is but an ill proof of its having furprized you.

Elvira. So little am I concerned at your fufpicions, that I will not fo much as condefcend to deny it.

D. Garcia. Go on with your heroic pride, and without hefitating, let your whole heart explain itfelf. Do not deny any thing, fince you have confeffed it; it is giving too much credit to diffimulation. Be brief, lay afide fcruples; fay that you are fenfibly touched with his paffion, that his prefence has fomething in it fo pleafing, that——

Elvira. And if I have a mind to love him, can you hinder me? can you pretend to any command over my heart? and am I to regulate my desires by your direction? know that too much pride has deceived you if you think you have the least power over me, and that my sentiments arise from too great a soul to submit to fiction: I will not tell you whether the count is beloved, but know that he is very much esteemed, that his high virtue deserves a princess' love better than you; that his ardour and assiduity make all the impression on me a soul is capable of, and that if the over ruling power of fate puts it out of my power to reward him with my person, it is at least in my power to promise him that I will never become the treasure of your flames. And without amusing you any longer with vain hopes, this is what I engage myself to, and I will keep my word. I have disclosed my thoughts to you, since you will have it so, and discovered to you my real sentiments. Are you satisfied? have I sufficiently explained myself? Consider whether there remains any thing else for me to do in order to clear up your suspicions. In the interim, Don Silvio, if you persist in your resolutions to please me, I freely tell you that I have occasion for your aid; and desire your utmost efforts to punish our tyrants. Value not the transports of a capricious man, be deaf to his fury, and consider who it is makes this request of you.

SCENE IV.

D. GARCIA, D. ALPHONSO.

D. GARCIA.

WITH you every thing flourishes, your soul proudly triumphs over my confusion. It is a pleasant thing to you to hear the noble confession of that victory which you obtain over a rival, but it must be an inexpressible addition to your happiness to have that rival a witness to it, and my stifled pretensions are illustrious trophies in your triumphant eyes. Enjoy this delight, taste it with deep draughts, but know that you have not yet gained your point: I have too much reason to be enraged, and numberless events may yet happen. Despair, when it breaks loose, goes a great way, and in him that is abused nothing is unpardonable. If the ungrateful woman, in flattery to you, has just now engaged never to be mine, my indignation will furnish me with means to prevent her ever being yours.

D. Alphonso. This obstruction does not in the least disturb me. We shall soon see who is like to be the happy man; each by his valour will be able to defend the glory of his flames, or revenge their misfortune. But as between rivals, the most sedate soul is easily transported beyond the limits of reason, and as I am unwilling that such a conversation should exasperate either of us, I desire you would shew me how I may retreat out of this place.

D. Garcia. No, no; do not fear that you will be forced to violate the order that was just now

prefcribed you.　Whatever juft fury oppreffes me
and flatters you, I know when it fhould break out;
this place is open for you; go then and exult in
the advantages you have obtained.　But take this
along with you, my head alone can put your conqueft into your hands.

D. Alphonfo. When things arrive at that pitch,
our difference will prefently be decided by fortune.

A C T IV. S C E N E I.

ELVIRA, D. ALVAREZ.

ELVIRA.

ALL you fay is to no purpofe, Don Alvarez,
I will never forget this offence, therefore
you may return; the wound is incurable, and all
endeavours to heal it make it but fefter the more.
Does he think I will yield to fome falfe refpects?
No, he has carried things too far, and his vain repentance, which brought you hither, follicits a pardon it fhall never obtain.

D. Alvarez. Madam, you would be very much
affected were you to fee how he is grieved; never
was any offence expiated with deeper remorfe.　It
is well known, the prince is of an age that forces
him to follow the firft movements of his foul, and
in fuch boiling blood as his, paffion leaves no room
for reflection.　D. Lopez, prejudiced by a falfe
report, was the occafion of his mafter's error: there
was a very confufed rumour concerning the count's
fecret arrival, and that you connived at it.　The

prince believed this report, and his love being se-
duced by this false alarm, has made this mighty
noise.   But being now recovered from his mistake,
he is perfectly sensible of your innocence, and his
turning away D. Lopez is a plain evidence of that
quick sense he has of his offending you.

Elvira. Alas! he too easily believes me too in-
-nocent; he has not an entire assurance of it yet.
Bid him weigh all things well, and not be too has-
ty, for fear of being deceived.

D. Alvarez. Madam, he knows too well——

Elvira. Good D. Alvarez, let us finish this
discourse; I am weary of it; it revives in me an
unseasonable gloominess, and disturbs other more
important affairs.   Yes, the surprize of a great
misfortune oppresses me, and the report of Agnesa's death has so strong a right in my sorrow, as
absolutely excludes all other concerns.

D. Alvarez. This may be false news, madam;
but my return carries a dismal piece of news to the
prince.

Elvira. The utmost torment he can suffer is
short of what he deserves.

SCENE II.

ÆLVIRA, ELIZA.

ELIZA.

I WAITED his departure, madam, to tell you
something that will revive you again, since
you will this moment be perfectly informed where
Agnesa is.   For this purpose a certain person unknown, has sent one of his servants to desire audience of you,

Elvira. Defire him to come immediately, Eli-za; it is proper I fhould fee him.

Eliza. But he begs that nobody may fee him but yourfelf.

Elvira. Well, we fhall be alone. I will give orders about that, while you introduce him. How great is my defire to know what news he brings! Whether, O heavens! do you fend me joy or grief?

SCENE III.

D. PEDRO, ELIZA.

ELIZA.

WHERE——————

D. Pedro. Here am I, madam, if you mean me.

Eliza. Where was your mafter when——

D. Pedro. He is hard by; fhall I tell him to come?

Eliza. Yes; tell him that he is impatiently ex-pected, and fhall not be feen by any body. [*alone.*] There is fome myftery in thefe precautions that I cannot penetrate. But here he comes.

SCENE IV.

AGNESA in a man's habit, ELIZA.

ELIZA.

WE have prepared, my lord—Butwhat do I fee? Ah! madam, do I really behold—

Agnefa. Do not difcover me, Eliza, but let my fad deftiny take vent under the fiction of having been my own murderer. This feigned death is what has delivered me from all my tyrants; for under that name I may comprehend my relations. I have thereby avoided the hateful match, which rather than have confented to, I would have fuffered a real death. Under this difguife, and the report of my death, I fhall keep my fate a fecret, and fecure myfelf from that unjuft perfecution which may follow me even to this place.

Eliza. My aftonifhment might have betrayed you in public; but go into the clofet there, and dry up the tears of the princefs. You will find her there alone: fhe has been very cautious in putting away all witneffes.

S C E N E V.

D. A L V A R E Z, E L I Z A.

E L I Z A.

IS not this Don Alvarez I behold?
D. Alvarez. The prince fends me to you, to beg that you would make ufe of your utmoft endeavours to procure him a moment's converfation with Elvira. He cannot live unlefs you favour him—but here he comes.

S C E N E VI.

D. G A R C I A, D. A L V A R E Z, E L I Z A.

D. G A R C I A.

ALAS! Eliza, pity my misfortunes, which weigh me down to the earth.
Eliza. I fhould regard your torments, my lord, with other eyes than the princefs does; but hea-

ven has so ordained it, that every one's opinion of things is quite different.   And since she blames you, and fancies your jealousy to be a deformed monster, I would be complaisant, and endeavour to conceal from her eyes what might be disagreeable to them.   A lover undoubtedly follows an useful method when he endeavours to accommodate his humour to ours; an hundred devoirs do less good than this one thing, for nothing is so much esteemed by us as what resembles ourselves.

D. Garcia. I know it, but, alas! the inhuman destinies oppose themselves to such well advised designs, and notwithstanding all my endeavours, are continually laying snares for me, which I cannot avoid.   Not but that the ungrateful woman did, in the presence of my rival, make a too fatal confession against my interest, and testified for him so much tenderness, that it was impossible for me ever to forget it; but in short, having too hastily believed that she had introduced him into the place, I should be very much dissatisfied to leave upon her mind any just cause of which she might complain against me.   Yes, if I am abandoned, it shall be only owing to the infidelity of herself; for I resolved, by excusing myself, and begging her pardon, not to leave her ingratitude the least pretence.

Eliza. Give a little time to her resentment before you see her, my lord.

D. Gracia. Ah! if thou lovest me let me see her; it is a liberty that must be granted me: I cannot stir till her cruel disdain at least——

Eliza. Pray, my lord, defer it a little.

D. Garcia. Do not trifle with me any longer.

Eliza aside.] I find the princess herself must send

him away. [To Don Garcia.] Stay here, my lord, I will go and speak to her.

D. Garcia. Tell her that I kept the person whose information was the occasion of the offence no long-er in my service, but immediately turned him a-way, and that Don Lopez shall never——

SCENE VII.

D. GARCIA, D. ALVAREZ.

D. GARCIA looking in at the door which Eliza left open.

GOOD heaven! what is this I see? may I believe my own eyes? Alas! they are but too faithful witnesses. Now my misery is compleat. This fatal blow fully makes my destruction appear, and when I found myself disturbed with suspicions, it was heaven that with mute threats foretold this horrible disgrace.

D. Alvarez. My lord, what have you seen that disturbs you so much?

D. Garcia. I have seen what I can hardly be-lieve; I would be less surprized at the overthrow of all nature than at this accident. It is done—— Fate—I cannot speak——

D. Alvarez. My lord, endeavour to compose yourself.

D. Garcia. I have seen——Vengeance, O heaven!

D. Alvarez. What sudden alarm——

D. Garcia. It will kill me, D. Alvarez, the thing is certain.

D. Alvarez. But, my lord, what can——

D. Garcia. Alas! all is over, I am betrayed; I

am murdered: a man——can I speak it without dying? a man in the arms of my treacherous Elvira.

.D. Alvarez. The princess, my lord, is so virtuous that——

D. Gracia. Oppose me not, Don Alvarez, after what I have seen. It is too much to defend
her after I have beheld so black an action.

D. Alvarez. Our passions, my lord, frequently make us mistake a deceiving object for a true
one, and so think that a virtuous soul can——

D. Garcia. Prithee leave me, Don Alvarez, a
counsellor is offensive upon this occasion; nothing
shall advise me but my passion.

D. Alvarez. There is no arguing with him in
this condition. [Aside.]

D. Garcia. O cruel wound! but I will see who
it is, and punish with my hand——But see, she is
coming, cannot thou contain thyself, my rage?

S C E N E   VIII.

E L V I R A, D. G A R C I A, D. A L V A R E Z.

E L V I R A.

WELL, what would you have? and what
hopes can your boldness flatter itself with
after such proceedings? Can you have the assurance
to appear again before me? and what can you say
that will become me to hear?

D. Garcia. I say, that all the wickedness of the
damned is not so bad as your disloyalty; that destiny, the devils, nor heaven in it's wrath never produced any thing so wicked as you are.

Elvira. What is the meaning of this? I expect-

ed an excufe for an affront, but I find I am deceived.

D. Garcia. Yes, you are deceived. You did
not think that by the accident of the door being o-
pen I faw the traitor in your arms, and beheld your
fhame and my own ruin. Is it the happy lover
returned? or fome other rival whom I know nothing of? Strengthen me, O heaven, to bear the
racking torture! Now blufh, for you have reafon;
the mafk of your treachery is now laid afide. This
is what the difturbances of my foul fo frequently
intimated; it was not without any juft reafon that
my flame was alarmed; my well-grounded fufpicions were feeking what now my eyes have met
with. But think not that I will bear this affront
unrevenged. I know that we have no power o-
ver our defires, and that love will every where grow
without dependance; that there is no forcibly entering into an heart, and that every foul is free to
name it's conqueror; and therefore I fhould have
no reafon to complain of you, if you had honeftly
expreffed yourfelf to me at firft, and my heart would
have laid all the blame upon fate alone; but to fee
my flame approved by a falfe and hypocritical confeffion, is fuch a piece of treachery, fuch a bafe action, that it can never be fufficiently punifhed.
No, no, after fuch an infult, hope for nothing; I
am not myfelf, I am all rage; being betrayed on
every fide, my love muft revenge itfelf to the purpofe; I muft, I muft facrifice every thing to my
rage, and put a period to my days and defpair at
once.

Elvira. Since I have been fo patient to all you
have faid, I hope I may now take the liberty to fpeak.

D. Garcia. And pray by what florid difcourfe, what artful fpeech—

Elvira. If you have any thing farther to fay to me, you may add it, I am ready to hear it ; if not, I hope you will pay a little attention to me.

D. Garcia. Well, then, I attend: ye heavens, what patience is mine!

Elvira. I bridle my wrath, and will, without the leaft anger, anfwer your mad difcourfe.

D. Garcia. You will perhaps—

Elvira. I have liftened to you as long as you pleafed; pray do the fame to me. I am aftonifhed at my deftiny, and I believe there never was any thing upon earth fo prodigious as it is; nothing more inconceivable for it's novelty, and nothing lefs fupportable with refpect to reafon. I have a lover who makes it his whole ftudy to perfecute me, who amidft all the amorous expreffions of his mouth, has no efteem for me in his heart; nothing that can do juftice to the blood I fprung from, nothing that can defend the innocence of my actions againft the leaft fhadow of a falfe appearance. Yes, I fee—[Don Garcia feems defirous of fpeaking.] Do not interrupt me—I fee, I fay, my unhappinefs carried to that pitch, that one who fays he loves me, and would make me believe that he would defend my reputation againft the whole fufpecting univerfe, is he that is the greateft enemy to it. He fufpects me on every occafion; he not only does fo, but, what wounds love, he makes a noife of it. Inftead of acting like a lover, who had rather die than offend what he loves, who calmly bemoans himfelf, and feeks with refpect to have his doubts fatisfied; he proceeds to extremities, and is all rage, invectives, threats. But I will now shut my eyes to every thing that may render him despicable to me, and by an act of mere goodness, will make this fresh affront an occasion of his future quiet. Your great rage proceeds from what you saw by mere chance; I should be in the wrong to contradict your sight, and I own you might have some reason to be uneasy at it.

D. Garcia. Is it not therefore——

Elvira. Stop a little, and you will know what I am resolved to do. It is neceffary that the fates of both of us should be accomplished: you are now upon the brink of a mighty precipice, and you will either miscarry or escape, according to the course you shall now take. If, prince, regardless of what you have seen, you act towards me as you ought, and require no other proof but me, to condemn the error of your uneasiness; if by a ready compliance of your sentiments, you are willing to believe me innocent upon my word alone, and laying aside all your suspicions, blindly believe what I tell you; this submission, this mark of esteem shall cancel, in my breast, all your past misbehaviour; I instantly recede from that indignation which I have justly declared against you: and I can hereafter chuse my own lot, without prejudicing what I owe to my birth; my honour, being content with this ready obedience, promises to your love both my heart and my hand; but remember what I am going to tell you; if this offer I now make you has so little prevalence with you, as not to obtain an entire sacrifice of your jealous suspicions; if what security my heart and birth can afford is not sufficient; and if the powerful umbrages of your spirit force me to convince your senses, and to produce an evident proof of my offended virtue, I am ready to

do it, and will satisfy you; but you muft depart
from me that moment, and never more have any
pretentions to me; and I take the Almighty Judge
of heaven and earth to witnefs, that, whatever we are deftined to, I will fooner chufe to put
a period to my days than to be yours. Make your
choice of thefe two propofals; fatisfy yourfelf, and
I fhall be fatisfied.

D. Garcia. Good gods! was ever any thing invented with more artifice and difloyalty? Has all
that the malice of hell ever ftudied any thing fo
horrid as this perfidy? Could a more cruel method be found out to perplex a lover? Ah! how
well you know to employ my own weaknefs againft
me! and to manage for yourfelf the furprifing
ftrength of that fatal love which your traiterous eyes
gave birth to! Becaufe fhe is furprized, and cannot excufe herfelf, fhe cunningly offers me a pardon. Her diffembled gentlenefs forges an amufe-
ment to divert the effect of my wrath; and by
means of the intricate knot of an election, would
ward off the blow that threatens a villainous traitor. Yes, madam, your artifices would gladly deprive me of that infight which would condemn you;
and your foul, pretending to be quite innocent, refufes to demonftrate itfelf fully, but upon fuch conditions, you think, as I will never accept; but you
are deceived if you think to furprize me. Yes,
yes, I am refolved to fee what you have to defend
yourfelf by; and what prodigy can juftify what I
have feen, and condemn my indignation.

Elvira. Remember that by this choice you cut
off all pretenfions to the heart of Donna Elvira.

D. Garcia. Be it fo, I agree to it all: in the
condition I am in I pretend to nothing farther.

Elvira. You will repent of the noife you have made.

D. Garcia. No, no, thefe are foolifh ftories, and I ought rather to tell you that fome-body elfe may foon repent of it. The traitor, whoever he be, fhall find it not eafy to efcape my rage with his life.

Elvira. This is too much, it cannot be born, my irritated heart can no longer preferve it's foolifh good nature. Let us leave the ungrateful villain to his caprice; and fince he will perifh, let him.
Eliza. [To Don Garcia.] You will force me to this difcovery, but I will let you fee the affront you put upon me.

S C E N E IX.

E L V I R A, D. G A R C I A, E L I Z A.

TEIL the lovely perfon to come forth—Go, you know my meaning, defire it as from me.
D. Garcia. And can I——
Elvira. Patience, you fhall be fatisfied.
Eliza afide going out.] Without doubt this is fome new touch of jealoufy.

Elvira. Take care at leaft that this noble indignation of yours perfeveres to the end; and above all, think well for the future at what price you would needs have your fufpicions cleared up.

S C E N E   X.

E L V I R A, D. G A R C I A, A G N E S A, E L I-
Z-A, D. A L V A R E Z.

ELVIRA to D. Garcia, shewing him Agnesa.

THERE, thanks to heaven, is what occasioned your obliging suspicions: behold that
face, and see if you do not observe the features of
Donna Agnesa.

D. Garcia. O heavens!

Elvira. If the rage which disturbs your soul does
at the same time hinder your sight; you have other
eyes to consult which will leave you no room to
doubt. Her death was a necessary piece of craftiness invented to avoid the authority of one who
persecuted her, and under this disguise she concealed herself, the better to enjoy the fruit of
her feigned death. [To Agnesa.] · You will forgive me, madam, if I have been forced to betray
your secrets, and act contrary to your expectation.
His temerity is so very great that he deprives my
actions of all manner of liberty, and my honour,
urged by his suspicions, is constantly reduced to a
necessity of defending itself. Our embracing each
other, which this jealous man accidentally saw, has
made him wreak his indignation on me. This
was the reason of his rage and my disgrace. [To
D. Garcia.] Now, like an absolute tyrant, enjoy
the discovery you would needs make. But know
that I will never blot from my memory the base
insult you have been guilty of. And if ever I forget my oaths, may heaven pour it's severest chas-
tisements upon my head; may a thunderbolt re-

duce me to aſhes when I reſolve to admit your
love.   Come, madam, let us depart, and avoid
this furious monſter; let us ſly from his infecti‑
ous looks and the eﬀects of his rage, and think of
nothing elſe but how to free ourſelves from his hands.

Agneſa to D. Garcia.] Even virtue itſelf, my
lord, has been wronged by the unjuſt violence of
your ſuſpicions.

S C E N E   XI.

D. G A R C I A, D. A L V A R E Z.

D. G A R C I A.

WHAT a cruel gleam of light diſſipates
my miſtake, and at the ſame time involves
my ſenſes in ſo profound an horror, that I can per‑
ceive nothing but the diſmal object of a remorſe
that kills me! Ah! Don Alvarez, I ſee you were
in the right; but hell has breathed it's curſed ve‑
nom into my ſoul, and by a fatal ſtroke of extreme
rigour, my greateſt enemy is within myſelf.   To
what end is it to love with the moſt ardent paſſion
that ever a conſumed ſoul diſcovered, if by reaſon
of it's tranſports, with which I am ſo much tor‑
mented, that love continually renders itſelf hate‑
worthy?   I muſt, I muſt revenge with my juſt
death, the offence I have committed againſt her
heavenly charms: what counſel can I follow! A‑
las! I have loſt the object for which alone life was
deſirable; If I were able to renounce the hope of
enjoying her, I can much more renounce life itſelf.

D. Alvarez. My lord————

D. Garcia. No, Don Alvarez, my death is
neceſſary; no endeavours ſhall turn me from it;

but at the fame time I muſt do ſome ſignal ſervice
to Elvira.   For this end, I will ſeek ſome glorious
means of ending my days, ſo that when I expire
for her ſhe may pity me, and ſay that my too great
love was the occaſion of my offending her.   My
hand muſt by a bold attempt give the death due
to Moorgat, and boldly prevent the blow that Caſtile threatens him with: thus, in my death, I ſhall
have the happineſs of ſnatching ſo great a glory from
my rival's hopes.

D. Alvarez. A piece of ſuch valuable ſervice,
my lord, may well make your offence be forgot,
but to hazard——

D. Garcia. Let me go then, that I may make
my deſpair ſubſervient to this glorious attempt, by
the performance of a juſt duty.

A C T V.   S C E N E I.

D. A L V A R E Z, E L I Z A.

D. A L V A R E Z.

MY maſter Don Garcia has formed a deſign,
the like of which was never heard of; deſpair
put him upon a new reſolution, which was to go and
ſacrifice Moorgat, aſſuring himſelf ſucceſs, and hoping in his death to find a pardon, and prevent the mortification of beholding his rival a ſharer of that glory.
As he was going out of theſe gates, unhappy ti-
dings came to him, that that rival had already obtained the honour he was going to ſnatch from him,
and had ſacrificed the traitor.   In reward for which
ſervice it is publicly ſaid that Don Alphonſo intends to give him his ſiſter in marriage; which is

not incredible, fince it was he that opened him a
way to the throne..

Eliza. Yes, Elvira has heard this news, and has
alfo had it confirmed by Don Louis, who writes her
word, that Leon is now waiting for the happy return of her and Don Alphonfo, and that fhe is there
to receive a fortunate turn; an hufband from the
hands of her brother. It is plain enough from
thefe words of his letter that Don Silvio is the hufband fhe is to have.

D. Alvarez. This blow to the prince's heart——

Eliza. Will without doubt ftrike deep: I cannot help pitying his diftrefs, and yet, if I have
any judgment, he has ftill a very good intereft in
her he has injured. I cannot find, notwithftanding the fuccefs which is boafted of, that the princefs fhewed very great fatisfaction at the news of
her brother's coming, or with the letter; but——

SCENE II.

ELVIRA, AGNESA, ELIZA, D. ALVAREZ.

ELVIRA.

DON Alvarez, tell the prince to come hither.
Allow me, madam, to fpeak to him in your
prefence concerning this accident which furprizes
my foul; and do not accufe me of too hafty a
change, if I lay afide my refentment againft him.
His unforefeen misfortune has extinguifhed it. He
is miferable enough, without the addition of my
hatred. Heaven, who thus rigoroufly treats him,
has but too well executed the oaths I have made.
I was obliged by the fentence of offended honour,
never to be his; but fince I fee fate is too fevere

to his love, the ill fuccefs of what he does in
my favour cancels the offence, and reftores him my
compaffion. Yes, fuch rough blows have feverely
revenged me, difarmed my indignation, and now,
by a compaffionate care, I am feeking to comfort
the misfortunes of a wretched lover; and I believe
his flame has well deferved that compaffion I would
fhew.

Agnefa. Madam, they would be in the wrong,
who fhould blame the tender fentiments you are
infpired with, what he has done for you—he comes,
and how much he is aftonifhed with this amazing
ftroke plainly appears by the palenefs of his face.

S C E N E III.

D. GARCIA, ELVIRA, AGNESA, ELIZA.

D. GARCIA.

HOW muft I appear before you, madam,
whom I have—

Elvira. No more of that, Don Garcia; your
deftiny has made a change in my heart; and confidering the difmal condition its rigour has thrown
you in, my wrath is appeafed, and your peace is
made. Yes, though you have deferved what heaven has afflicted you with, though your jealous fufpicions have fullied my fame with moft incredible
indignities, yet I cannot but own that I pity your
misfortune to that degree as to be fomewhat difpleafed with our fuccefs. I defpife the favours of
that fervice, when my heart muft be facrificed to
reward it, and I could wifh it were in my power
to redeem the moments when deftiny made me
curfe you fo much. But in fhort, you know that

it is the fate of such as we, to be ever chained down to the public interests, and that heaven has ordained that the brother, who is concerned in the disposal of my hand, is also my sovereign. Yield as I do, prince, to this violence, to which those of my birth are subject; and if the uneasinesses of your love be great, let it comfort itself with the share that I have therein, and not make use of the power which your valour gives you in this place against this surprizing stroke; it would undoubtedly be an act unworthy of you to struggle against fate; and when it is to no purpose to oppose one's self to its rage, a ready submission shews a greatness of soul. Therefore make no resistance, but set wide the gates of Astorga to my brother, who is coming; let me render him those rights which he has a pretence to from me, and which I am resolved not to fail in; and perhaps that fatal homage which, contrary to my inclination, I offer him, may not go so far as you think.

D. Garcia. You are too good, madam, in endeavouring to sweeten the bitter draught that is prepared for me; you may, without any such reluctance, suffer the cruel thunder of your whole duty to fall on me. I have nothing to say, in the condition I am in, to you. The most severe punishments which have been invented are not too severe for me; and I know that I should be in the wrong to murmur at any thing that may befal me. Alas! in what manner could I authorize the boldness of the least complaint against you? my love has numberless times been guilty of outrages, and rendered itself hateful to you, and when, by a just sacrifice, my arm was preparing to do some service to your family, my stars abandoned me, and made

me taſte the bitter grief of being prevented by my
rival's arm.   After this, madam, I can pretend to
nothing, I deſerve the blow which I expect, and I
ſee it coming, without daring to tempt the favourable aid of your heart againſt it.   What remains
for me in this my utmoſt infelicity, is to ſeek a remedy in myſelf; and by a death propitious to my
wiſhes deliver my troubled heart from all its woes.
Yes, Don Alphonſo will ſoon be in this place, and
my rival already begins to appear.   He ſeems to
have flown hither from Leon, to receive the re-
compence of a ſacrificed tyrant.   Fear not that a-
ny reſiſtance ſhall ſhew the power I have here;
there is no human force which I would not defy
for your ſafety, if you gave me your conſent to do
it; but I dare not preſume to expect that glorious
conſent, I who needs muſt appear ſo deſpicable to
you, and I would not, by vain efforts, throw the
leaſt obſtacle in the way of your juſt deſigns.   No,
madam, I do not in the leaſt conſtrain your ſentiments; I will leave you in full liberty, I will o-
pen the gates of Aſtorga to that victorious happy
prince, and patiently undergo the laſt cruelty of
my fate.

S C E N E IV.

E L V I R A, A G N E S A, E L I Z A.

E L V I R A.

IMAGINE not, madam, that the deſpair which
his deſtiny expoſes him to is the occaſion of
my uneaſineſs.   You will be juſt to me, if you
believe that your intereſt has no ſmall ſhare in the

grief with which my heart is difturbed. I am no lefs fenfible of friendfhip than of love, and if I complain of any dire difgrace, it is that the dreadful wrath of heaven has from me borrowed thofe fhafts it lances againft you, and has rendered my eyes guilty of a flame which gives unworthy treatment to the goodnefs of your heart.

Agnefa. This, madam, is an accident which your eyes ought not to be angry with heaven for. If my weak attractions have expofed me to the ill fortune of having to do with an inconftant, heaven could not better alleviate that misfortune, than by making ufe of you to deprive me of that heart; I ought not at all to be afhamed of an inconftancy which demonftrates the difference between your attractions and mine. If I figh for this change, it is becaufe I forefee it fatal to your wifhes, and in this grief which my friendfhip excites in me, I blame my want of merit in your behalf, not being able to retain an heart, the image whereof fo much difturbs your defires.

Elvira. Rather accufe yourfelf of that unjuft filence, which has concealed the underftanding there was between you two; this fecret, had it been fooner known, might, perhaps, have fpared both of us thefe uneafy troubles, and my juft coldnefs toward him might, in their birth, have ftifled the defires of a rover, and fent back—

Agnefa. Madam, he is coming.

Elvira. You may remain here, without looking at him. Do not go away, madam, but ftay, and be a witnefs to what I fhall fay to him.

Agnefa. I confent, madam, yet I very well know, that were another in my place they would avoid fuch a converfation.

Elvira. You will not have the least reason to be ſorry at it, madam, if the gods ſecond my wiſhes, I aſſure you.

SCENE V.

ALPHONSO, ELVIRA, AGNES.

ELVIRA.

I Beg, my lord, that you would attend to what I am going to ſay, before you ſpeak. Fame has already brought to our ears the news of your victorious atchievements, and I admire, as all do, at the ſpeedy and happy turn which they have given to our deſtiny. I know very well that a ſervice of ſo much importance can never receive a reward adequate to its deſerts, and that every thing is due to you for the immortal exploits which replaces my brother on the throne of his anceſtors. But tho' he offers you the homages of his heart, make a generous uſe of your advantages; and ſuffer not, my lord, this glorious blow to bring me under an imperious yoke. Do not allow your love, which knows what intereſt I eſpouſe, obſtinately to triumph over a juſt refuſal. Do not permit my brother to begin his reign by an act of tyranny over his ſiſter: Leon has abundance of rewards, which may do more honour to your high valour; an heart forcibly given you, would be too mean a preſent for your virtues. Can a man ever be ſatisfied in himſelf when, by conſtraint, he obtains what he loves? It is a woful advantage, and a generous lover diſdains to be happy upon ſuch conditions. He will not owe any thing to that violence which the right of birth exerciſes over our hearts, and is al-

ways too zealous for the object he loves, ever to
suffer it to be sacrificed to it as a victim. Not that
this heart of mine intends to reserve that for another's merit, which it refuses to yours. No, my
lord, I will promise you no person shall ever have
power over me, a sacred retreat shall to every other
pursuit—

D. Alphonso. Madam, I have been very attentive to all that you have said, and would, by two
words, have prevented it all, if your false alarm had
prevailed less over you. I know that a common
report which is generally believed, ascribes to me
the glory of having slain the tyrant, but in short,
the people alone, as we are informed, being stirred
up by Don Louis to do their duty, bore away the
honour of that heroic act, which I was reported to
be the author of. The cause of which was this: Don
Louis, the better to carry on his noble designs, had
caused it to be reported, that I and my men had
seized the city, and by this news he pushed on the
people to cut off the usurper as soon as possible.
He knew how to conduct the whole by his prudence and zeal, and has just now sent one of his
servants to inform me of the whole affair. But at
the same time reveals me a secret, at which I dare
say you will be as much surprized as I was. You
expect a brother, and Leon its true master, and
now heaven presents him to your eyes. Yes, I am
Don Alphonso, and being preserved and bred up
under the name of the Prince of Castile, a man illustrious effect of that sincere friendship, which was
between Don Louis and the king my father. Don
Louis has all the proofs of this secret, and will difplay the truth of it to every body; and now my
thoughts are taken up with other cares; not that

they are croffed with refpect to your love, that my paffion quarrels with fuch a difcovery, and that the brother, in my heart, is troublefome to the lover. My flame has received, without the leaft murmur, from this fecret, the change which nature prefcribes to it, and the blood which conjoins us has fo entirely detached me from the affection for you with which my heart was touched, that it now longs for nothing fo much as the pleafing tranfports of its firft chain, and the means of rendering to the amiable Agnefa that which her exceffive goodnefs has deferved. But her uncertain deftiny renders mine miferable, and if all be true that is faid, in vain does Leon invite me, in vain does a throne wait for me; it is not in the power of a throne to make me happy; it has no other charms to me, than as it would let me tafte the joy of placing it on that object that heaven has recalled me to, and by that means to repair, as much as poffible, the injury I have done her noble virtues. It is from you, madam, I have reafon to expect to be informed what has become of her. Pray inftruct me in it, and by your difcourfe either render me for ever happy, or miferable.

Elvira. Be not furprized if I delay anfwering you; for this news, my lord, confounds me. I will not take upon me to fay whether Agnefa be dead or alive, but this gentleman here, than whom fhe cannot have a more faithful friend, will give you fuch information as you may depend upon.

D. Alphonfo knowing Agnefa.] Ah! madam, how happy am I in thefe perplexities to fee the gleaming of your heavenly charms! But with what eye can you behold an inconftant, whofe crime——

Agnefa. Ah! fay not that a heart which I e-
fteem could be inconftant. I cannot bear the
thought, and the excufe troubles me. Nothing
could offend me, fince you loved this princefs, becaufe her high merit is a fufficient excufe for any
ardour fhe might caufe. The love you bore her
does not make you in any wife guilty with refpect
to me; but had it been otherwife, know that you
would in vain endeavour to make me forget fuch
an affront, and that no force, no repentance fhould
be able to cancel it in my heart.

Elvira. Ah! dear brother, the joy you give me
is infinite, I love your choice, and blefs the accident which caufes you to crown fo pure a friendfhip, and of two noble hearts that I dearly love—

SCENE THE LAST.

D. GARCIA, ELVIRA, AGNESA, D. ALPHONSO, ELIZA.

D. GARCIA.

LET me not behold, madam, your great con-
tentment, but fuffer me to die in full per-
fuafion that your duty is what commits fome violence upon you. I know you have it in your power to difpofe of yourfelf, and I do not defire to oppofe your inclinations; I am all obedience. But
I muft own your gaiety amazes me, and fhakes my
refolution. It tranfports me fo much, that I am
afraid I fhall not be able to command. I would
punifh myfelf if it would deprive me of that fubmiffive refpect, which is owing to you. Yes, your
commands have made me bear patiently the mifery of my love; they are fo powerful, that I would

rather die than difobey them. Still I am fhocked at your prefent joy, and cannot fee it without concern; the moft prudent people cannot anfwer for their conduct on fuch occafions. I beg you may for a moment fupprefs your joy, and fhew fome compaffion for my misfortune. I cannot bear to fee the happinefs of a rival. I think this the fmalleft favour I can afk, as my difgrace gives place to another lover. I do not defire it, madam, for a long time. My abfence will fatisfy your wifhes. I fhall go where I fhall only hear the account of your marriage by report, which will induce me to haften the end of an unhappy life.

Agnefa. Suffer me, my lord, to blame your complaining, as the princefs has compaffion for your misfortunes. The joy at which you are difpleafed arifes intirely from the good which is prepared for you. Your profperity gives her pleafure, and fhe has found in your rival a brother. The fecret is juft now difcovered; this is Don Alphonfo, who has been fo much talked of.

D. Alphonfo. Thank heaven, my heart has all that it defires, after a long fuffering, without abridging your happinefs, and has the greater pleafure from being able to affift your love.

D. Garcia. Your exceffive goodnefs, my lord, in offering to bear a part in my wifhes, confounds me: heaven has diverted the ftroke I dreaded, and any other perfon would imagine himfelf happy. But the lucky difcovery of this pleafing fecret makes me blameable towards the adorable object of my love; having fallen again into thefe treacherous fufpicions, which I have been fo often warned of to no purpofe, I fhould defpair of ever being happy. I deferve her hatred, and do not deferve a pardon; whatever fuccefs fortune may give me, I deferve death, and expect it alone.

Elvira. No, no, prince, my pity is moved by your forrow and fubmiffion. I can perceive your fincere love fhine through all your actions; I fee the weaknefs of my oaths; fince the influence of the heavens is the caufe of your defects, we fhould indulge them a little, and whether jealous or not, my king may give me to you without force.

D. Garcia. Good heavens, enable me to bear the joy this confeffion gives me.

D. Alphonfo. I beg, my lord, that this marriage may for ever join our hearts and kingdoms, after all our vain debates; but time preffes, and Leon expects us, therefore let us go and chearfully fatisfy its zeal, and give the laft ftroke to the tyrant's party by our prefence.

T H E   E N D.

T H E

SCHOOL FOR HUSBANDS.

A

C O M E D Y.

E 3

COMEDY

The SCHOOL *for* HUSBANDS, *a Comedy of Three Acts, acted at Paris, at the Theatre of the Palace-Royal, June 24th, 1661.*

THE Comedy of the SCHOOL for HUSBANDS is so copious, so polished, and so simple, that few pieces, especially of three acts, can be put in competition with it; a fresh incident appears in every scene, which are artfully unfolded, and infensibly lead to one of the most excellent cataftrophe's that ever appeared upon the French ftage. The hint of this comedy is taken from the Adelphi of Terence; in which two old men, of oppofite humours, one an uncle, and the other a father, gave a very different education, the one to his nephew, and the other to his fon. In the SCHOOL for HUSBANDS are two guardians; one of an indulgent temper, the other of a rigid one, each of whom are intrufted with the education of a young girl. Moliere has improved upon Terence, in giving to his two charaɛters not only the concern of fathers, but of lovers alfo, an intereft fo rare and lively, that it forms an entire new piece upon the ancient poet's fimple plan.

A C T O R S.

SGANAREL, ⎫
ARISTO,   ⎬ Brothers.

ISABELLA, ⎫
LEONORA,   ⎬ Sisters.

VALERE, Lover to Isabella.
LISETTA, Leonora's Waiting Woman.
ERGASTE, Valere's Footman.
A COMMISSARY.
A NOTARY.
TWO VALETS.

SCENE, a public place in Paris.

THE

SCHOOL FOR HUSBANDS.

ACT I. SCENE I.

SGANAREL, ARISTO.

SGANAREL.

I BEG we may not talk fo much, brother, but let each of us live according to his own manner of thinking; notwithftanding you are older, and may be wifer, I will not be reproved by you, my fancy alone fhall direct me.

Arifto. But your manner of living is condemned by every body.

Sganarel. Yes, brother, by fools like yourfelf.

Arifto. I am obliged to you for this kind compliment.

Sganarel. Since all muft be difcovered, I would gladly know what there is in me for thefe fine cavillers to find fault with.

Arifto. That morofe temper, which avoids all pleafures of fociety, gives a whimfical air to all

E 5

your actions, and makes yourfelf and every thing about you appear barbarous.

Sganarel. Do you think I would make myfelf a flave to fashion? Certainly I fhould drefs myfelf for my own pleafure; you would by your trifling ftories, Mr. Elder Brother, (for, to be plain, fo you are by twenty years) perfuade me into the fafhions of young fops; infift upon my wearing thofe fmall hats, which allow their weak brains to evaporate, and the large powdered bufhy wigs, which darken the figure of a human countenance; thofe jerkins but juft below the arms, and large bands hanging down, very long fleeves to dip in the fauce at table, and petticoats in imitation of breeches; thofe hand-fome fhoes dreffed out with ribbons, which appear like rough-footed pigeons, and thofe large rollers, where the captive legs are confined every morn-ing, as if they were in the ftocks, and which make thofe fine gentlemen walk with a ftrad-dle, as if they were flying?— It would undoubt-edly give you great pleafure to fee me dreffed out in the manner as I obferve you always do.

Arifto. One fhould not make themfelves parti-cular, but comply with the majority. An extreme on either fide is offenfive; no wife man fhould have any thing affected either in his words or cloaths, but follow what is introduced by cuftom. One fhould not imitate people who are fo fond of being in extremes, that they would be uneafy if another perfon were a ftep beyond them. But I think it wrong upon one's fingle opinion obftinate-ly to avoid what every other perfon does; it is cer-tainly better to be among the number of fools, than fo be the only one the reverfe of every other perfon.

Sganarel. This is the opinion of an old fellow, who conceals grey hairs under a black periwig, to impofe himfelf upon the world for younger than he really is.

Arifto. It is very odd that you muft always upbraid me with my age, and rail againft decency as well as chearfulnefs, as if old people were to think of the grave only, and not enjoy the pleafures of this world at all: old age is attended with difagreeable circumftances enough, without being flovenly and ill-tempered.

Sganarel. I am refolved to make no alteration in my drefs, be it as it will. I will have a hat with a brim for to fhelter my head, a long doublet, buttoned clofe as it fhould be, to keep the ftomach warm for digeftion; a pair of breeches made to fit my thighs, and fhoes that will not pinch my toes, fuch as wife people wore formerly, in fpite of the fafhion; and whoever does not like my drefs may clofe his eyes.

S C E N E II.

LEONORA, ISABELLA, LISETTA, ARISTO and SGANAREL whifpering together at the further part of the ftage, without being feen.

LEONORA to Ifabella.

I WILL take it all upon me to prevent your being found fault with.

Lifetta to Ifabella.] What, always in a room without being feen by any body?

Ifabella. Such is his temper.

Leonora. I pity you for it, fifter.

Lifetta to Leonora.] It is lucky for you, madam, that his brother is quite of a different temper; and fate was very kind to you in throwing you into the hands of a reasonable man.

Isabella. It is a miracle, that he has not locked me up, or taken me with him to-day.

Lisetta. Faith I would send him to the devil with his ruff, and——

Sganarel being run against by Lisetta.] By your favour, whither are you going?

Leonora. We do not know yet; I was advising my sister to walk out and enjoy the benefit of this fine weather. But——

Sganarel, to Leonora.] For your part, you may go where you will; [*pointing to Lisetta.*] you have nothing to do but ramble, both of you together; [*to Isabella.*] but as for you, madam, if you please, I desire you may not go.

Aristo. Ah! brother, let us give them leave to go and entertain themselves.

Sganarel. I am your servant, brother.

Aristo. Young people would——

Sganarel. Young people are foolish, and old ones too sometimes.

Aristo. Do you think there is any harm in her going with Leonora.

Sganarel. No, but I would rather have her stay with me.

Aristo. But——

Sganarel. But her actions shall be under my direction: in short, I know it is my interest to take care of them.

Aristo. Am I less concerned in those of her sister?

Sganarel. Alas! every one judges and acts as he chuses. They have no relations, and our friend, their father, in his laft moments, committed the care of them to us, defiring us to marry them our-felves, or if that was not agreeable, to difpofe of them to others at a proper age; by this contract he chofe to give us over them from their child-hood the authority of father and hufband. You took the care of bringing up one, and I the other: you manage your charge as you think proper, pray let me do the fame.

Arifto. I think—

Sganarel. I think, and will fpeak it freely, that I talk right upon this fubject. You fuffer yours to flaunt about taudry and fine:—I am fatisfied. Let her jaunt about, love idlenefs, allow coxcombs to pay compliments to her;— with all my heart:—but I am determined mine fhall live as I pleafe, and not have her own will; fhe fhall be dreffed in a de-cent ftuff gown, wear black on holidays, go little abroad, but prudently apply herfelf to houfewife-ry; at her fpare hours mend my linen, or for her entertainment knit ftockings; fhe fhall not hear the flattery of fops, nor go abroad without fome-body to take care of her: in fhort, the flefh is weak, I know what is faid concerning thefe matters, and will not wear horns if I can avoid it; and as it is her fate to marry me, I will be as fure of her per-fon as my own.

Ifabella. You have no reafon, I believe—

Sganarel. Be filent; I will let you know whe-ther you are to go abroad without me.

Leonora. What then, Sir,—

Sganarel. Lord, madam, no words; I do not talk to you, for you are too wife.

Leonora. Are you angry to fee Ifabella with us?

Sganarel. Why really yes, you spoil her for me. Your visits here displease me, and you will oblige me if you will make no more of them.

Leonora. Must I also tell you my real sentiments? I do not know how she puts up with this; but I know what effect suspicion would have on me; and though both one woman's daughters, we can hardly be sisters, if your usual behaviour induces her to love you.

Lisetta. So many cautions are shameful: are we in Turkey, to be locked up? It is said women are kept like slaves there, and that those people are accursed of heaven on that account. Our honour is very weak indeed, if it is necessary to watch it continually: do you think you can prevent our intentions by these precautions? No, no, the utmost craftiness is to no purpose when we take any thing into our head; upon my word, the best way is to confide in us. Confinement puts our inventions on the stretch, and he that takes it in hand brings himself into great danger, for our honour is always for guarding itself. When we are so carefully watched, we have the greater desire to do imprudent things; and were I restrained by a husband, I would be vastly inclined to realize his suspicions.

Sganarel to Aristo.] This is your manner of education, good Mr. Teacher; and you can bear it without being concerned.

Aristo. One should only laugh at what she says, brother; yet there is reason in it. Her sex loves liberty, and will not be kept from it by severity; bolts and grates, and distrustful cares will not make virtuous wives or girls; it is not authority, but honour, that will keep them to their duty. A woman, who is prudent by force only, is a ftrange thing indeed. It is to no purpofe to attempt to govern their actions; in my opinion the heart muft be gained; and with all poffible care, I fhould not think my honour very fafe in the hands of a perfon, who wants only an opportunity of tranfgreffing amongft the affaults of temptation.

Sganarel. It is all nonfenfe.

Arifto. Well, be it fo; but it is my opinion, that young people fhould always be inftructed with good humour; their failings fhould be reproved with meeknefs, and the name of virtue not made terrible to them. By thefe maxims I have guided my cares for Leonora; I have always complied with her youthful defires, and have not looked upon fmall liberties as criminal; and it gives me pleafure that I have no reafon to repent of my indulgence. I have introduced her into genteel company, allowed her to attend balls, plays, and all diverfions, which I think neceffary to form the minds of young people; in my opinion, the world is a fchool, which teaches the ways of life better than can be taught by books. She takes pleafure in fpending money upon fafhionable cloaths and linen; what would you have me do? Thefe pleafures fhould be granted to young women, when one can afford it; and I am willing to gratify her wifhes. She is obliged to marry me by her father's defire, but I never will be a tyrant to her. I am fenfible that there is no equality in our ages, therefore I give her her own choice; and if a great deal of tendernefs, polite refpect, and a thoufand pounds a-year, can in her opinion make up for the difference in age, fhe may have me for a hufband; if not, let her pleafe herfelf; if fhe can be happier with another perfon, I fhall agree to it: it will give me more pleafure to fee her happy with another, than to be poffeffed of her againft her inclination.

Sganarel. He is all fweetnefs.

Arifto. Indeed it is my temper, and I am thankful for it; I will never follow thofe rigid rules which induce children to wifh their parents dead.

Sganarel. But liberties of youth are not eafily laid afide, and you will not be of the fame way of thinking when her manner of living is changed.

Arifto. And why muft it be changed?

Sganarel. Why?

Arifto. Yes, why fhould it?

Sganarel. I cannot tell.

Arifto. Is there any thing in it to hurt a perfon's honour?

Sganarel. And if you marry her, will fhe pretend to the fame liberties which fhe took while fhe was unmarried?

Arifto. Why fhould fhe not?

Sganarel. Will you be fo complaifant as to allow her ribbons and patches?

Arifto. Undoubtedly.

Sganarel. Allow her to attend all balls and affemblies like a mad creature?

Arifto. Certainly.

Sganarel. And fhall the beaux come to your houfe?

Arifto. And what then?

Sganarel. To make merry, and give entertainments?

Arifto. I confent to it.

Sganarel. And fhall your wife hear their fine fpeeches?

Aristo. Ay.

Sganarel. And you will behold these coxcombs visits in such a manner, as may shew you do not in the least regard them?

Aristo. Certainly.

Sganarel. Go, you are an old fool.—[to Isabella.] Get you in, that you may not hear this infamous conduct.

S C E N E III.

A R I S T O, S G A N A R E L, L E O N O R A,
L I S E T T A.

A R I S T O.

I WILL commit myself to the fidelity of my wife, and intend always to live as I have done.

Sganarel. How greatly will I be rejoiced when he is made a cuckold!

Aristo. I cannot tell to what fortune I am born; but I know, that for your part, if you fail to be one, the fault must not be laid on you, for you have used every precaution to avoid it.

Sganarel. Laugh on, giggler; O what a pleasure it must give one to see a buffoon of almost sixty.

Leonora. I engage to preserve him from the fate you talk of, if I marry him; he may assure himself of it: but know that my heart would be answerable for nothing, was I to be your wife.

Lisetta. There is a conscience due to those who confide in us; but it is delightful, really, to cheat such people as you.

Sganarel. Be gone with your foolish ill-bred tongue.

Aristo. You bring this ridicule upon yourself, brother. Farewell, alter your temper, and be fore-warned, that locking up a wife is the worst step you can take.—Your servant.

Sganarel. I am not your's.

SCENE IV.

SGANAREL alone.

O HOW excellently they are all suited one to another! what a hopeful family; a foolish old dotard, who acts the fop in a crazy worn-out carcase, a girl that is mistress, the arrantest coquet that can be, and impertinent servants!————No, not even wisdom herself could bring it about, she would be destitute of all sense and reason to endeavour the regulation of such a family————Isabella may lose those principles of honour she has imbibed with me amongst such acquaintance; and, in order to prevent this misfortune, I intend shortly to send her back again to my cabbages and my turkies.

SCENE V.

VALERE, SGANAREL, ERGASTE.

Valere at the further part of the stage.

THERE is the Argus that I detest, Ergaste; the rigid guardian of her I love.

Sganarel thinking himself alone.] Is not the corruption of manners now-a-days very astonishing?

Valere. I will speak to him, if I can, and endeavour to get acquainted with him.

Sganarel. Inftead of feeing that feverity prevail, of which in former times virtue fo properly confifted, the young people hereabouts, debauched, without reftraint, do not take——

Valere. He does not perceive that we are bowing to him.

Ergafte. His blind eye is on this fide, perhaps; let us get to the right fide of him.

Sganarel. I muft leave this place.—A city life can only produce in me the——

Valere approaching him.] I muft endeavour to gain admittance to his houfe.

Sganarel hearing a noife.] How! I thought I heard a voice—in the country, heaven be praifed, I am not plagued with thefe fafhionable fooleries.

Ergafte to Valere.] Go up to him.

Sganarel ftill hearing a noife.] What would he be at? my ears tingle.—There, all the amufements of our young women are——[*Seeing Valere bow.*] Is that to me?

Ergafte. Go nearer.

Sganarel not minding Valere.] Here no coxcomb comes.— [*Valere bows again.*] What the deuce!—[*Turns and fees Ergafte bow on the other fide.*] Again?—What mean thefe bows?

Valere. Accofting you in this manner, Sir, interrupts you, perhaps?

Sganarel. May be fo.

Valere. But why fo? I was fo much delighted with the honour of your acquaintance, that I defired vaftly to pay my refpects to you.

Sganarel. Be it fo.

Valere. To wait on you, and assure you, without any dissimulation that I am wholly at your service.

Sganarel. I believe so.

Valere. I am so fortunate as to be one of your neighbours, for which I am thankful to my happy destiny.

Sganarel. That is well done.

Valere. Have you heard the news, Sir, which is current at court, and thought to be true?

Sganarel. What does it concern me?

Valere. True; however, a man, sometimes, may be curious after novelties. Will you go, Sir, and see the grand preparations for the birth of our Dauphin?

Sganarel. If I think fit.

Valere. Paris, we own, affords us numberless amusements which are no where else. The country is a solitude in comparison. How do you pass away the time?

Sganarel. About my business.

Valere. The mind should have some relaxation; it flags by too earnest an attention to serious things. In what manner do you pass the evening before bed-time?

Sganarel. As I chuse.

Valere. Certainly; nothing could be said better; it is a reasonable answer, and good sense appears in never doing any thing but what one chuses. If I thought you was not too much taken up, I should come sometimes to your house, after supper, to pass away the time.

Sganarel. Your servant.

SCENE VI.

VALERE, ERGASTE.

VALERE.

WELL, what do you think of this whimsical fool?

Ergaste. He has a furly way of anfwering, and receives people very favagely.

Valere. Ah! how vexed I am!

Ergaste. At what?

Valere. At what?—It provokes me to fee her I love in the power of a barbarian, a watchful dragon, whofe feverity will not allow her the leaft liberty.

Ergaste. That makes for you, and on the effect of it your paffion muft build its fureft hopes. Know, for your encouragement, that a woman that is watched is half won, and the peevifhnefs of fathers and hufbands always forwards the bufinefs of lovers. I intrigue very little, it is my leaft accomplifhment, and I have not the leaft pretenfions to galantry: but I have affifted twenty of your fportfmen, who often faid, they were beft pleafed to meet with thofe churlifh hufbands, who never come home without grumbling, thofe fullen fellows, who without thought or reafon condemn the conduct of their wives in every thing, and haughtily affuming upon the name of hufband, fall out with them for nothing in the company of their admirers.—One knows, fay they, to make the beft of thefe advantages; and the lady's indignation at fuch kind of ufage, the foft complaining, the obliging condolence of the lover upon the occafion, afford an op-

portunity to pufh things far enough.   In fhort
the furlinefs of Ifabella's guardian is a circum
ftance fufficiently favourable for you.

Valere. I could never find the leaft opportuni
ty of converfing with her thefe four months that
have been in love with her.

Ergafte. Love quickens people's wits; though
it has little effect on yours: if I had been——

Valere. Why, what could you have done? wher
fhe is never to be feen without that brute, and
there are neither maids nor footmen in the houfe
whom I might influence to affift my paffion by the
flattering temptation of a reward.

Ergafte. Does fhe not know yet that you are in
love with her?

Valere. That is a matter which my heart is not
yet informed of; where-ever that churl has carried
the fair one, fhe has feen me continually after her
like a fhadow, and my looks have always endeavoured to declare to her the violence of my paffion.   My eyes have fpoke loudly to her; but who
can tell me whether they could make their language
be underftood?

Ergafte. That language, it is true, may fometimes prove unintelligible, if it has neither writing
nor fpeech for its interpreter.

Valere. What fhall I do to get out of this ex-
tream uneafinefs, and learn if the fair one knows
I love her?—Let me know by fome means.

Ergafte. That is what muft be contrived. Let
us go into your houfe a little, that we may confider of it better.

ACT II. SCENE I.

ISABELLA, SGANAREL.

SGANAREL.

YOU need go no farther, I know the house and person by the marks alone that you give me.

Isabella aside] Be favourable to me now, ye gods! and let the artful contrivance of an innocent passion succeed.

Sganarel. His name is Valere, I think you say people tell you?

Isabella. Yes, they told me so.

Sganarel. Go, be easy: get you in, and leave me to do it. I will go talk immediately to this young rake.

Isabella going.] The project I am now about is a very bold one for a young girl; but every considerate person will readily forgive me, when they know how severely I am treated.

SCENE II.

SGANAREL alone, knocking at the door, thinking it is Valere's.

LET us lose no time: this is the place.—Who is there?—Well, I am thinking.— Soho, I say, soho, somebody. I am not surprized, after this discovery, that he came thither just now in so complaifant a manner; but I will be expeditious, and his foolifh hope——

S C E N E III.

VALERE, SGANAREL, ERGASTE.

SGANAREL to Ergafte, who comes out haftily.

DEUCE take the lubberly afs, who plants himfelf like a poft directly before me, in order to throw me down.

Valere. Sir, I am forry for that——

Sganarel. Ah! it is you I look for.

Valere. Me, Sir?

Sganarel. Yes you; is not your name Valere?

Valere. Yes.

Sganarel. I come to fpeak with you, if you pleafe.

Valere. I fhall do all in my power to ferve you.

Sganarel. I am obliged to you, but I myfelf intend to do a good turn for you; and that is what brings me to your houfe.

Valere. To my houfe, Sir?

Sganarel. To your houfe; need you be fo aftonifhed at that?

Valere. I have great reafon to be fo, and the honour you do me is——

Sganarel. Pray talk no more of honour.

Valere. Will not you walk in?

Sganarel. There is no occafion for it.

Valere. Sir, pray go you firft.

Sganarel. No; I will not go a ftep farther.

Valere. I cannot hear you whilft you remain here.

Sganarel. I will not ftir.

Valere. Well, I muft fubmit:————Since the gentleman is refolved upon it, bring a chair hither, quickly.

Sganarel. I will talk ftanding.

Valere. Can I fuffer you in this manner!

Sganarel. Oh! it is a terrible force upon you!

Valere. Such rudenefs would be too inexcufable.

Sganarel. Nothing can be fo rude as not to pay attention to people that would fpeak to us.

Valere. I obey you then.

Sganarel. You cannot do better. [They ufe abundance of compliments about putting on their hats.] So much ceremony is needlefs.————Will you hear me?

Valere. Undoubtedly, and with a great deal of pleafure.

Sganarel. Anfwer me then;—Do you know that I am the guardian of a handfome young woman, called Ifabella, who lodges in this neighbourhood?

Valere. Yes.

Sganarel. If you know it, I need not inform you—but do you know likewife, that being fenfible of her charms, I am concerned for her in another manner than as a guardian, and that fhe is deftined to the honour of my bed?

Valere. No.

Sganarel. Then I inform you of that; and, that it is very fit you fhould not difturb her with your paffion.

Valere. Who, I, Sir?

Sganarel. Ay, you:—you need not diffemble.

Valere. Who told you that I had a paffion for her?

VOL. II.   F

Sganarel. People that one may believe.

Valere. But who, pray?

Sganarel. She herself.

Valere. She!

Sganarel. Ay, she: Is that saying enough?——
Like an honeft girl, that has loved me from her
infancy, she told me all, juft now; and more than
that, charged me to let you know, that fince she
has been followed every where by you, her heart,
which your purfuit exceedingly offends, has underftood but too well the language of your eyes;
that she very well knows your fecret wifhes; and
that it is giving yourfelf a needlefs trouble to endeavour at explaining a paffion farther, which is
contrary to that affection she referves for me.

Valere. Is it she, do you fay, that from herfelf
made you——

Sganarel. Ay,——come to give you this frank and
faithful account; and that having obferved the violent love which difturbs your mind, she would
have made known her intentions to you, if, under
fuch emotion of foul, she could have found any
body to fend this meffage by; but that, at laft,
the vexation of being under a ftrict confinement,
brought her to make ufe of me, to apprize you, as
I have told you, that her affection muft be granted to nobody but me; that you have ogled her long
enough, and that, if you have ever fo little underftanding, you will take fome other meafures.——
Adieu, till I fee you again——this is what I had to
tell you.

Valere low.] What think you of this adventure,
Ergafte?

Sganarel low afide.] He is greatly amazed.

Ergafte low to Valere.] 'Tis my opinion, there

is nothing in it to difpleafe you, but that fome fub-
tile myftery is concealed under it: and in fhort,
that this meffage does not come from one who
would deftroy the love fhe infpires in you.

Sganarel afide.] He takes it right.

Valere low to Ergafte.] You judge it to be myfterious.

Ergafte low.] Yes—but we are obferved by him;
let us get out of his fight.

S C E N E   IV.

S G A N A R E L alone.

HIS confufion plainly fhews that he expected no fuch meffage! But—let us call Ifabella; fhe fhews what effect education has upon
the mind.   So virtuous is fhe, that fhe is difpleafed at the very looks of a man.

S C E N E   V.

I S A B E L L A, S G A N A R E L.

ISABELLA to herfelf entering.

MY lover I am afraid does not underftand the
intention of my meffage, fo full he is of
my paffion; and fince I am fuch a prifoner, I will
run the rifque of another that may fpeak my meaning plainer.

Sganarel. Here I am returned.

Ifabella. Well.

Sganarel. Your meffage has had its full effect;
your man's bufinefs is done.   At firft he would
not confefs that his heart was fick with love, but
when I affured him I came from you, he was ftruck

immediately dumb and confounded, and I do not think he will come any more hither.

Ifabella. Ha! what do you fay? I very much apprehend the contrary, and that he is again cutting out more work for us.

Sganarel. What makes you think fo?

Ifabella. No fooner was you got out of doors, than, putting my head out at the window to take the air, I faw a young fellow at yonder turning, who came very furprifingly, to wifh me a good morning from that impertinent fellow, and flung a box directly into my chamber, in which was a letter fealed like a billet-doux.—I would immediately have thrown it back to him, but he was got to the end of the ftreet, and my heart fwells with vexation at it.

Sganarel. Obferve the cunning, the knavery!

Ifabella. It is my duty to fend back immediately the box and letter to this woeful lover, and I fhall want fomebody for that purpofe, for to make bold with you————

Sganarel. On the contrary, dearee, it convinces me the better of your affection and fidelity; my heart joyfully accepts the office, and I cannot exprefs how much you oblige me by it.

Ifabella. Take it then.

Sganarel. Well, let us fee what he could write to you.

Ifabella. O heavens! be fure not to open it.

Sganarel. For what reafon?

Ifabella. Would you give him the leaft occafion to imagine it was I?——A woman of honour ought always to avoid reading the letters a man fends her; the curiofity one then difcovers, fhews a fecret pleafure in hearing one's felf praifed; and I think it proper this letter fhould immediately be carried to him, fealed up as it is, that he may fo much the better learn how I hate him; that his paffion may not have the leaft hope henceforward, and no more attempt the like extravagance.

Sganarel. She has certainly reafon for what fhe fays.————Well, I am delighted with your virtue and difcretion.   I perceive that my inftructions are rooted in your foul: and, in a word, you fhew that you deferve to be my wife.

. Ifabella.   I would not, however, balk your curiofity: you have got the letter, and you may open it.

Sganarel. Alas: I have not the leaft curiofity; —no, your reafons are too good for that, and I am juft going to difcharge the truft you put in me; afterwards, I fhall ftep a little way to fpeak a word or two, and then return to make you eafy.

S C E N E · VI.

SGANAREL alone.

HOW happy am I in finding her fuch a prudent girl! She is a treafure of honour in my family! to take the glances of love for treafon, receive a billet-doux as a very great injury, and fend it back again to her gallant by me! I have a great defire to know, whether upon fuch an occafion my brother's damfel would have acted thus. Faith, girls are juft what they are taught to be—— Soho.   [Knocking at Valere's door.

F 3

SCENE VII.

SCANAREL, ERGASTE.

ERGASTE.

WHO is there?

Sganarel. Take this; and tell your mafter that he muſt not any more impertinently prefume to write letters and ſend them with golden boxes, and that Iſabella is very vexed at it. See, ſhe has not ſo much as opened it. He will find how much ſhe regards his paſſion, and what happy ſucceſs he ought to expect from it.

SCENE VIII.

VALERE, ERGASTE.

VALERE.

WHAT have you got from that peeviſh fellow?

Ergaſte. This letter, Sir, which, with this box, he pretends that Iſabella received from you, and about which, he ſays, ſhe is very angry. She ſends it back to you without ſo much as opening it; read it quickly, and let us ſee if I am miſtaken.

Valere reads.] " You will undoubtedly be ſur
" prized at this letter: and both the deſign of writ
" ing, and the manner of getting it to you, may be
" thought very raſh in me: but I find myſelf in a
" ſituation not to obſerve forms any longer. The
" juſt dread of a marriage wherewith I am threaten
" ed in ſix days, makes me run all riſques: and
" being reſolved to free myſelf by ſome means or

" other, I believe, that I ought rather to choose
" you than defpair. However, you need not think
" that you are wholly obliged to my evil deftiny:
" it is not the conftraint I am under that gives birth
" to the fentiments I have for you; but it is that
" which makes me difcover them, and forces me
" to pafs over thofe formalities which the decency
" of my fex requires. It depends on yourfelf a-
" lone to have me fpeedily yours, and I wait you
" till you fhew me what your love defigns, before
" I let you know the refolution I have taken: but
" above all, remember that time is preffing, and
" that half a word is enough for two hearts in
" love."

Ergafte. Well, Sir, is not this contrivance an o-
riginal? For a young creature, her underftanding
in this affair is not amifs. Who would imagine
her capable of thefe love ftratagems?

Valere. Ah! She is an amiable creature! This
ftroke of her wit and friendfhip even doubles my
paffion for her; and adds to the fentiments wherewith her beauty infpires me.

Ergafte. The ruffian is coming; confider what
you muft fay to him.

S C E N E IX.

SGANAREL, VALERE, ERGASTE.

SGANAREL thinking that he was alone.

OTHRICE and four time bleft be this e-
dict which prohibits extravagance in drefs!
The uneafinefs of hufbands will be no more fo grievous, and wives will now be limited in their demands.
Oh! how I am obliged to the king for this de-

crec! And, for the satisfaction of the said husbands, how I wish that coquettry was prohibited as well as laces and embroidery. I have bought the edict on purpose for Isabella to read to me; and that, for want of other employment, shall be our diversion by and by after supper. [seeing Valere.] Will you send love-letters wirh golden boxes again, Mr. Fribble? You surely thought to find some young coquette, fond of intrigues, and easily melted down by flattery; but you see with what an air your presents are received; and be assured, it is spending your powder to kill sparrows. She is discreet; she loves me; and she is affronted at your passion; away, bag and baggage, therefore, and form your designs elsewhere.

Valere. Ay, indeed, Sir, your merit, to which every body yields, is too powerful an obstacle to my addresses; and however sincere my passion be for Isabella, it is in vain to contend with you.

Sganarel. It is true, it is a folly.

Valere. Nor should I have devoted my heart to the pursuit of her beauty, could I have foreseen that this miserable heart should find a rival so formidable as you.

Sganarel. I believe it.

Valere. I now, Sir, yield to you, without murmuring, as I can no longer hope for any favour.

Sganarel. You do well.

Valere. Reason will have it so; for you are so virtuous, that I should be in the wrong to behold with an angry eye the tender sentiments Isabella has for you.

Sganarel. That is to be supposed.

Valere. Yes, yes, I yield to you. But, Sir, I beseech you, (and it is the only favour a wretched lover begs, whofe prefent torment you are the fole reafon of:) I conjure you then, to affure Ifabella, that if for three months paft my foul has loved her, its paffion has been pure and fpotlefs, and never had a thought which her honour could reafonably be difpleafed at.

Sganarel. Ay.

Valere. That having nothing but my own inclinations to gratify, all my defigns were to obtain her for a wife, if, in you, who are now the fole poffeffor of her heart, fate had not oppofed an obftacle to this juft paffion.

Sganarel. Mighty well.

Valere. That, happen what will, fhe muft not imagine I can ever forget her charms; that in what manner foever I muft fubmit to the degrees of heaven, 1 am deftined to love her as long as I live; and that, if any thing ftifles my addreffes, it is the juft regard I have for your merit.

Sganarel. That is wifely faid, and I am going to inform her of this difcourfe, at which fhe will not be difpleafed; but if you will truft to me, endeavour earneftly to drive this paffion out of your head.——Adieu.

Ergafte. Excellent bubble!

SCENE X.

SGANAREL alone.

I AM very forry for this poor good-natured fellow; but it was unhappy for him to think of taking a fort that I had fubdued.

[Sganarel knocks at his door.

SCENE XI.

SGANAREL, ISABELLA.

SGANAREL.

NEVER did a letter returned unopened give a lover more uneasiness: his hopes, in short, are quite deftroyed, and he is withdrawn: but he begged me to tell you, that in loving you, his paffion has been pure and fpotlefs, and never had a thought which could in the leaft difpleafe your honour; and that having only his own inclinations to gratify, all his defires were to obtain you for a wife if fate had not, by making me poffeffor of your heart, oppofed him; that, let what will happen, you muft not imagine that he can ever erafe your charms out of his mind; that whatfoever decrees of heaven he muft fubmit to, he is deftined to love you even to the lateft gafp: and that, if any thing ftifles his addreffes, it is the juft regard he has for my merit. Thefe are his own words, and fo far from blaming him, I think him an honeft fellow, and pity him for loving you.

Ifabella foftly.] I have not been miftaken in my belief of his paffion; his looks affured me always of its innocence.

Sganarel. What do you fay?   -

Ifabella. That it is unkind to me to pity a man fo much whom I hate fo much; and that if you loved me, as you fay you do, you would be fenfible how I am affronted by his addreffes.

Sganarel. But he did not know your mind; and for the honefty of his intention, his love does not deferve————

Ifabella. Is it a good intention, pray now, to think to run away with people? Is it acting like a man of honour to form defigns of taking me from you, and marrying me by force, as if I was a creature that could bear life after fuch infamy being thrown upon me?

Sganarel. How?

Ifabella. Yes, really, this bafe lover, I underftand, talks of running away with me; but I cannot imagine, for my part, by what fecret means he learned fo foon that you intended to marry me at fartheft in eight days, fince it was but yefterday you told me fo; but, it is reported, he will prevent that day which fhould unite your fate and mine.

Sganarel. That fignifies nothing.

Ifabella. O! pardon me; he is a very honeft man, and does not retain for me————

Sganarel. He is in the wrong, and this is carrying the jeft too far.

Ifabella. Come, your mildnefs encourages his folly. If, juft now, he had found you talk ill-naturedly to him, he would have been afraid of your rage and my refentment, for it is even fince his letter was rejected, that he fpoke of this fcandalous defign; and, as far as I can fee, his paffion makes him ftill imagine that my heart approves of him, that I avoid marrying, whatever the world may think of it, and that I fhould with joy find myfelf out of your clutches.

Sganarel. He is a fool.

Ifabella. He knows how to difguife himfelf before you, and his intention is to amufe you: But be certain the traitor impofes upon you with his fair fpeeches. I am very unhappy, I am fure, that notwithstanding all my endeavours to live with honour, and repulse the addresses of a vile seducer, I must be exposed to the vexation of his infamous attempts upon me.

Sganarel. Well, fear nothing.

Isabella. For my part, I assure you, that unless you shew yourself exceeding angry at so impudent an attempt, and quickly find out some way to free me from the persecutions of such a rash creature, I will give up every thing, and not endure the affronts I receive from him.

Sganarel. Come, be not so much vexed, my love; I will go find him out and tell him what you say.

Isabella. However, tell him, that it is in vain for him to deny it, for I was credibly informed of his design; and that after this notice, I dare defy him to surprise me, whatever he may atrempt. In a word, that without farther loss of time and trouble, he may be sensible what my sentiments are towards you, and that, if he would avoid making mischief, he must not want being told the same thing twice.

Sganarel. I will give him a right answer.

Isabella. But do it in such a manner that he may be sensible it comes from my very soul.

Sganarel. Fear nothing, I will tell him every thing.

Isabella. I am impatient for your return, pray make all possible haste. I languish if you are from my sight one moment.

Sganarel. Go, my heart's delight, I will return immediately.

SCENE XII.

S. GANAREL. alone.

IT is impoffible to find a difcreeter or better young woman.——Ah! how I am. rejoiced. in find-ing a wife according to my. own wifh! Ay, thus wives ought to be,. and not like fome I. know, down-right coquettes, that fuffer themfelves to be court-ed,.and make their honeft hufbands be pointed at thro' all the town. [Knocking at Valere's door.] Soho, there, where is Valere, that enterprizing youth?

SCENE XIII.

VALERE, SGANAREL, ERGASTE.

VALERE.

WHAT brings you here now, Sir?
Sganarel. Your follies.
Valere. What do you mean?
Sganarel. You know well enough what I want to fpeak to you about. I tell you plainly, I took you to be a more fenfible young man than you are. You came to amufe me with your fine fpeeches, and fecretly retain your own foolifh hopes. I was inclinable to ufe you gently, but at laft you will. force me into a paffion. Are you not afhamed, confidering who you are, to invent fuch projects as you do, to intend running away with a woman of honour, and interrupting a marriage on which depends her whole happinefs?

Valere. Who told you this wonderful news, Sir?

Sganarel. You need not diffemble. I have it

from Isabella; who, for the last time, sends you word by me, that she has plainly enough discovered to you whom she chuses; that her heart, which is wholly mine, is enraged at such an invention; that she had rather die than be so grosly insulted; and that you will occasion terrible doings, unless you put an end to all this uneasiness.

Valere. If she really said what you inform me, I confess my passion can pretend to nothing farther. These expressions are clear enough to let me see all is over, and I must revere the sentence she has passed.

Sganarel. You need not in the least doubt it. Do you imagine all the complaints I have brought from her to you are mere pretences? Would you have her come herself and tell you? If you will not believe it, follow me, you shall see if I have added any thing, and if her youthful heart is in suspense between us.

[Going to knock at his own door.

SCENE XIV.

ISABELLA, SCANAREL, VALERE, ERGASTE.

ISABELLA.

WHAT do you mean? Do you take his part, and bring him to me? Do his noble qualities charm you so much, that you will force me to love him, and endure his visits?

Sganarel. No, dearee, I set too great a value on your heart for that; but he imagines what I told him to be an errant fiction, he believes it is all my own invention, and that I cunningly represent you full of hate towards him, and tenderneſs for me; wherefore, from your own mouth I would cure him infallibly of an error which encourages his paſſion.

Iſabella. What, does not my ſoul fully declare its meaning to you, and can you ſtill be doubtful whom I love?

Valere. Indeed, madam, I might well be ſurprized at whatever the gentleman ſaid to me from you. I was in doubt, I own, and that final ſentence which determines the fate of my unbounded paſſion, muſt be ſo ſenſibly felt by me, that you cannot be in the leaſt offended if I deſire the repetition of it.

Iſabella. No, no; you muſt not be ſurprized at ſuch a ſentence; he told you my real thoughts, and I conceive them founded on reaſon ſufficient to prove how ſincere they are. Yes indeed, I would have it known, and I ought to be credited, that fate here preſents two objects to my view, which inſpiring me with different ſentiments, agitate all the paſſions of my ſoul. One, by a reaſonable choice, whereto honour engages me, poſſeſſes all my eſteem and love; and the other, in return for his affection, has all my rage and abhorrence. I am delighted with the preſence of the one, but the ſight of the other inſpires my heart with ſecret emotions of hatred and horror. I deſire nothing better than to be the wife of the one; but I had rather loſe my life than be married to the other. But it is ſufficient that I declare my real ſentiments, and languiſh too long under theſe cruel torments; the perſon I love muſt now exert his diligence to deſtroy intirely the expectations of him I hate, and deliver me by a happy marriage from a puniſhment I dread much more than death.

Sganarel. Ay, my dearee, I intend to satisfy thy wish..

Isabella. I cannot be easy unless you do it.

Sganarel. You shall be so shortly.

Isabella. I know it is indecent for young women to declare their love so freely..

Sganarel. No, no.

Isabella. But these liberties may be allowed in the condition I am at present; and I can, without a blush, make this tender acknowledgment to him whom I already look upon as my husband..

Sganarel. Ay, my lovely child, my soul's delight.

Isabella. Then pray let him think of proving his passion for me.

Sganarel. Ay, there, kiss my hand.

Isabella. Without further courtship, let him conclude a marriage, which I earnestly desire; and accept the assurance I now give him that I will never hearken to the vows of any other person.

[She pretends to embrace Sganarel, and gives her hand to Valere to kiss.

Sganarel. Ha, ha, my pretty-face, my amiable dearee: you shall not pine very long, I promise you. Go, say no more. [To Valere.] You see she speaks freely, and loves none but me.

Valere. Well, madam, very well, your meaning is plain enough: I learn by this discourse what it is you urge me to; and ere long, I shall be able to remove from your presence him who is the occasion of so much uneasiness to you.

Isabella. You cannot oblige me more agreeably; for, in short, the sight of him is grievous to endure; I hate him, and am——

Sganarel. So so.

Isabella. Are you displeased with what I say?
Do I———

Sganarel. Alas! by no means, I do not say that;
but, without lying, I pity his condition, and your
aversion shews itself too violently.

Isabella. I cannot shew it too much on such an
occasion.

Valere. Well: you shall be satisfied; and after three days never more shall your eyes behold the
hated object.

Isabella. I wish it may be so.   Farewel.

Sganarel. I am very sorry for you: but———

Valere. Nay, you shall hear no complaint at all
from me; the lady certainly does justice to us both,
and I will endeavour to satisfy her wishes.——Farewel.

Sganarel. Unhappy youth! how much he is
grieved! Come embrace me, for I am your second
self.

S C E N E XV.

ISABELLA, SGANAREL.

SGANAREL.

I THINK he is greatly to be pitied.
    Isabella. Pho! not at all.

Sganarel. I am greatly charmed with your love,
my dearee, and I wish it was rewarded. Eight
days are too long to stay, considering your impati-
ence; I will marry you to-morrow, and will not
invite-------

Isabella. To-morrow?

Sganarel. You pretend reluctance out of modesty, but I know what joy my saying so gives you, and you wish it was already concluded.

Isabella. But—

Sganarel. Let us go prepare every thing for this wedding.

Isabella aside.] How shall I now, ye gods! prevent this fatal match?

ACT III.   SCENE I.

ISABELLA.

DEATH, when compared to this fatal marriage, to which I am forced, is nothing; and whatever I do to avoid the terrors of it, ought to find some favour with those who censure me. Time presses: it is night: let me therefore go boldly, and commit my safety to the fidelity of a lover.

SCENE II.

SGANAREL, ISABELLA.

Sganarel speaking to the people in the house.
I AM returned, and to-morrow I will send——

Isabella. O heaven!

Sganarel. Is it you, my love? Whither do ye go so late? When I went out you said you was much fatigued, and would shut yourself up in your chamber: nay, you begged that I would let you be quiet at my return, and not trouble you till to-morrow morning.

Isabella. It is true; but—

Sganarel. But what?

Isabella. I am perplexed, you see, nor do I know what excuse to make to you for it.

Sganarel. How so? What can this mean?

Isabella. A wonderful secret: The reason of my going abroad at this present is, because my sister has, with a design for which I very much blame her, desired my chamber of me, where I have shut her up.

Sganarel. For what purpose?

Isabella. Why, this very youth whom we have discarded is beloved by her.

Sganarel. Who? Valere?

Isabella. She is desperately in love with him. Her coming to me at this hour of the night to disclose her passion plainly shews how violent it is: she says that she shall certainly die if she does not obtain what she so much desires; that their amour has been carried on above a year; and that they made each other mutual promises of marriage at the very beginning of their fondness.

Sganarel. A villain!

Isabella. That being informed to what despair I have driven the man she loves, she came to beg I would suffer her passion, to prevent a separation which would much grieve her, and allow her to entertain her galant this evening in my name at my chamber window which looks into the little street, where, counterfeiting my voice, she may talk a little kindly to him, and thereby tempt his stay; in short, that she may dexterously manage to her own advantage the regard he is known to have for me.

Sganarel. And can you imagine that----

Isabella. For my part, I am provoked at it. What, sister, said I, are you out of your wits? Are you not afhamed to be thus in love with a man who is inconftant, and changes every day? To forget your fex, and deceive the hopes of a man whom heaven has appointed for you?

Sganarel. He well deferves it, and I am very glad of it.

Ifabella. In fhort, I ufed every method to diffuade her from making fuch a requeft; but fhe begged fo earneftly, wept and fighed to fuch a degree, and told me that I would drive her to defpair if I denied to gratify her paffion, that I was obliged to yield; and to juftify this night's intrigue, which a tendernefs for my own blood made me give way to, I was going to get Lucretia to come and lie with me, who is fo much praifed by you for her virtue; but your fpeedy return has greatly furprized me.

Sganarel. No, no, I will not have this juggling at my houfe; 1 could agree to it fo far as it concerns my brother, but they may be feen by fomebody in the ftreet, and fhe whom I honour with my perfon fhould not only be modeft and well-bred, but fhe muft not even be fufpected. Let us us go turn out the fhamelefs creature; and for her paffion---

Ifabella. For God's fake do not do that; you will greatly confound her, and fhe may juftly complain how badly I can keep a fecret. As you will not allow me to countenance her defign, ftay here at leaft till I let her out.

Sganarel. Well then, do fo.

Ifabella. But above all things conceal yourfelf, I befeech you, and let her go without fpeaking one word to her.

Sganarel. Well, for thy fake I will reftrain my

wrath; but as soon as she is gone, I will go and tell the whole affair to my brother.

Isabella. Pray do not mention my name. Good night to you, for I am going to shut myself up this moment.

Sganarel. Until to-morrow, dearee. [Alone.] How impatient am I to see my brother, and inform him of this accident? The good man is bubbled, with all his wisdom, and I would not be without this discovery for an hundred crowns.

Isabella in the house.] Yes, sister, I am sorry to incur your displeasure, but it is impossible for me to gratify you; my honour, which is dear to me, runs too great a risque by it; farewell; begone immediately.

Sganarel. There she goes; she's a sweet baggage, I warrant ye: let us lock the door, for fear she should come back again.

Isabella entering.] Desert me not, good heavens! in my enterprize.

Sganarel aside.] Whither can she be going? I will follow her a little.

Isabella aside.] The night, however, favours me in my distress.

Sganarel aside.] To Valere's lodgings! What a gypsey is this!

S C E N E III.

VALERE, ISABELLA, SGANAREL.

VALERE coming out hastily.

YES, yes, I will try some way this very night to speak—Who is there?

Isabella. Softly, Valere, it is Isabella who now

speaks to you, therefore trouble yourself no farther.

Sganarel. You lie, buffy, it is not she. She follows closely those laws of honour which you forsake, and you assume falsely both her name and voice.

Isabella. But if I thought that you would not by the most sacred ties——

Valere. Indeed, that is the only purpose of my destiny; and I here solemnly declare to you, that to-morrow, I will go where-ever you please to perform the ceremony.

Sganarel aside.] Poor self-cozened fool!

Valere. Go in, and fear nothing: I now defy your fantastical guardian's power; and sooner shall this arm pierce his heart, than he shall again be in possession of thee.

S C E N E IV.

SGANAREL alone.

I Have not the least inclination, I assure you, to take from you such a scandalous gypsey, enslaved to her passion; your promise to her does not make me jealous, and you have my free consent to take her. Ay, let us catch him with this impudent creature: the memory of her father, well worthy of respect, together with the great interest I have in her sister, requires my endeavours at least to preserve her honour.—Scho!

[Knocking at a commissary's door.

SCENE V.

SGANAREL, the COMMISSARY, the NOTARY,
Attendant with a Flambeau.

COMMISSARY.

WHO is there?

Sganarel. Your servant, Mr. Commissary; we want a cast of your office; please to follow me with your light.

Commissary. We are going to—

Sganarel. The affair is in great haste.

Commissary. What is it?

Sganarel. To go in there, and surprize two people together, who must be honestly married: it is a girl of ours whom a youth called Valere has deceived, and got into his house by promising her marriage; she is descended from a noble and virtuous family, but—

Commissary. If it is for that, our meeting is very lucky, for here is a Notary with us.

Sganarel. Sir.

Notary. Yes, Sir, a public Notary.

Commissary. And also a man of honour.

Sganarel. That is to be supposed. Go in at the door, make no noise, but mind that no body gets out: you shall be fully satisfied for your pains: but do not suffer yourselves to be greased in the fist however.

Commissary. How? Do you imagine that officers of justice—

Sganarel. I do not say it as a reflection upon your office. I will fetch my brother hither this

moment. Let the flambeau light me. [Afide.]
I will go congratulate this Solomon. Soho.
[Knocking at Arifto's door.

SCENE VI.

ARISTO, SGANAREL.

ARISTO.

WHO knocks?—Oh! brother, what brings
you here at this time of the night?

Sganarel. Come along, poor fuperannuated fop,
I will fhew you fomething that is pretty.

Arifto. What do you mean?

Sganarel. I bring you good news.

Arifto. What is it?

Sganarel. Where is your Leonora, pray?

Arifto. What is the reafon of your afking? She
is at a friend's houfe, I believe, at a ball.

Sganarel. Hey! ay, ay, follow me: you fhall
fee what kind of ball fhe is at.

Arifto. I do not underftand you.

Sganarel. She now plainly maketh it appear how
well you have brought her up. It is cruel to be
conftantly finding fault; the mind is eafily won by
gentlenefs; and neither maids nor wives are rendered virtuous by bolts, grates, and diftruftful
cares. The fex requires a little liberty, and by
feverity we occafion them to do amifs. She has
really taken her fill of it, a cunning baggage, and
virtue with her is grown exceeding gentle.

Arifto. I cannot in the leaft apprehend what you
mean by this difcourfe.

Sganarel. Come, Mr. Elder-brother of mine, it
is what you well deferve; and I would not for

twenty piftoles, but that you fhould have this fruit of your filly maxims.   It is plain what effect our inftructions have produced on two fifters: one fhuns galants, and the other runs after them.

Arifto. If you do not fpeak plainer I cannot—

Sganarel. Why then you muft know, that her ball is at Valere's, that I myfelf faw her go thither, not an hour ago, and that he juft now has her in his arms.

Arifto. Who?

Sganarel. Leonora.

Arifto. Leave off your bantering, I befeech you.

Sganarel. Bantering! it is very good to hear him talk of bantering: poor foul! I tell you again and again, that your Leonora is juft now with Valere, and that they were engaged by a mutual promife before he thought of following Ifabella.

Arifto. So improbable is this ftory, that----

Sganarel. He will not believe it, though he fees it. It makes me mad. When people are defective here, years avail nothing.

[Pointing to his forehead.

Arifto. Do you think, brother, that----

Sganarel. No, no, only follow me, your mind fhall prefently be made eafy. You fhall fee if I impofe upon you, and if they have not been contracted for more than a year paft.

Arifto. Is it likely fhe fhould confent to this engagement without apprizing me of it! me, who always from her infancy upon every occafion have practifed towards her a compliance, and have times innumerable told her that I would never force her inclinations, but let her chufe whom fhe pleafed!

Sganarel. In fhort, your own eyes fhall judge of the matter: I have already fetched a Commiffary and a Notary, it is our intereſt that the honour ſhe has loſt ſhould be repaired upon the ſpct by marriage; for I do nct imagine you will be ſo mean-ſpirited as to make her your wife with this ſtain upon her, unleſs you have ſome new arguments toplace you above ridicule.

Ariſto. I ſhall never, I hope, be ſo weak, as to deſire to poſſefs a heart which inclines more to any other perſon than to me. Nevertheleſs, I cannot believe————

Sganarel. What a talking you make! come along, this diſpute would laſt for ever.

S C E N E   VII.

. C O M M I S S A R Y, ʼN O T A R Y, S G A N A-
RE L, A R I S T O.

COMMISSARY.

IF you deſire that they ſhould be married, gentlemen, you need make uſe of no compulſion, for they are both equally inclined to it. And, as to what concerns you, Valere has given it under his hand already, that he deſigns for his wife her who now is with him.

Ariſto. The girl————

Commiſſary. She is locked up, and unleſs you premiſe to gratify their deſires, will not ſtir a foot.

SCENE VIII.

VALERE, COMMISSARY, NOTARY,
SGANAREL, ARISTO.

VALERE at the window.

NOT a foul shall enter here, gentlemen, till you let me know what you want. You know very well who I am, and I have done my part in figning the inftrument, which they may fhew you: if you intend to confent to the match, you muft likewife fet your hand to a confirmation of it; but, if not, depend upon it, you fhall kill me fooner than take from me the object of my love.

Sganarel. Nay, we do not defign to feparate you from her. [Afide] He is ftill ignorant who it is that he has got, he thinks it is Ifabella; let us take advantage of his error.

Arifto to Valere.] But is that Leonora?

Sganarel to Arifto.] Hold your tongue.

Arifto. But——

Sganarel. Be quiet.

Arifto. I would know——

Sganarel. What, again? hold your tongue, I tell you.

Valere. In fhort, whatever be the confequence, Ifabella has my folemn promife, as I have her's, and I am not a match, confidering every thing, which you fhall be admitted to difapprove.

Arifto to Sganarel.] What he fays is not——

Sganarel. Hold your tongue: I have a reafon for it: and you fhall know the fecret. Well, without any more ado we both agree that you are to marry her who is now with you.

Commiffary. The thing is drawn in thofe terms, and a blank is left for the name, as we did not fee her—Come, fign, the lady will make you all agree afterwards.

Valere. I confent to it in that way.

Sganarel. I am very fond of it, for my part: [*Afide.*] We fhall have fine diverfion prefently. Here, brother, you have the honour to fet your name firft.

Arifto. But why all this myftery----

Sganarel. Pox take your impudence! Come, fign your name, you fool.

Arifto. He talks of Ifabella, and you of Leonora.

Sganarel. Do not you confent, brother, if it is her, to allow them to make their nuptial promifes good?

Arifto. Certainly.

Sganarel. Sign then, and I will do fo too.

Arifto. So let it be, I do not underftand it.

Sganarel. You fhall be informed of the affair.

Commiffary. We will be back again foon.

Sganarel to Arifto.] Well, now I will tell you the fubtlety of this intrigue.

[*They retire to the farther part of the ftage.*

S C E N E IX.

LEONORA, SGANAREL, ARISTO, LISETTA.

LEONORA.

HOW I have been plagued with the impertinence of thefe young coxcombs!

They obliged me to flip away from the ball privately.

Lifetta. They all endeavoured to make themselves agreeable to you.

Leonora. In short, I never met with any thing more troublesome; and would be much happier in the meaneft converfation, than in all their flattering difcourfes : they imagine all muft be given up to their powdered periwigs; they think themfelves the wifeft people in the world, when, with a ftupid banteriug tone, they rally one in a filly manner about the love of an old man : but I fet more value upon the affections of fuch an old man, than all the giddy raptures of a young fellow. But I fee---

Sganarel to Arifto.] Well, the affair ftands in this manner. [feeing Leonora.] O! yonder fhe comes, attended by her maid.

Arifto. I am not angry, Leonora, but have reafon to complain : you are fenfible I never laid any reftraint upon you, and have a hundred times told you, that you fhould gratify your own wifhes; and notwithftanding this, your heart has engaged itfelf, both by promife and affection, without my knowledge. I do not repent the indulgence I have given you, but your behaviour affects me fenfibly; my fondnefs for you did not deferve this return.

Leonora. I do not underftand the reafon of your talking in this manner; but you may be certain I am the fame I ever was; nothing can leffen my efteem for you: I fhould think it a crime to have a regard for any other perfon, and if you are willing to compleat my wifhes, the facred knot fhall make us one to-morrow.

Arifto. Upon what foundation then, brother, came you----

Sganarel. What! have not you come from Valere's lodgings? Have you not been in love with him for a year paft, and declared your paffion for him this very day?

Leonora. Who has taken the pains to invent fuch lies, and given you this account of me?

SCENE THE LAST.

ISABELLA, VALERE, LEONORA, ARISTO, SGANAREL, COMMISSARY, NOTARY, LISETTA, ERGASTE.

ISABELLA.

I HOPE, fifter, you will forgive me freely, if by the liberty I have taken I may have hurt your character.   I was forced into that fcandalous contrivance by the confufion the great furprize put me into. Fate deals very differently with you and me. Your example condemns my paffion. [to Sganarel.] I will make no apology to you, Sir, as I am doing you a piece of fervice, rather than ufing you ill. I found myfelf unworthy of your love, and chofe rather to give myfelf to another, than prove unworthy of fuch an heart as yours; heaven never intended us for each other.

Valere to Sganarel.] To receive her from your hands, Sir, is happinefs and glory.

Arifto. Indeed, brother, nobody will be forry for you, though they know you are cheated; your own behaviour is the occafion of it, and you muft fubmit to it peaceably.

Lifetta. This reward of his miftruft is an exemplary ftroke, and I am very glad of it.

Leonora. For my part, I cannot blame this ftra-

tagem; I do not know whether it fhould be commended or not.

Ergaſte. He is a lucky fellow to efcape being a
cuckold, when his ſtars expofed him to the danger
of it.

Sganarel. Really I cannot recover myfelf from
my aſtoniſhment; this deviliſh trick confufes my
underſtanding: after this, he that truſts in women
is wretched. I believe the devil himfelf could not
be fo wicked as this jilt; I thought that I could
have engaged my life that ſhe would never have
behaved fo. Women are continually hatching mifchief; they were made for a curfe to the world.
I give up the treacherous fex, for ever, and wiſh
them all at the devil heartily.

Ergaſte. Well faid.

Ariſto. Let us all go to my houfe. Come, Mr.
Valere, to-morrow we will endeavour to appeafe
his rage.

Lifetta to the audience.

You who churliſh hufbands know that want mend-
    ing,
Ours is the fchool to which you may fend them.

T H E   E N D.

G 4

THE
SCHOOL FOR WIVES.

A

COMEDY.

COMEDIE

EN QUATRE ACTES

The SCHOOL *for* WIVES, *a Comedy of Five Acts;
acted at Paris, at the Theatre of the Palace-
Royal, December 26th,* 1662.

AT the first reprefentation of the SCHOOL for
WIVES, all Paris flocked to Moliere's
Theatre; however, the immenfe number of fpectators could not fecure him againft feveral criticifms being publifhed againft his piece, though it
afforded him comfort in it. So inveterate were
they againft it, that they took notice of the fmalleft neglects, and exclaimed againft the flighteft
faults; but the moft effential of all was overlook-
ed, I mean fome dangerous images in it, which
fhould always be banifhed from the ftage. But if
we confider only how artfully the piece is contrived, we cannot but confefs, that this comedy is
one of the moft excellent·productions of human
genius. The repeated confidence which Horace·
places in the jealous Arnolph, who, notwithftanding all his precautions, was always duped by a filly innocent young girl; the excellent character of
Agnes, the humour of the under characters which
were chofen to attend her, together with the natural and quick tranfition from one furprize to another, are excellent comic productions. What di-
ftinguifhes the SCHOOL for WIVES ftill more
particularly is, that the whole appears to be related, and yet at the fame time is all in action; a
fpecies of comedy of which neither the ancient nor
modern ftages have given us the leaft model. E-
very relation, by its proximity to the incident
which gave occafion to it, traces it over again in
fo lively a manner, that the fpectator thinks him-

self present at it, and by a peculiar advantage which the relation of this piece has over the action, we enjoy the effect which the fact produces, at the same time that we learn it; for the person who is concerned to be instructed learns everything which there is the greatest reason should be concealed from him. The great resemblance which appears in the School for Husbands and the School for Wives, with regard to Sganarel and Arnolph being both deceived by the very measures they took to prevent it, must turn to Moliere's reputation, who discovered the secret of varying what appeared to be so much alike. The subtil strokes of Isabella, which sprang from no other principle but the constraint her guardian kept her under, are very different from those natural ones of the witty Agnes, who offended against decorums only because Arnolph had kept her in ignorance of them.

A C T O R S.

Arnolph, otherwise Mr. de la Souche.
Agnes, daughter to Henriques.
Horace, lover to Agnes.
Chrisaldus, Arnolph's confident.
Henriques, brother-in-law to Chrisaldus.
Orontes, Horace's father, and a friend to Arnolph.
A Notary.
Allen, a country fellow, Arnolph's man.
Georgetta, a country girl, Arnolph's maid.

SCENE PARIS, a square in the suburbs.

THE
SCHOOL FOR WIVES.

ACT. I. SCENE I.

CHRISALDUS, ARNOLPH.

CHRISALDUS.

YOU are come to marry her, you say?

Arnolph. Yes, to-morrow I will finish the affair.

Chrisaldus. We are alone here, and I dare say, may speak freely, without being heard by any body. Would you have me to speak sincerely as a friend? Your intentions make me anxious for you, for I think it a piece of madness in you to marry, in whatever light you may consider it.

Arnolph. I believe it is true, my friend. Probably your own experience makes you apprehensive for me; perhaps your brows make you imagine, that matrimony and horns are inseparable.

Chrisaldus. Accidents of that sort nobody can avoid, and it appears to me very foolish for people

to be fo careful about it.   My uneafinefs for you
is on account of the raillery which a thoufand hufbands indure the fting of.   You know very well
that every body fuffers by your reflexions, and to
exclaim againft fecret intrigues, has been your greateft delight in every place you go.

Arnolph. Very well.   Are hufbands fo tame
any where as in this city? We fee them of every
degree treated at home with difrefpect.   One heaps
up riches, which his wife can difpofe of to a perfon who is endeavouring to make a cuckold of him;
another, not lefs infamous, but more eafy, fees his
wife accept of prefents every day, and is not in the
leaft uneafy, as fhe tells him it is ont of refpect for
her virtue.   One makes a great buftle, which ferves
but to little purpofe: another, quite eafy, fees the
fpark vifit at his houfe, walks out, and lets affairs
take their courfe.   One wife, with female cunning,
pretends to make a confident of her faithful hufband, who fleeps quietly under the delufion, pitying the poor galant for giving himfelf the trouble
—which anfwers his intentions.   Another, to a-
void the appearance of extravagance, pretends the
money fhe expends is won at play, and the poor
weak hufband returns God thanks for it, without
fufpecting at what game fhe wins it.   In fhort, you
will find thefe fubjects of ridicule every where, and
may not I as a looker on laugh at them? May not
I amongft our fools——

Chrifaldus. Very true; but he who makes a jeft
of another, may be afraid of being laughed at himfelf.   I hear what the people fay, how they amufe
themfelves with tattling things that happen; but
whatever is difcovered in places where I am, no
body ever heard me rejoice at them.   I am clofe

enough in that refpect; and if I happened on thefe occafions to think certain degrees of forbearance wrong, and my intention were not to fuffer what fome hufbands bear quietly, yet I never attempted to fay this; for after all, it is to be dreaded that fatire will come home, and a perfon fhould never fay pofitively that he would do fo and fo, in fuch a cafe. By which means, if fate fhould deftine my brows to a difgrace of that fort, my behaviour would induce people to pity me, or, at leaft, privately to laugh at me. But, my dear friend, your cafe would differ widely, and I really think you run a very great rifk, as you have always been ready to ridicule tame hufbands. In fhort, you have been a devil let loofe upon them, and to avoid being a fubject of jeft, you muft walk upright indeed: if they get the fmalleft hold of you, they will make your fhame public, even at the market-crofs. And——

Arnolph. Alas! friend, do not give yourfelf any trouble about that point. He muft be very cunning indeed who catches me. The perfon I am to marry is fo innocent, that my forehead cannot be in any danger. I know all the artful contrivances, and the ftratagems they fall upon to plant horns upon us.

Chrifaldus. Hey, what do you pretend? that a a fool, in one word——

Arnolph. A perfon is no fool, to marry an ignorant wife. I believe, as a good chriftian, your other half to be very wife, but an artful wife is a very bad prefage, and I am fenfible what certain people have loft by marrying women with great abilities. Shall I plague myfelf with the care of a witty wife, who loves to talk of nothing but the ring and the drawing room? who can write tender things both in verse and profe? who is visited by the marquises and the wits, while I, under the name of the lady's husband, am like a saint, whom nobody calls upon? No, no, none of your high flown genius's for me; a woman who writes, understands more than she should do. I intend mine with so little of the sublime in her, that she shall be ignorant what rhime is. If one happen to play at the basket with her, and in one's turn ask her, what is put into it? Let her answer be, a cream-tart. In short, I would chuse to have her very ignorant: to say the truth, it is enough if she can love me, know how to sew, spin, and say her prayers.

Chrifaldus. Then your choice would be a stupid wife?

Arnolph. I would prefer an ugly fool to a handsome wit.

Chrifaldus. And wit——

Arnolph. Virtue is enough.

Chrifaldus. After all, a fool may not know what it is to be virtuous; and I should think it very insipid to live all one's life with a fool. To be serious, even that will not secure one from horns: a sensible woman may deviate from her duty, but she must do it knowingly; whereas a fool, without ever thinking of it, may fail in the common course of her's.

Arnolph. I will answer as Pantagruel did to Panurgus, to this fine argument. Endeavour to prevail upon me to marry a wealthy woman, and talk from January to June, when you are done you will be amazed, that all your advice is to no purpose.

Chrifaldus. I will say no more to you on that subject.

Arnolph. Every one to his own way.   In a wife, as in other things, I will follow my own humour. I have money enough, and can afford to marry a woman that has nothing, whofe dependence upon me will prevent her from reproaching me either with her birth or fortune.   When I firft faw her amongft the children, her grave and mild look in-fpired me with a love for her, though fhe was then but four years old.   Her mother was in a very low ftation, and I thought I would beg her from her; and the good woman very readily gave up her charge. I had her brought up at a little convent, according to my own directions, diftant from all company. I defired them to ufe all their endeavours to make her as great an idiot as they could.   Thank hea-ven they fucceeded to my wifh, and as fhe grew up, I found her filly, and was thankful for it.   I brought her home, but as my houfe is always open to a hundred forts of people, (precaution being al-ways neceffary) I have her placed out of the way in this other houfe, that her agreeable difpofition may not be fpoiled by people who come to vifit me: I have no body near her but people as ignorant as herfelf.   You will be furprized at my troubling you with fo long a ftory, but it is to acquaint you with the care I have taken————And I invite you this evening, as a faithful friend, to fup with her: obferve her well, and you will certainly approve my choice.

Chrifaldus. I will.

Arnolph. And by this converfation you will judge of both her innocence and perfon.

Chrifaldus. As to that article, what you have told me cannot————

Arnolph. The defcription I give you, is even

short of the truth.   Her simplicity on all occasions is admirable; I am often like to die with laughing at some questions she asks.   The other day, (could you suppose it?) she was uneasy, and with an ignorance which nothing can equal, came to ask me if children come into the world by the ear.

Chrisaldus. It gives me pleasure, Mr. Arnolph——

Arnolph. How! Will you always give me that name?

Chrisaldus. I really cannot avoid it, it comes always into my mouth; and I never think of Mr. de la Souche.   What the deuce has put it into your head to change your name, at forty-two years of age; to take a title from an old rotten stump belonging to your farm?

Arnolph. Besides the house being known by that name, la Souche is a more agreeable name to me.

Chrisaldus. It is shameful to give up the name of one's ancestors, to take another founded on fancy; and yet it is the whim of a great many people, without mentioning you.   I know a country fellow, named fat Peter, who had only a quarter of an acre of land, he made a muddy ditch round it, and assumed the name of Mr. de L'Isle.

Arnolph. Repeat none of those instances: if you call me by any other name than la Souche, you will disoblige me; I have a pleasure in it, and will be called so.

Chrisaldus. Few people will submit to it, and I still see the directions of your letters——

Arnolph. From those who are not acquainted with it I bear it easily, but for you——

Chrisaldus. Be it so.   We shall not differ about

that; I will accustom myself to say Mr. de la Souche.

Arnolph. Farewel.   I knock here only to say good-morrow, and acquaint them that I am re-turned.

Chrisaldus aside, going away.] Really I think him an accomplished fool.

Arnolph alone.] He is a little touched as to some particular things.   It is surprizing to see how much every man is wedded to his own opinion!

       [Knocking at his door.] Soho.

S C E N E II.

ARNOLPH, ALLEN and GEORGETTA
in the house.

ALLEN.

WHO is there?
    Arnolph. Open the door. [aside.] They will be very well pleased to see me, I suppose, af-ter ten days absence.

Allen. Who knocks?

Arnolph. I.

Allen. Georgetta.

Georgetta. Well.

Allen. Open the door below there.

Georgetta. Do it yourself.

Allen. You go do it.

Georgetta. I will not go, indeed.

Allen. Nor will I go.

Arnolph. A pretty sort of ceremony, while I am standing without!—Soho, soho there; pray—

Georgetta. Who knocks at the door?

Arnolph. Your master.

Georgetta. Allen.

Allen. What do ye say?

Georgetta. It is my master. Open the door immediately.

Allen. Do you open it.

Georgetta. I am blowing the fire.

Allen. I cannot stir, lest my sparrow should get out, and the cat eat it.

Arnolph. Which ever of you two will not open the door, shall not have a bit of victuals for above these four days.

Georgetta. What occasion have you to come, when I am going?

Allen. Why you more than I? A fine contrivance truly!

Georgetta. Stand out of the way.

Allen. I will not, stand you out of the way.

Georgetta. I will open the door.

Allen. And I will open it.

Georgetta. You shall not open it.

Allen. No more shall you

Georgetta. Nor you.

Arnolph. I had need have great patience here.

Allen entering] However, it is my business, Sir.

Georgetta entering.] I am your servant for that; it is mine.

Allen. Was it not out of respect to my master here, I'd————

Arnolph receiving a blow from Allen.] Plague!

Allen. I beg your pardon.

Arnolph. See that loggerhead there.

Allen. She is so too, Sir————

Arnolph. Hold your tongues, and mind what I am going to say to you. How are all here?

Allen. Why Sir, we we—[*Arnolph pulls off*

Allen's hat three times.] Sir, we we are——thank God—— we we——

Arnolph. Foolish blockhead, who taught you to talk to me with your hat upon your head?

Allen. You do well, Sir, I was in the wrong.

Arnolph to Allen.] Tell Agnes to come down to me.

SCENE III.

ARNOLPH, GEORGETTA.

ARNOLPH.

WHEN I was away did she appear melancholy?

Georgetta. Melancholy? No.

Arnolph. No!

Georgetta. Yes, yes.

Arnolph. Why then·······

Georgetta. Yes she was; she expected you every moment, and never a horse, mule, or ass passed by which she did not take for you.

SCENE IV.

ARNOLPH, AGNES, ALLEN, GEORGETTA.

ARNOLPH.

HER work in her hand is a good sign—— Well, Agnes, are you glad to see me come back again?

Agnes, Yes, Sir, thank heaven.

Arnolph. And I too am glad to see you again.

Your face plainly shews you have been well since I went from home.

Agnes. Fleas have disturbed me very much in the night.

Arnolph. O, in a little time you shall have some body to catch them for you.

Agnes. You will do me a kindness.

Arnolph. So I can easily imagine. What are you about there?

Agnes. I am making myself some head-clothes. Your night-shirts and caps are done.

Arnolph. Very well, go up stairs again, I will be with you presently, and will discourse with you about some affairs of consequence.

SCENE V.

ARNOLPH alone.

THIS modest and virtuous ignorance far surpasses all your knowledge, your romances, your verses, and your love-letters, ye learned ladies, and heroines of the age. One ought not to be tempted by riches; and provided a girl be virtuous——

SCENE VI.

HORACE, ARNOLPH.

ARNOLPH.

WHO is this I see? Is it he?—Ay. I am mistaken. No, no. But it is. Nay, it is he himself. Hor——

Horace. Mr. Ar——

Arnolph. Horace.

Horace. Arnolph.

Arnolph. O, joy extreme! How long have you been here?

Horace. Nine days.

Arnolph. Really————

Horace. As soon as I came I went to your houfe, but you was not to be found.

Arnolph. I was in the country.

Horace. Ay, you had been gone two days.

Arnolph. What an alteration a few years make in children! I am furprized to find him grown fo, after having known him when he was fo little.

Horace. You fee how it is.

Arnolph. But, pray, how does my dear friend Orontes your father, whom I refpect and revere? Is he hearty ftill? He knows I bear a part in every thing which concerns him; it is four years fince we faw each other, and a letter has not paffed between us all that time.

Horace. He is even heartier than we are, Mr. Arnolph:—I have got a letter for you from him: but by another fince he fends me word of his own coming, though I am yet ignorant of the reafon of it.——Do you know who of your townfmen it fhould be, that is upon his return hither with immenfe riches, which he has been fourteen years acquiring in the Weft-Indies?

Arnolph. No. Did you hear his name?

Horace. Henriques.

Arnolph. No.

Horace. My father fpeaks to me of him and his return, as if I was perfectly acquainted with him; and writes me word they are fetting out together upon an important affair, which his letter does not mention.

[*Giving Orontes's letter to Arnolph.*

Arnolph. I shall certainly be extremely glad to see him, and will do every thing in my power to entertain him.   [After having read the letter.] Letters amongst friends should be less ceremonious; all these compliments are superfluous; you might freely have used my fortune, without his taking the pains to write to me on that score.

Horace. I am one who take people at their word: and I have just now occasion for an hundred pistoles.

Arnolph. Why really you oblige me in making use of me in this manner, and I am glad I have got them ready for you;—take purse and all.

Horace. It must————

Arnolph. Let us talk about something else, and drop this discourse.   Well, what do you think of this city?

Horace. Its inhabitants are numerous, its buildings very magnificent, and I believe its diversions admirable.

Arnolph. Every man has his pleasures suitable to his taste; but as for those people, who go under the name of galants, they have all they can desire in this country; for the women are made for coquettry, you will find them of gentle temper, both the fair and the brown, and the husbands are withal the most complaisant creatures you ever saw. It is an entertainment for a king, it is a meer comedy to me to see the pranks I do.—You have perhaps already smitten some-body.—Have you had no luck yet? people formed like you are of more value than gold;—you are of a shape to be a cuckold-maker.

Horace. Why, to tell you the truth, I have had

here a certain love adventure, and I am obliged in friendſhip to acquaint you with it.

Arnolph aſide.] Very well, here is ſome new waggiſh ſtory to minute down in my pocket-book.

Horace. However, I beg you would not tell it to any body.

Arnolph. Oh!

Horace. You are not ignorant that on theſe occaſions, if a ſecret gets air it fruſtrates all our deſigns. I will freely tell you then, that my heart is captivated by a certain young lady in this city. My ſmall endeavours have immediately had ſo much ſuccefs, that I have obtained a free admittance to her; and without boaſting of myſelf too much, or in the leaſt injuring her, my affairs with her are in a mighty good poſture.

Arnolph laughing.] Ha, ha, who is it?

Horace pointing to Agnes's lodging.] A very charming young creature, who lives in that brick houſe there. Simple indeed ſhe is, through the matchleſs folly of a man who ſhuts her up from all company; but amidſt that ignorance to which he would enſlave her, ſhe diſplays charms that would throw one into raptures; an air moſt engaging, and I know not what of tendernefs, which no heart is proof againſt. But, perhaps you have often ſeen this young ſtar of love, adorned with ſuch numberleſs perfections. Agnes is her name.

Arnolph aſide.] Oh! I burſt.

Horace. As for the man, it is I think la Zouſſe, or Source, that they call him; no matter which He is rich by what they told me, but not over-wiſe. They talked to me of him as a ridiculous fellow. Are you acquainted with him?

Arnolph aſide.] A bitter pill!

Horace. Why do not you anſwer?

Arnolph. O, ay——I know him.

Horace. He is a fool, is not he?

Arnolph. Heh——

Horace. How now? what do you ſay to it? Heh! that means yes. Ridiculouſly jealous: Fool? I find he is juſt as I was told. In ſhort, the love-ly Agnes has made a conqueſt of me; to tell you the truth, ſhe is a lovely creature, and it would be a ſin to let a beauty ſo extraordinary remain in the power of this fantaſtical old fellow. For my part, all my endeavours, all my moſt paſſionate wiſhes are, to make her mine, notwithſtanding this jealous wretch; and the money I was ſo free to borrow of you, is for no other purpoſe but to bring about this laudable enterpriſe. You know better than I, that money does everything in ſuch undertakings; and that it procures the victory in love as well as war. But methinks you do not ſeem pleaſed: does my ſcheme diſpleaſe you?

Arnolph. No, I was conſidering——

Horace. You are tired with this converſation: Farewell. I will come preſently to your houſe, to thank you.

Arnolph thinking himſelf alone.] What! muſt it——

Horace coming back.] Once more, I beg you would take care, and not let any one know what I have been ſaying to you.

Arnolph thinking himſelf alone] What my ſoul now feels——

Horace coming back.] Eſpecially my father, who would perhaps be angry at it.

Arnolph thinking he will come back again.] Oh!—— [*alone.*] Oh! what have I ſuffered during

this difcourfe! never was any body fo vexed as I
have been! With what imprudence and what ex-
tremehafte he came to give an account of this bufinefs to me myfelf! Though my other name keeps
him in an error, yet did ever any hair-brains run
on fo furioufly? but having fuffered fo much, I
fhould have been more peaceable, till I had difcovered what I have reafon to apprehend; I fhould
have encouraged his foolifh babbling, by which I
might thoroughly have informed myfelf of what is
carrying on privately between them.   I will endeavour to join him again, he is not got far, I be-.
lieve, and get out of him the whole fecret of this
matter.   I tremble for fear of the misfortune that
may befal me by fo doing; we often feek after
what we would not find.

ACT II. SCENE I.

ARNOLPH.

MY miffing the way he went is really very
lucky, for I do not think I could have
concealed my perturbation of mind, which I am
not willing he fhould know at prefent. But I am
not a man that can put up this matter, and leave
the fpark at liberty to purfue his defign.   I am
refolved to fruftrate it, and be informed how matters have been carried on between them.   I take
it, that my honour is deeply concerned therein:
as the cafe ftands, I confider her as a wife already.
I fhall be blamed, and no one elfe, for whatever

she does amiss. O wretched journey! unhappy absence!

[Knocking at the door.

SCENE II.

ARNOLPH, ALLEN, GEÓRGETTA.

ALLEN.

AH! Sir, this time——

Arnolph. Be quiet. Come hither both of ye: That way, that way. Come along, come along, I say.

Georgetta. Ah! you frighten me! my blood runs chill in my veins!

Arnolph. Is this the way you have obeyed me in my absence? and have you both betrayed me by agreement?

Georgetta falling at Arnolph's feet.] Oh! pray, Sir, do not eat me.

Allen aside.] I am certain some mad dog has bit him.

Arnolph aside.] Ugh! I cannot speak I came so fast, I am stifled; would I could throw off all my clothes. [*To Allen and Georgetta.*] Ye base vipers, you have suffered a man to come then, have ye—What, would you run away?—You must this instant—if you stir— I will have you tell me. Ugh! Ay, I will have you both—S'death! stir not a foot, else I will kill you—How came that man into my house? Heh!—speak, [*panting.*] make haste, quick, dispatch, in a moment, without considering; will ye tell me?

Allen and Georgetta. Oh! Oh!

Georgetta falling at Arnolph's feet.] I swoon.

Allen falling at Arnolph's feet.] I die.

Arnolph aside.] I am all over in a sweat: Let me breathe a little. I muſt walk and cool my-ſelf. Could I have imagined when I ſaw him a little one, that he would grow up for this! Hea-vens! what my heart endures! It would be bet-ter I think to draw from her own mouth by kind uſage an account of what concerns me. Let me try to moderate my paſſion. Softly, my he art, be not in ſuch a flutter, [To Allen and Georget-ta.] Riſe, get ye in, and tell Agnes to come to me. Stay. [Aſide.] They will go tell her the uneaſineſs I am under, and ſhe will be the leſs ſurpriſed. I will fetch her out myſelf. [To Al-len and Georgetta.] Wait here for me.

S C E N E III.

ALLEN, GEORGETTA.

GEORGETTA.

WHAT a frightful look he has! I never ſaw a man appear ſo terrible.

Allen. That gentleman has angered him, I told you ſo.

Georgetta. I cannot imagine what makes him conceal our young lady ſo much, and will not let her ſee any company.

Allen. It is becauſe this affair makes him jea-lous.

Georgetta. But how comes this fancy into his head?

Allen. It comes—it comes, becauſe he is jea-lous.

Georgetta. Ay; but what makes him fo? and why this paffion?

Allen. It is becaufe jealoufy . . . do ye underftand me right, Georgetta? is a thing—which makes people uneafy—and drives them all round the houfe. I will give you a comparifon, that you may conceive it better. Now tell me fincerely, when you have got a mefs of porridge, if fome greedy gut fhould come to eat it from you, would it not vex you, and make you ready to beat him?

Georgetta. Ah, I underftand that.

Allen. It is juft in the fame manner. Woman really is a man's porridge; and when a man fees other people endeavouring to dip their fingers in his porridge, he flies immediately into a rage.

Georgetta. Ay; but why does not every body do fo alike? What is the reafon that fome hufbands appear pleafed, when their wives are in company with fine gentlemen?

Allen. Becaufe every body has not this gluttenous love, that would keep all to itfelf.

Georgetta. If my eyes are not dazzled, I fee him coming.

Allen. Your eyes are good: it is he.

Georgetta. Obferve how penfive he is.

Allen. He is very much vexed juft now.

SCENE IV.

ARNOLPH, ALLEN, GEORGETTA.

ARNOLPH afide.

THE emperor Auguftus was told by a certain Greek, as a maxim equally reafonable and ufeful, that when we happened to be put in a paffion by any accident, we fhould firft of all repeat the alphabet; that in the mean while our anger may abate, and we may do nothing which we ought not to do. I have purfued this advice with regard to Agnes, and I have brought her on purpofe hither, under pretence of taking a walk, in order that the fufpicions of my difordered mind may artfully bring this difcourfe about fo as to dive into her heart, and clear up the matter gently.

SCENE V.

ARNOLPH, AGNES, ALLEN, GEORCETTA.

ARNOLPH.

COME, Agnes, [To Allen and Georgetta.] Get ye in.

SCENE VI.

ARNOLPH, AGNES.

ARNOLPH.

IT is fine walking.
  Agnes. Very fine.
Arnolph. A delightful day!
Agnes. Indeed it is.
Arnolph. What news have ye?
Agnes. The little cat is dead.
Arnolph. That is a great pity; but we are all mortal, and every one for himfelf. Had you any rain when I was in the country?
  Agnes. No.
Arnolph. Were you not tired?

Agnes. I never am tired.

Arnolph. But what have you employed yourself with these nine or ten days?

Agnes. I have made six shirts, I think, and likewise six caps.

Arnolph having mused a while.] This is a strange world we live in, my dear Agnes. Observe how scandalous people are! I have been told by some of the neighbours, that when I was from home, you suffered a young man to come to my house, to see and talk with you. But I gave no credit to these slandering tongues, and would have laid a wager it was false——

Agnes. Lack-a-day, do not lay, you will certainly lose.

Arnolph. What! was there really a man——

Agnes. It was really so. He scarce stirred out of our house, I will swear.

Arnolph aside.] That she is not in jest, this sincere declaration plainly shews. [Aloud.] But, methinks, Agnes, if I remember right, I forbad your seeing any body.

Agnes. Yes: but although I saw him, you are ignorant of the reason of it. Had you been in my place, you would certainly have done the same.

Arnolph. That may be; but, in short, tell me how this matter was.

Agnes. It is very amazing, and I dare say you will hardly believe it. As I was working in the balcony one fine day, I saw a well-made young man pass along under the tree just by, who observing that I looked at him, immediately bowed to me very respectfully: I, in civility, not to be behind hand with him, returned him a courtsy. He soon bowed to me again, I took care to make him another curtfy: and he bowing to me a third time, I alfo anfwered with a third curtfy. He walked to and fro, making me every time the handfomeft bow imaginable, and I, who looked at him earneftly all the while, made him as many curtfies: fo that if night had not come on, I fhould ftill have continued in that manner, being unwilling to give over, or to lie under the diffatisfaction of having him imagine, that I was not fo complaifant as he.

Arnolph. Very well.

Agnes. The next day, as I was ftanding at the door, there came an old woman up to me, who thus fpoke: May heaven long preferve thee in all thy beauty, my child, and pour forth its bleffings upon thee! Becaufe it has made thee fo lovely, thou art not therefore to mifemploy its gifts; know therefore, that thou haft wounded an heart, which now is obliged to complain of it.

Arnolph afide.] Ah! agent of the devil! damned curfed jade!

Agnes. I! have I wounded any body? replied I, very much furprized. Wounded! Ay, thou haft wounded him indeed, cries fhe; and it is the gentleman thou faweft from the balcony yefterday. Alas! fays I, how could I poffibly do it? Did I throw any thing down upon him carelefly? No, replies fhe, thine eyes have given the fatal ftroke, and all his hurt proceeds from their glances. Alas! fays I, you furprize me much; can my eyes hurt any body? Ay, daughter, cries fhe, thine eyes have a deadly poifon in them which thou doft not know of. In a word, the poor wretch is languifhing away, and if fo be, continues the charitable old woman, thy cruelty refufes him affiftance, he will

be a dead man in two days time. Blefs me! I
fhould be very forry for it, fays I; but what affiftance does he require of me! my child, cries fhe,
he only requefts the happinefs of feeing thee, and
talking to thee: thine eyes alone are able to prevent his ruin, and remedy the mifchief they have
produced. Good lack! fays I, with all my heart,
and fince it is fo, he may come and fee me as often
as he chufes.

Arnolph afide.] O curfed forcerefs! may hell
reward thy charitable wiles!

Agnes. He therefore came, faw me, and was
cured. Do not you yourfelf think now, that I
acted but reafonably in doing fo? and after all,
could I have the confcience to lethim die for want
of help? I who am fo full of pity for thofe that
fuffer, that I cannot forbear crying when a chick-
en dies?

Arnolph afide foftly.] All this is only the effect of an innocent mind; and I muft blame my
own indifcreet abfence for it, which left this perfect goodnefs expofed to the defigns of artful fedu-
cers, without any advifer. I fear the rafcal, by
his impudent pretences, has carried the matter
fomewhat beyond a jeft.

Agnes. What is the matter? methinks you are
a little out of humour. Is it that I did amifs in
what I told you?

Arnolph. No. But tell me what followed upon
this interview, and in what manner the young
man behaved in his vifits.

Agnes. Lack-a-day! did you but know how he
was tranfported, how foon his illnefs left him
when he faw me, the prefent he has made me of a
fine cafket, and the money our Allen and Georget-

ta have had of him, you would certainly be in love with him, and fay as we do.

Arnolph. Well, but when you was alone with him, what did he do?

Agnes. He faid he loved me with an unequalled paffion, and told me in the fineft language in the world, things that nothing ever can come up to; the agreeablenefs whereof delighted me every time I heard him fpeak, and raifed within me a certain inexpreffible emotion, with which I was vaftly delighted.

Arnolph afide.] O tormenting enquiry into a fatal fecret, where the enquirer only fuffers all the pain! [Aloud.] Befides all this talk, all thefe pretty ways, did not he kifs you too?

Agnes. Yes he did, moft lovingly! he took my hands and arms, and was never weary of kiffing them.

Arnolph. Did he take nothing elfe from you, Agnes? [Seeing her at a lofs.] Hah!

Agnes. Why, he did—

Arnolph. What?

Agnes. Take—

Arnolph. How!

Agnes. The—

Arnolph. What do you mean?

Agnes. I dare not tell you; for perhaps you will be angry with me.

Arnolph. No, I will not.

Agnes. Yes but you will.

Arnolph. Indeed I will not.

Agnes. Swear faith then.

Arnolph. Well, faith.

Agnes. He took—You will be in a paffion.

Arnolph. No.

Agnes. Yes.

Arnolph. No, no, no, no: What the deuce do you mean? What did he take from you?

Agnes. He——

Arnolph aside.] I suffer damnation.

Agnes. Well then, to tell you the truth, he took away the ribbon you gave me, but I could not help it.

Arnolph recovering himself.] No matter for the ribbon. But I want to know whether he did nothing but kiss your hands.

Agnes. Why! do people do other things?

Arnolph. No, no. But did not he desire of you some other remedy to cure the disorder he said had seized him?

Agnes. He did not, but if he had, I should have given any thing to do him good.

Arnolph aside.] Heaven's goodness be praised, I am come cheaply off. If I fall into the like mistake again, I will consent to be ill used. [*Aloud.*] Peace, it is an effect of your innocence, Agnes: I will say no more of it: What is done is done. I am sensible that by flattering you, the spark only wants to impose upon you, and afterwards to laugh at you.

Agnes. Oh, no, he told me so above twenty times.

Arnolph. You ought not to believe him. It is committing a great sin to accept of caskets, and hearken to those powdered beaux, to suffer them, in a languishing tone, to kiss your hands and charm your heart in this manner.

Agnes. Do you call it a sin? For what reason, pray?

Arnolph. For what reason? Why the reason is,

becaufe it is declared that heaven is offended at fuch doings.

Agnes. Offended! But why fhould it be offended? Alas! it is fo fweet, fo pleafant! I admire at the delight one finds in it, and was ignorant of thefe things before.

Arnolph. Ay, there is a great deal of pleafure in all thefe tenderneffes, thefe complaifant difcourfes, thefe fond embraces; but they fhould be tafted in an honeft manner, and the fin fhould be taken away by marrying.

Agnes. After one is married is it not a fin?

Arnolph. No.

Agnes. Then, pray, marry me immediately.

Arnolph. If you defire it, I defire it too, and came back on purpofe to marry you.

Agnes. Did you really?

Arnolph. Yes.

Agnes. How glad you will make me!

Arnolph. Ay, I do not queftion but matrimony will pleafe you.

Agnes. Will you have us two——

Arnolph. Nothing more certain.

Agnes. If it be fo, I fhall embrace you.

Arnolph. And I fhall do the fame by you.

Agnes. For my part, I do not underftand when people are in jeft.   Do you fpeak ferioufly?

Arnolph. Ay, you fhall fee I do.

Agnes. We fhall be married then?

Arnolph. Yes.

Agnes. But when?

Arnolph. This very evening.

Agnes, laughing.] This very evening?

Arnolph. This very evening.   Are you glad at it?

Agnes. Yes.

Arnolph. It is my defire to fee you happy.

Agnes. I am very much obliged to you: what fatisfaction fhall I enjoy with him!

Arnolph. With whom?

Agnes. With—him there.

Arnolph. Him there — I do not talk of him there; you are a little forward, methinks, to choofe an hufband. In a word, it is another body I have got ready for you; and as for that gentleman there, I intend, by your favour, (even though the malady he amufes you with fhould kill him) that hence-forward you fhall break off all acquaintance with him: that when he comes to the houfe, your com-pliment fhall be civilly to fhut the door upon him, and if he knocks, throw a ftone at him out of the window, and oblige him in good earneft never to come there again. Do you underftand me, Agnes? I will lie concealed in a corner, and obferve how you behave.

Agnes. Alack! he is fo genteel, it is—

Arnolph. Heh! what a fpeech!

Agnes. I fhall not have the heart----

Arnolph. No more difputing. Go up ftairs.

Agnes. Will you really----

Arnolph. Hold your tongue; I am mafter, therefore you fhall obey.

{*}{*}{*}{*}{*} . {*}{*}{*}{*}{*}{*}

ACT III. SCENE I.

ARNOLPH, AGNES, ALLEN,
GEORGETTA.

ARNOLPH.

BY following my directions, you have confounded the handsome seducer; in short, every thing has succeeded to my wishes, and I am vastly pleased. This it is to have a discreet adviser:
your innocence, Agnes, had been infnared; and
fee what a condition you would have been in, before you were aware of it. You were running directly on in the high road to hell and destruction,
had not I set you right. The ways of these sparks
are but too well known; they have fine stockings,
ribbons and feathers in abundance, large wigs, good
teeth, and a smooth tongue; but I assure you,
there is a cloven foot underneath, and they are devils in reality, whose voracious appetite endeavours
to make a prey of female honour. However, this
time, thanks to the care that has been taken, you
are escaped with your virtue. The air wherewith I
saw you throw that stone at him, which has rendered all his designs hopeless, makes me still more
resolved not to delay the marriage, for which I told
you to prepare yourself. But it is proper, first of
all, to have a little talk with you, that may be to
your advantage. [to Georgetta and Allen.] Bring
out a chair hither. If you ever——
Georgetta. We will remember all your instruc

tions perfectly: The other gentleman there impof-
ed upon us: But----

Allen. May I die, if ever he get in again. Befides, he is a blockhead, he gave us two crown pieces the other day that were not weight.

Arnolph. Get what I ordered for fupper, and
as for our contract which I fpoke of, let one of you
fetch the Notary hither, that lives at the corner of
the market-place.

S C E N E II.

A R N O L P H, A G N E S.

ARNOLPH fitting.

LAY afide your work, Agnes, and pay attention to what I am going to fay to you: hold
up your head, and look at me whilft I am fpeaking, and be fure remember every thing I fay to
you. I intend to marry you, Agnes, and you ought
an hundred times a-day to blefs your happy fate,
to remind yourfelf of the pitiful condition you were
in, and at the fame time to admire my goodnefs,
which raifes you from the mean ftation of a poor
country-wench to the honourable rank of a citizen's wife; to enjoy both the bed and the embraces of a man who has fhunned all fuch engagements, and whofe heart has refufed the honour it
will do you, to twenty people very capable of pleafing. You ought, I fay, continually to remind
yourfelf how infignificant you would be without
this glorious alliance, to the intent that confidera-
tion may the better teach you to deferve the ftation I fhall place you in, and make you always know
yourfelf, fo that I may never repent of what I do.

Matrimony, Agnes, is not a trifling thing; severe
duties are required of a wife; and I do not defign
to exalt you to that condition, for you to be a Li-
bertine and to take your pleafure. Your fex is
merely dependant in that ftate, the whole power is
on the hufband's fide; though they are two parts
of the fame body, yet thofe two parts are far from
being equal; one is the fuperior part, and the o-
ther the fubordinate; the one is in all cafes fubject to the other that governs: and that obedience
which the well-difciplined foldier fhews to his general, the fervant to his mafter, a child to his father, or the loweft monk to his fuperior, comes e-
ven very fhort of the tractablenefs, the fubmiffion,
the humility, and the profound veneration which
a wife fhould have for her hufband, her chief, her
lord and mafter. When he looks ferioufly upon
her fhe fhould turn her eyes immediately upon the
ground, and never prefume to look him in the face,
till he favours her with a gracious glance. Our
wives, in this age, are ignorant of this, but be not
you corrupted by the example of other people. Beware of imitating thofe foolifh jilts, whofe pranks
are talked of all the city over; and do not let the
devil tempt you, that is to fay, hearken to no young
coxcomb. Confider, Agnes, that by making you
part of myfelf, I give you up my honour, which
honour is tender, and eafily offended; that there
is no trifling on fuch an occafion as this, and that
in hell there are boiling cauldrons wherein wives
that live wickedly are plunged for ever and ever.
Thefe are not foolifh ftories which I am telling you,
and thefe leffons fhould be imprinted in your heart.
If you practife them fincerely, and avoid being a
coquette, your foul will be always as white and

spotless as the lily, but if you forfeit your honour, it will become as black as a coal; you will appear as a terrible monster to every body, and in time you will be the devil's property, and boil in hell to all eternity, from which I heartily pray you may be preserved. Make a curtsy. As a probationer in a convent must know her duty by heart, so she that marries should do the very same: and I have a writing of great importance in my pocket, which will teach you the duty of a wife. Some good body has wrote it, who is now unknown, and I would have you study it constantly. [He gets up.] Hold: Let's see if you can read and understand it. [Agnes reads.

MAXIMS of WEDLOCK, or the duties of a married woman; together with her daily exercise.

I. MAXIM.

" THE woman who intends to be married
" ought to remember, that the man who
" takes her, takes her only for himself, notwith-
" standing the vast numbers of admirers which o-
" ther women have in these our days.

Arnolph. I shall explain to you what that means; but for the present let us only read.

[Agnes goes on.

II. MAXIM.

" She ought to consult her husband about her
" dress; it being for him alone she should take care
" of her beauty, and be regardless whether other
" people think her handsome or not.

III. MAXIM.

" She muſt lay aſide the practice of ogling, and
" muſt uſe no paints, pomatums, beauty-waſhes,
" nor the numberleſs ingredients that are made
" uſe of to ſet off the complexion. Theſe are
" always mortal poiſons to honour, and the pains
" beſtowed to appear beautiful are ſeldom for
" the huſband's ſake.

IV. MAXIM.

" When ſhe goes abroad, ſhe ought, as honour
" requires, to prevent the wounds her eyes might
" give, by concealing them under her hood: for
" ſhe ſhould ſtudy to pleaſe her huſband, and no
" one elſe.

V. MAXIM.

" Decency prohibits her from receiving any
" friends whatever, except ſuch as come to ſee her
" huſband: thoſe people of gallantry that have no
" buſineſs but with the wife, are very diſagreea-
" ble to the huſband.

VI. MAXIM.

" She muſt not accept any preſents from men,
" for they always expect ſome favour in return.

VII. MAXIM.

" Amongſt her moveables ſhe muſt have neither
" ſcrutoir, ink, paper, nor pens. The huſband, ac-

" cording to good cuſtom, ſhould write all that is
" written in his family.

VIII. MAXIM.

" She ſhould not go to thoſe diſorderly ſocieties
" called aſſemblies, which tend to corrupt wo-
" men's mind; for at theſe places they invent the
" deepeſt plots againſt their huſbands.

IX. MAXIM.

" If a woman intends to preſerve her honour,
" ſhe muſt ſhun gaming as a terrible thing; for
" play is very bewitching, and often drives a wo-
" man to the laſt ſtake.

X. MAXIM.

" She muſt never go to public walks, nor ac-
" cept of treats in the country, for it is thought
" the huſband generally is at the expence of ſuch
" jaunts."

Arnolph. You may read the reſt of it when a-
lone, and by-and-by I will explain theſe matters
to you, as they ſhould be, line by line. I have a
little affair come into my head, it is only to ſpeak
a word, and I ſhall not tarry long. Go in, and
take a ſpecial care of that book. If the Notary
comes, tell him to wait till I come.

SCENE III.

ARNOLPH alone.

THIS girl is fo pliant in my hands, that I can turn her any way, therefore I cannot do better than make her my wife. I very narrowly efcaped being choufed in my abfence through her over innocence; but to fay the truth, one's wife's failings had much better be from that caufe; for fuch fort of miftakes are eafily amended. Simple people pay great attention to their advifers, and if they chance to be deceived, a word or two will put them right again. But it is quite otherwife with a witty wife; our fate depends on her judgment only; nothing can divert her from purfuing what fhe is once fet upon, and all our precepts, in this cafe, prove abortive. Her wit enables her to ridicule our maxims, to make virtues of her faults, and find out ways of deceiving the moft dexterous, in order to bring about her wicked defigns. We labour in vain to turn afide the blow; a witty woman is a plague in intrigue, and after her caprice has filently paffed fentence on our honour, it muft be fubmitted to. A great many honeft people are able to declare as much. But my blunderbufs fhall find no caufe to laugh; he has met with what he deferves for tattling. This is the common fault of our countrymen, in the poffeffion of good fortune they are never eafy, while it is a fecret, and this fenfelefs vanity is fo valuable to them, that they would rather lofe their happinefs than not talk of it. Sure the devil muft be very ftrong in women when they choofe fuch rattle-pates! and——But here he comes: let me be upon my guard, and discover how greatly he is mortified.

SCENE IV.

HORACE, ARNOLPH.

HORACE.

I Have just been at your house, where fate seems resolved I should never meet with you; but I will go so often, that some moment at last shall---

Arnolph. Pray use not these silly compliments, than which nothing is more tiresome to me, and could I prevail, all manner of ceremony should be wholly laid aside. It is a wretched custom, wherein most people waste two parts in three of their time. Let us leave it off then without any more ado. [*Puts on his hat.*] Well, as to your love intrigue, Mr. Horace, may I be informed how you go on in it? I was taken off before by some business that came into my head, but I have been considering of it since: I admire the quick progress you have made at the beginning, and am solicitous for the event.

Horace. My passion has been unfortunate, Sir, since I discovered it to you.

Arnolph. Ay! how so?

Horace. The master of my fair one is unhappily returned from the country.

Arnolph. What a misfortune!

Horace. And besides, to my very great sorrow, he knows what has passed in private between us two.

Arnolph. How the deuce could he learn this affair fo foon?

Horace. I really cannot tell, but fo it really is. At my ufual hour, I went to the houfe to fee her, when both the man and maid, with a voice and countenance quite altered from what they ufed to be, oppofed my entrance, and fhut the door to my face with a Get you gone, you are troublefome.

Arnolph. The door to your face!

Horace. To my face.

Arnolph. That is a little hard.

Horace. I would have talked to them through the door, but to all that I could fay their anfwer was, You fhall not come in, my mafter has forbid it.

Arnolph. Did they not let you in then?

Horace. No. And Agnes confirmed her mafter's return to me from the window, by bidding me be gone in a very angry tone, and throwing a ftone at me.

Arnolph. How! a ftone?

Horace. A ftone that was none of the leaft neither, by which with her own hand fhe received my vifit.

Arnolph. The devil! Thefe are no jokes: your affair is in no very flourifhing way.

Horace. Very true, this return of his has greatly hurt me.

Arnolph. Really I am forry for you, I proteft I am.

Horace. This man breaks all my meafures.

Arnolph. Ay, but that is nothing; you will find a way of fetting yourfelf to rights again.

Horace. I muft endeavour by fome intelligence to baffle the ftrict vigilance of her jealous mafter.

Arnolph. You will eafily do that, for when all is done the girl loves you.

Horace. I really believe fhe does.

Arnolph. You will bring matters to bear.

Horace. I hope fo.

Arnolph. That ftone has perplexed you, but you fhould not be aftonifhed at it.

Horace. That's certain, for I prefently difcovered that my rival was there, and managed the whole affair without being feen in it. But what furprized me, and what you will wonder at, was another accident I am going to tell you of, a bold ftroke of the lovely girl, which one would not have expected from her fimplicity. Love, it muft be owned, is a fkilful mafter; he teaches us to be what we never were before, and frequently an intire alteration in our manners becomes by his leffons only a moment's work. He breaks through the obftacles of nature in us, and his fudden effects have the appearance of miracles. A coward is by him in an inftant rendered courageous, a mifer liberal, and a churl obliging; he infpires the greateft blockhead with wifdom, and makes him capable of doing every thing. Agnes is a furprizing inftance of this, for fnapping me up in thefe very words, Get you gone, I am refolved never to fee you more. I know all you have to fay, and there is my anfwer. This ftone, or this pebble, at which you would wonder, fell down with a letter at my feet; and what I admire is to find this letter adapted exactly to the meaning of her words, and the ftone fhe threw. Are not you furprized at fuch an action as this? Does not love know the art of quickening the underftanding? And can it be denied that his powerful flames have wonderful effects upon the mind? What do ye say to all this? What think ye of the letter? Heh! do not you admire this crafty contrivance? Is not it comical to observe what a part my jealous rival has been acting with all this foolery? Are not—

Arnolph. Ay, very comical.

Horace. Why, I think, it does not make you laugh. [Arnolph forces a laugh.] This military man, who fortifies himself in his own house against my passion, and seems provided with stones, as tho' I meant to enter by storm, who in a whimsical fright encourages all his servants to drive me away, is imposed upon before his face, even by his own instrument, by her whom he would keep in the utmost ignorance. I confess, for my part, though his return has thrown my affair under a very great difficulty, I think it is so very droll that I cannot forbear laughing whenever it comes into my head, and methinks you do not laugh at it enough.

Arnolph with a forced laugh.] I beg your pardon, I laugh at it as much as I am able.

Horace. But I must shew you her letter as a friend, in which she has writ down all that her heart felt, in terms so affecting, so perfectly full of goodness, of innocent tenderness and sincerity! in a word, in the very manner that pure nature expresses the first wound love gives.

Arnolph aside.] This is the consequence of your writing, you gypsey: it was contrary to my intention that you was taught it.

Horace reads.] " I have a mind to write to you, " but I know not where I shall begin. I have " some thoughts which I am desirous you should " be acquainted with; but I am at a loss how tell " them you, and distrust my want of words. As

" I begin to underſtand that I have always been
" kept in ignorance, I am afraid of writing ſome-
" thing that would be wrong, or ſaying more than
" I ſhould do.   I do not know what you have
" done to me, but I find that I am ready to die
" with vexation for what I am forced to do againſt
" you, that it would give me all the uneaſineſs in
" the world to loſe you, and that I ſhould be great-
" ly delighted to be yours.   There is harm, per-
" haps, in ſaying ſo, but really I cannot forbear,
" though I wiſh it could have been brought about,
" and no harm had been in it.   I am informed,
" that all young men are falſe, that what they ſay
" muſt not be minded, and that every thing you
" tell me is only to deceive me: But I aſſure you,
" I cannot yet imagine that of you, and I am ſo
" affected by your words, that I do not know how
" to believe they are lies.   Tell me generouſly
" if they be; for as I am devoid of any ill de-
" ſign, you would do the greateſt injury in the
" world ſhould you deceive me, and I believe the
" vexation of it would kill me.

Arnolph aſide.] Um, Bitch!

Horace. What do ye ſay?

Arnolph. I? Nothing   I only coughed.

Horace. Did you ever ſee more tenderneſs of
expreſſion? notwithſtanding all the curſed endeavours of unreaſonable power, is it poſſible to find a
better natural capacity? and is not it certainly a
mortal ſin villainouſly to ſpoil ſuch an admirable genius? to be deſirous of obſcuring the brightneſs
of ſuch a mind in ignorance and ſtupidity? But
love has begun to pull off the maſk; and if by the
favour of ſome lucky ſtar I can be able to deal with

this mere animal, this blockhead, this fcoundrel, this brute----

Arnolph. Good bye to ye.

Horace. Why in fuch a hurry?

Arnolph. I have juft thought of an important affair, which----

Horace. Can you not tell me of any body (as you live in the neighbourhood) that could get admittance into this houfe? I make free with you, and it is not un-ufual for friends to ferve one another on fuch occa-fions. At prefent I have no body in it but people to watch me; the man and maid both, as I found juft now, in fpight of all that I could do, would not be fo civil as to hear me. I had a certain old wo-man in my intereft for fome time, of a genius, to fay the truth, more than human. She was very ferviceable to me at the beginning; but four days ago the poor woman died. Cannot you put me in fome way?

Arnolph. No, really; you will find out fome without me.

Horace. Farewel then. You fee what confidence I put in you.

S C E N E V.

A R N O L P H alone.

WHAT a reftraint I am obliged to put upon myfelf before him! What! a fimpleton have fo much ready wit! fuch the huffy has pretend-ed to be in my fight. How the deuce has her foul fucked in this fubtility? After all, that fatal letter is the death of me. I find the villain has corrupted her mind, and has fixed himfelf there in my place: This gives me defpair and mortal pain. I fuffer doubly by being robbed of her heart; for thereby love is injured as well as honour. It diftracts me to fee my prudent meafures defeated, and my place ufurped. I am fenfible that to punifh her guilty paffion, I need only leave her to her evil deftiny, and that fhe herfelf would revenge me upon herfelf; but to be deprived of the thing one loves is terrible. Heavens! after making ufe of fo much philofophy in my choice, why muft I be fo mightily bewitched by her charms? She is deftitute of parents, friends, and money; fhe abufes my care, my favours, my tendernefs; and yet I love her, even after this bafe affair, fo much that I am unable to throw off this fondnefs. Fool! haft thou no fhame? Oh I burft! I am mad, and I could tear myfelf in pieces. I will ftop in a little, but only to fee how fhe looks after fo enormous a crime. Heaven grant that my brows may be free from difhonour! but if it is decreed that I muft fuffer it, beftow upon me at leaft that fortitude which fome people are endowed with to bear fuch accidents!

ACT IV. SCENE I.

ARNOLPH.

WHerever I go my mind diftracts me, it is greatly perplexed how to manage things both within doors and without, fo as to fruftrate the defigns of this young fop. With what effrontery did the traitrefs bear the fight of me! what fhe has done does not in the leaft concern her; and though she has brought me within an inch of the grave, one would swear, to look at her, that she had not the least hand in it. The more she appeared compofed when I faw her, the more was I vexed, and thofe boiling tranfports which inflamed my heart, feemed only to redouble my ardent paffion. I was incenfed againft her, and yet I never faw her appear fo beautiful; her eyes, methought, never were before fo piercing, never did they before infpire me with fuch violent defires: and I perceive it would kill me fhould my evil deftiny bring this difgrace upon me. What? Have I brought her up fo tenderly, and with fo much care? Have I taken her to me from her infancy? Have I indulged the fondeft hopes? Muft I build upon her growing charms? And during thirteen years have I fondled her to be my own, as I imagined, for an hair-brained youth whom fhe is in love with to come and run away with her before my face, and that even when fhe is half married to me? No, by heavens, my foolifh young friend; by heavens, no: you muft be a cunning fellow to overturn my project; or elfe by my faith, I fhall render all your hopes abortive, and you will find no caufe to laugh at me.

S·C E N E II.

A NOTARY, ARNOLPH.

NOTARY.

O There he is! Good-morrow to ye: I am ready to draw up the contract as you defire.

Arnolph not perceiving or hearing him.] In what manner muft it be done?

Notary. It muſt be done in the uſual form.

Arnolph not perceiving him.] I will uſe all poſſible precaution.

Notary. I will do nothing contrary to your intereſt.

Arnolph not perceiving him.] I muſt guard againſt any ſurprize.

Notary. It is enough that your affairs are put into my hands. You muſt by no means ſign the contract before you receive the portion, for fear of being cheated.

Arnolph not perceiving him.] I am afraid, ſhould I make the leaſt diſcovery, it would become a public town-talk.

Notary. But it is very eaſy to prevent a diſcovery; your contract may be tranſacted privately.

Arnolph not perceiving him.] But how ſhall I ſettle the point with her?

Notary. The jointure ſhould be in proportion to the fortune ſhe brings you.

Arnolph not perceiving him.] I love her, and that love is the greateſt difficulty I labour under.

Notary. In that caſe the wife may have ſo much the more.

Arnolph not perceiving him.] How to behave to her on ſuch an occaſion?

Notary. The law ſays, the huſband that is to be ſhall ſettle upon the wife that is to be the third part of her portion; but the law ſignifies nothing at all, you may do a great deal more than that if you have a mind to it.

Arnolph not perceiving him. If----

[Seeing the Notary.

Notary. As for the preſents to be made, let them agree together. I ſay the huſband that is to be may give the wife that is to be what jointure he chufes.

Arnolph. Heh!

Notary. He may give her fo much and more, if he loves her greatly, and is defirous to oblige her, and that by way of jointure or fettlement as they call it, to be left and go away intirely to the right heirs of the faid wife that is to be, upon her deceafe; or elfe according to the ftatute, as people have a mind; or as a gift, by a deed in form, which may be made either fingle or mutual. Wherefore do you fhrug? Do not I talk very learnedly? Do you think that I do not underftand the manner of a contract? Who is it can teach me? No body, I prefume. Do not I know that when they are married they have in law an equal right to all moveables, monies, immoveables and acquifitions, unlefs they give it up by an act of renunciation? Do not I know that a third part of the portion of the wife that is to be, becomes in common, for——

Arnolph. I do not in the leaft doubt but that you know all this; but no body is talking to you about it.

Notary. Why, do you feem to take me for a fool, by fhrugging up your fhoulders, and making faces at me?

Arnolph. Pox take the fellow with his puppy's face. Adieu, that is the way to make you hold your peace.

Notary. Was not I fetched hither to draw up a contract?

Arnolph. Yes, I fent for you; but the affair is put off, and I will fend for you again when the

time is fixed.   What a noife the fellow makes!
Notary alone.] I dare fay the man is mad.

SCENE III.

NOTARY, ALLEN, GEORGETTA.

NOTARY.

DID you come to fetch me to your mafter?
Allen. Yes.

Notary. I do not know what you may take him for, but go and tell him from me, that he is a mad fool.

Georgetta. We fhall not fail to do it.

SCENE IV.

ARNOLPH, ALLEN, GEORGETTA.

ALLEN.

SIR,———
Arnolph. Come hither, you are my trufty, my good, my real friends, and I have fome news for you.

Allen. The Notary———

Arnolph. No matter, fome other time for that. A wicked defign is contrived againft my honour; and what a difgrace would it be for you, children, to have your mafter robbed of his honour? After that you would not dare to appear in any place, for whoever fees you would point at you.   Therefore, fince the affair concerns you as much as me, you muft take fuch care, for your part, that this gallant may not———

Georgetta. You have taught us our leffon already.

Arnolph. But beware of paying the least attention to his sly speeches.

Allen. O! to be sure.————

Georgetta. We know how to deny him.

Arnolph. Suppose he should come now in a
coaxing manner; Allen, my dear heart, cheer up
my drooping spirits by a little of your affistance.

Allen. You are a blockhead.

Arnolph. Right. [To Georgetta.] Georgetta,
my pretty-face, you seem so sweet-tempered, and
so good a body.

Georgetta. You are an oaf.

Arnolph. Right. [To Allen.] Do you think there
is the least harm in an honest and virtuous design?

Allen. You are a villain.

Arnolph. Very well. [To Georgetta.] I shall
certainly die, if you take no pity on the pains I suffer.

Georgetta. You are a fool, an impudent rascal.

Arnolph. Mighty good. [To Allen.] I am not
a person that desires something for nothing; I know
how to remember services that are done me: However, Allen, there is somewhat to make you drink
before-hand; and there is to buy you some ribbons,
Georgetta. [Both hold out their hands and take
the money.] This is only an earnest of my kindness; and all the favour I request of you is only to
let me see your handsome mistress.

Georgetta pushing him.] None of your tricks
upon us.

Arnolph. That is good.

Allen pushing him.] Begone.

Arnolph. Right.

Georgetta pushing him.] Immediately.

Arnolph. Very well. Hold, enough.

Georgetta. Do not I do right?

Allen. Is this the way you would have us behave to him?

Arnolph. Yes, you do extremely well, except as to the money, which you muſt not take.

Georgetta. We did not think of that.

Allen. Would you have us begin again juſt now?

Arnolph. No; it is enough, go in both of you.

Allen. You need only ſpeak.

Arnolph. No, I tell you, go in when I deſire you. You may keep the money; go, I will come to you again; look circumſpectly to every thing, and ſecond my endeavours.

S C E N E V.

ARNOLPH alone.

THIS ſpark ſhall be mighty cunning indeed, if he can now get either letter or meſſage conveyed to her. I will get the cobler who lives at the corner of our ſtreet to be a ſpy for me. I intend never to let her out of doors, and will baniſh all milliners, tire-women, and glove-makers, who make it their conſtant cuſtom to help on love-intrigues. I who underſtand matters, and have ſeen the world, know all the tricks of it.

S C E N E VI.

HORACE, ARNOLPH,

HORACE.

I HAVE juſt now made a very narrow eſcape, and am very glad to find you here. Juſt after I ſaw you laſt, I unexpectedly ſaw Agnes all alone in the balcony, enjoying the fresh air. After having made me a sign, she came down and let me in by the garden door. But I was hardly in her chamber, before she heard her watchful Argus upon the stairs; upon which she shut me up in a closet which luckily happined to be in the room. He came into the room immediately: I did not see him, but I heard him walk to and fro at a great rate, without uttering one syllable, but sighing grievously now and then, and sometimes giving great thumps upon the table, beating a little dog that fawned upon him, and overturning every thing that came in his way; he broke in his passion the very flower-pots with which the fair one had set out her chimney; and without doubt the trick she has played must have come to his ear. At last, after having by twenty such tricks discharged his fury on things that could not help it, he without saying what made him uneasy, left the chamber, and I my prison. We durst not venture to stay together any longer for fear of somebody, it would have been running too great a risque: But she is to admit me into her chamber to-night, when it is late; the sign for her to know me is to be three hems, and then the window will be opened, out of which Agnes is to put a ladder, whereby I will enter. This I tell to you as my only friend: Joy increases by being revealed; and should one taste the most consummate joys an hundred times over, it would not be satisfactory unless it were known by some-body. You will take part, I believe, in the success of my affairs. Farewell, I am going about some other business just now.

I 6

SCENE VII.

ARNOLPH alone.

AM I never to be at reft, but be conftantly per-
fecuted by my evil deftiny? Is my vigilance
and wifdom to be for ever defeated? And am I
always to be the fport of this fimple wench and
raw-brained fop? I have been contemplating the
wretched fate of married men for thefe twenty years
and upwards, and have carefully informed myfelf
of all the accidents whereby the moft wary are diftrefs-
ed: I have profited by the difgraces of others, and
have endeavoured to fecure my brows from all affronts, and prevent their being like other foreheads,
it being my intent to marry: For this noble purpofe I thought I had made ufe of every project
that could be thought of, but cruel fate feems
to have decreed that no mortal fhould be exempt-
ed from it; after all the light and experience that
I could poffibly gain in thefe matters, after more
than twenty years ftudying how to conduct myfelf
cautioufly through the whole affair, have I acted contrary to the practice of fo many hufbands, to find
myfelf in the very fame condition as they are? Ah!
cruel deftiny, thou haft proved falfe! I am ftill in
poffeffion of the defired object; and if her heart is
ftolen from me by this unlucky fpark, I will prevent him however from feizing any thing elfe, and
they fhall not fpend this night fo agreeably as they
imagine. This blunderer, by entrufting his fecret
with me, puts it in my power to defeat all his projects, which is however fome fmall comfort.

SCENE VIII.

CHRISALDUS, ARNOLPH.

CHRISALDUS.

WELL, shall we sup before we walk?

Arnolph. No, I do not intend to take any supper to-night.

Chrisaldus. Pray what is the reason of this?

Arnolph. I have a reason for it.

Chrisaldus. Is not the wedding you resolved upon to be performed?

Arnolph. You interfere too much in other people's affairs.

Chrisaldus. How sharp you are! I suppose you have been crossed in your love-affair.

Arnolph. Let what will befal me, I shall at least have the advantage of being unlike certain people, who peaceably suffer galants to make their visits.

Chrisaldus. It is very odd, that you should always take fright upon this affair, that you should place your sovereign happiness in this, and imagine no other kind of honour in the world: To be a miser, a villain, a bully, and coward, is nothing in your opinion, compared with this blot; and in whatsoever manner a man may have lived, he is a man of honour if he is not a cuckold. To speak seriously, what makes you think that all our glory is dependent on such an accident? And that a virtuous mind has any thing to reproach itself for the injustice of a vicious one which it could not help? Why will you, I say, imagine that in marrying one deserves either praise or blame for the choice one makes, and form a moſt horrible monſter of the affront that is done one by a wife's falſhood? Be perſuaded that a man of honour need not be ſo frighted at cuckoldom; that none being ſecure from the ſtrokes of fortune, this accident ſhould be thought in itſelf indifferent; and in a word, that all the harm of it, let the world pretend what it will, lies only in the manner of our bearing it. To behave well under theſe difficulties, one muſt, as well as in all others, avoid extremes: not be like thoſe over-good natured people, who, proud of ſuch affairs, are continually bringing galants to viſit their wives, and telling their good qualifications to everyone; who appear exactly of their humour, come to all their treats and meetings, make every one wonder at their having the aſſurance to ſhew their faces there. This way of acting is certainly highly blameable, but the other extreme is not leſs ſo. As I do not approve of ſuch as are friends to their wives' galants, I am no more for thoſe violent people whoſe indiſcreet reſentment, full of rage and fury, draws the eyes of every one upon them by its noiſe, and who, by the buſtle they make, appear unwilling that any body ſhould be ignorant what they are. There is a medium between theſe two extremes, where a wiſe man ſtops upon ſuch an occaſion: when a body knows how to take it, there is no cauſe to be aſhamed for the worſt a wife can do. In a word, people may ſay of it what they pleaſe, but it may be eaſily made to appear not ſo frightful, and, as I told you before, all the dexterity lies in knowing how to turn the fair ſide outwards.

Arnolph. The whole fraternity ought to return you thanks for this excellent ſpeech, and any bo-

dy that hears you fpeak muft rejoice to find himfelf enrolled amongft the number.

Chrifaldus. I do not fay that, for it is what I
blame: but as a wife is the gift of fortune, one
fhould do, I fay, as at dice, where if what you expect do not come up, you muft make ufe of dexterity and temper to amend your luck by good conduct.

Arnolph. That is to fay, always eat and fleep
quietly, and perfuade yourfelf it fignifies juft nothing.

Chrifaldus. You think to make a jeft of it: but
in my opinion there are a hundred things worfe
than this accident which you dread fo much. If
I were forced to make my choice, I would rather
chufe to be one of that fraternity you fo much defpife, than to be married to one of thefe modeft women
whofe perverfenefs makes a quarrel out of nothing;
thofe dragons of virtue, thofe honeft fhe-devils, pique
themfelves continually upon their wife conduct,
who, becaufe they do not do us a flight injury, take
upon them to behave haughtily, and expect from
their being true to us, that we fhould bear every
thing from them.—Let me tell you, friend Arnolph, once again, that cuckoldom is really nothing
but what one makes it, that it is even defirable on
fome accounts, and that it, as well as other things,
has its pleafures.

Arnolph. If you are of a temper to be contented under it, I have not the leaft inclination to experience it for my part, and rather than fubmit to
fuch a thing———

Chrifaldus. Swear not, I befeech you, for fear
of being perjured. If fate ordains it fo, your pre-

cautions are all to no purpofe; you will not be confulted about the matter.

Arnolph. Shall I be a cuckold?

Chrifaldus. You are grievoufly hurt: A thoufand people are fo, without difparagement to you, who for perfon, courage, wealth, and family, would be affronted to be compared with you.

Arnolph. For my part, I fhall make no comparifons with them. But, in one word, this raillery is foolifh, let us have done with it, if you pleafe.

Chrifaldus. You are at prefent enraged, therefore I bid you adieu for the prefent: but remember, whatever your honour may make you imagine as to this affair, that it is being half what we were talking of, to fwear you will not be fo.

Arnolph. I fwear it again, and will go immediately and endeavour to prevent this misfortune.

[Goes to knock at his door.

SCENE IX.

ARNOLPH, ALLEN, GEORGETTA.

ARNOLPH.

NOW is the time, my friends, that I beg you would affift me. I really believe you have a regard for me, but now you muft make it appear; if you are honeft and faithful you may be certain of a reward. The young fpark intends to trick me this very night, and get by a ladder into Agnes's chamber, but pray keep it very fecret; we three muft lay a trap for him. Each of you muft be ready with a good heavy club, and when he is almoft at the top of the ladder, (for I will open the window at the nick of time) both of you muſt fall upon him in ſuch a manner, that his back may be ſure to make him remember it, and teach him never to come there again. However, do not mention me at all, nor make any appearance of my being behind. Will you have the courage to execute my reſentment?

Allen. If he is only to be thraſhed, Sir, depend upon us, you ſhall ſee whether I ſtrike with a dead man's arm or not.

Georgetta. 'Tho' mine ſeems not ſo ſtrong, in thraſhing him it ſhall not be lazy.

Arnolph. Go you in then, and above all things, be careful of ſpeaking about it. [alone.] This is a uſeful leſſon for my neighbour, and there would not be ſo many cuckolds, if every huſband was to give his wife's galant the ſame reception.

ACT V. SCENE I.

ARNOLPH, ALLEN, GEORGETTA.

ARNOLPH.

WHO commanded you to beat him in that manner, wretches? you have murdered him.

Allen. We followed your directions, Sir.

Arnolph. I ordered you to beat his back, but not to murder him, therefore it is in vain for you to make that excuſe. Heavens! into what a condition has fortune now reduced me! what can I think of doing, to ſee the man dead? Get into the houſe, and be ſure you ſay not a word of the innocent order

I gave you. [alone.] It will foon be light, and I will go afk advice how I fhall manage this affair. Alas! what will become of me? And what will the father fay, when he comes to know of this fatal misfortune?

S C E N E II.

ARNOLPH, HORACE.

HORACE afide.

I MUST go afk who it is.

Arnolph thinking himfelf alone.] It was impoffible to forefee——[being run againft by Horace.] Who is there pray?

Horace. Is it you, Mr. Arnolph?

Arnolph. Yes, but who are you?——

Horace. I was going to your houfe to beg a favour of you. You are very foon abroad this morning.

Arnolph low afide.] Surprifing! Is it an enchantment? Is it a vifion?

Horace. To fay the truth, I have been very much troubled, and I thank heaven's great goodnefs for meeting you here thus luckily. I am going to tell you how every thing has fucceeded even much better than I could have expected, and that too by an accident which might have ruined all. I do not know how the affignation we had made could poffibly come to be fufpected; but juft as I was got to the window I faw fome people appear, who ftriking furioufly at me, made my feet flip, and I tumbled to the ground: which fall, at the expence of a bruife, faved me from a hearty drubbing. Thefe people, (amongft whom my jealous-pate, I fuppofe, was one) imagined my fall to be occafioned by the force of their blows; and as my pain made me lie a confiderable time motionlefs on the fpot, they really thought I was dead; which immediately a-larmed them all. I heard their noife with a profound filence; they accufed one another of the violence, and complaining of their hard fate, came foftly, without any light, to feel if I was dead. It being very dark, I eafily affumed the appearance of a dead man. They went away very much terrified: and as I was confidering how to get off, young Agnes, whom my pretended death had frighted, came to me in great concern: (For fhe had heard what the people faid to one another, and being lefs obferved during all this fray, fhe eafily flipped out of the houfe.) But finding I was not hurt, fhe was greatly delighted. What fhall I fay more to you? At laft this amiable fair one has followed the dictates of her love, and being unwilling to go home any more, has committed herfelf intirely to my truft. You may find a little by this harmlefs proceeding, how much the grofs impertinence of a fool expofes her, and what danger fhe might have been in, had I a lefs fincere regard for her; but my heart burns with teo pure a flame, and I would rather die than injure her. I fee charms in her which are worthy of a happier fate, and nothing but death fhall part us. I forefee my father's anger, but we fhall find a time to appeafe his wrath. I yield to her tender charms, and in fhort, we muft pleafe ourfelves in life: The favour, therefore, I would beg of you, (relying on your fecrecy and fincerity) is, that I may put her into your hands, and that you will fo far affift my paffion, as to conceal her in your houfe for a day or two at leaft.

For, besides that, her going off should be kept an intire secret, to prevent any certain pursuit after her; you are sensible that a girl of her beauty would be strangely suspected in the company of a young man; and as I have disclosed the whole secret of my passion to you, being well assured of your prudence, so I can entrust this valuable prize to no friend so sincere as you.

Arnolph. You may be assured that I am wholly devoted to your service.

Horace. And will you do me this kind office?

Arnolph. Very readily, I assure you; I am overjoyed at this opportunity of serving you, and thank heaven for giving it me. Never did any thing afford me more pleasure.

Horace. How greatly am I indebted to you for your goodness! I was afraid you would make a difficulty of doing it; but you know the world, and your wisdom can excuse the heat of youth. She is at the corner of this street, with one of my servants.

Arnolph. But it now begins to grow light, how shall we manage? Perhaps I shall be seen if I take her here, and the servants will tattle if you should come to my house. Therefore, to be safe, she must be brought to me in some darker place. I will go stay for her in my alley, it is very convenient.

Horace. It is very right to use these precautions; for my part, I shall do no more than put her into your hands, and then get me home immediately without saying any thing.

Arnolph alone.] All the mischief thou hast done me, cruel fortune! is repaired by this single accident.

[Throws his cloke over his face.

SCENE III.

AGNES, HORACE, ARNOLPH.

HORACE to Agnes.

I AM carrying you to a very safe lodging, therefore be not in the least uneasy; it would ruin all for you to be with me. Go in at this door, and he will conduct you.

[Arnolph takes her hand without her knowing him.

Agnes to Horace.] Wherefore do you leave me?

Horace. Dear Agnes, it must be so.

Agnes. Pray then do not stay long, but come back as soon as possible.

Horace. I will return to you immediately.

Agnes. I feel no joy but when you are present.

Horace. I too am melancholy when you are out of my sight.

Agnes. Alack! If that was true, you would not leave me now.

Horace. What! can you doubt of my excessive love?

Agnes. Nay, you do not love me so much as I love you. [Arnolph pulls her.] Oh! you pull me too hard.

Horace. Dear Agnes, that is because it is not safe for us two to be seen here; and this faithful friend who pulls you so, is prudently zealous for our service.

Agnes. But to follow a stranger, who——

Horace. Fear nothing, you cannot be in better hands.

Agnes. I fhould think myfelf much better in Horace's; and I fhould——[*To Arnolph, who pulls her again.*] Stay a little.

Horace. The day drives me away. Adieu.

Agnes. When fhall I fee you then?

Horace. Very foon, you may be certain:

Agnes. How uneafy I fhall be till that time comes!

Horace. My happinefs now, thank heaven, is fecure, and I may fleep fafely.

SCENE IV.

ARNOLPH, AGNES.

ARNOLPH *concealed under his cloke, and altering his voice.*

COME along, I have prepared a lodging elfe-where for you, and you fhall not ftay here; I intend to put you in a place where you may be fafe enough. [*Difcovering himfelf.*] Do you know me?

Agnes knowing him.] Hah!

Arnolph. You are frightened, I think, hufly, at feeing me, and are undoubtedly very much difpleafed at finding me here: I have very luckily interrupted the love-contrivances you have in your head. [*Agnes looks if fhe cannot fee Horace.*] Think not that your eyes can call back your fpark to your affiftance, he is gone too far for that. Ha! ha! fo young, and yet to play thefe pranks! Your extraordinary feeming ignorance enquired if children were produced at the ear, though you are not ignorant how to make affignations by night, and fteal away very filently to run after a galant. Odfbobs,

how flippant your tongue was with him! fure you
muft have been at fome rare fchool: Pray who has
taught you all this fo fuddenly? You are no longer it feems afraid of ghofts? This galant has given
you courage in the night-time. Ah! baggage,
to arrive at this deceit! to form fuch a defign, re-
gardlefs of all my kindnefs: Thou art a little fer-
pent that I have warmed in my bofom, which when
it comes to its feeling, ungratefully tries to kill
him who preferved its life.

Agnes. Why do ye fcold at me?

Arnolph. I am very much to blame, indeed.

Agnes. I do not know any harm in all this that
I have done.

Arnolph. Is not running after a galant a fcandalous action?

Agnes. It is a man that fays he will take me
for his wife. I followed your directions; for you
told me one muft marry to take away the guilt.

Arnolph. Ay, but I intended to make you my
own wife, and methinks I let you know my meaning plain enough.

Agnes. Yes, but to tell you the truth, I love
him better than you; matrimony with you is a
troublefome uneafy thing, and you give a frightful
defcription of it; but alack-a-day! he reprefents it
fo delightful, that it makes one have a mind to be
married.

Arnolph. Ah! traitrefs! that is becaufe you
love him.

Agnes. Really I do love him.

Arnolph. And have you the impudence to tell
me fo?

Agnes. Why may not I fay fo, if it is true?

Arnolph. Ought you to love him, impertinence?

Agnes. Alas! can I help it? He only is the cause of it; I did not think of it till it was over.

Arnolph. But you should have discarded that amorous desire.

Agnes. How can a body discard what is delightful?

Arnolph. And are you ignorant that I am displeased at it?

Agnes. Not at all; What harm can it do you?

Arnolph. Very true, I have reason to be glad at it. You do not love me then at this rate?

Agnes. You!

Arnolph. Ay,

Agnes. Indeed I do not

Arnolph. How! no?

Agnes. Would you have me tell you a falshood?

Arnolph. What is the reason that you do not love me, madam impudence?

Agnes. Lack-a-day, you should not blame me! Why did not you make yourself beloved as he did? If I hindered you, it was without my knowledge.

Arnolph. I endeavoured it all I could, but my pains were in vain.

Agnes. Then he understands it better than you do, for he made me love him without the least pains.

Arnolph aside.] Observe how the slut answers and argues! None of your witty ladies could have said more. Ah! I did not well know her, or else, by my faith, in these cases a simple woman understands more than the wisest man. [*To Agnes.*] Since you are so good at reasoning, Mrs. Chop-Logick, is there any reason why I should maintain you so long a time at my own charge for him?

Agnes. No, he will repay you every thing.

Arnolph aside.] She hits upon certain words which give me double vexation. [To Agnes.] Is he able, gypfey, to repay me the obligations you have to me?

Agnes. I have no fuch great ones as you think.

Arnolph. Is it nothing to take care of your e-ducation from your childhood?

Agnes. You have been at great pains about that matter truly, and have caufed me to be bravely in-ftructed in every thing. Do ye imagine I flatter myfelf fo far as not to know in my own mind that I am intirely ignorant? I am afhamed of it my-felf, and at this age will not pafs any longer for a fool, if I can help it.

Arnolph. You defpife ignorance, and are re-folved, whatever it cofts, to learn fomething of your galant?

Agnes. To be fure. He has taught me what I do know, and I think myfelf more obliged to him than you.

Arnolph. I cannot tell what fhould prevent me from revenging this faucy language with my fift. I am diftracted at the fight of her provoking cold-nefs, and beating her would be a fatisfaction to me.

Agnes. If that will pleafe you, you are very welcome to do it.

Arnolph aside.] That fpeech and that look dif-arm my rage, and produce a return of tendernefs which effaces all her guilt. What ftrange effects does love produce! and how weak do men make themfelves appear, for thefe gypfies! Every body knows their imperfection; they are nothing but ex-travagance and indifcretion; their mind is wicked and their underftanding weak; nothing is more frail, nothing more unfteady, nothing more falfe, and yet for all that one does the greateft abfurdities for their fake. [To Agnes.] Well, let us make peace: Go, thou little rogue, I forgive thee every thing, and now am fond of thee again: Learn by this how much I love thee, and feeing I am fo good, love thou me in return.

Agnes. I would very willingly oblige you, if it was in my power.

Arnolph. My dear life, thou canft if thou wouldft. Do but hear that amorous figh, behold this dying look, view my perfon, and lay all thoughts afide of this young coxcomb, and the love he offers thee. He muft certainly have put fome fpell upon thee, and thou wilt be a hundred times more happy with me. Thou delighteft in being fine and gay, and I proteft thou fhalt always be fo. I fhall be fondling thee continually; I fhall hug thee, and kifs thee. Thou fhalt do every thing thou chufeft, which is faying all that can be faid without coming to particulars. [Afide.] How far will my paffion go? [Aloud.] Nothing really can be equal to my love. What proof of it wouldft thou have me give thee, ungrateful wench? Wouldft thou behold me weep? Wouldft thou have me beat myfelf? Wouldft thou have me tear off my hair? Would'ft thou have me murder myfelf? Ay; fay if thou wouldft have me do it; I am intirely ready, cruel creature, to convince thee of my love.

Agnes. Hold; I am not in the leaft affected at all you fay; Horace with two words would have wrought upon me more than you.

Arnolph. Heh! this is too great an infult, provoking my rage too far: I will purfue my defign, you untractable brute, and pack you out of town immediately. You vex me, and reject my addresses, but depend upon it, if you do not behave better, I will send you to a convent.

SCENE V.

ARNOLPH, AGNES, ALLEN.

ALLEN.

I Know not how it is, Sir, but methought the dead corps and Agnes went away together.

Arnolph. Here she is: Go confine her in my chamber. [Aside.] He will not come there to seek her. Besides, it is only for half an hour. I will go get a coach, that I may secure her in a more convenient place. Fasten yourselves in well, and be sure do not let her be out of sight. [Alone.] It is some comfort to me, that I can easily turn her head from this love-affair, when she is out of town.

SCENE VI.

HORACE, ARNOLPH,

HORACE.

WHAT woeful news have I now to tell you, dear friend! Fate is determined that I never shall be happy, and is going again to wrest my beloved Agnes from me. I just now saw my father arrive, who tells me that he has made a match for me, without writing me a word about it, and is come to this place to celebrate the nuptials. You are sensible what a great disappointment this is to me. That Henriques of whom I spoke to you yesterday is come with my father, and it is to his daughter that they intend to marry me. I almost fainted when I first heard it, and not caring to hear any more of it, (as my father talked of coming to see you) I hasted hither beforehand, very much perplexed. Do not tell him a word, I beg of you, of my engagement, which might incense him; and endeavour to dissuade him from this fresh engagement, for no one's words have greater power over him than yours.

Arnolph. I shall do all in my power.

Horace. Advise him to put it off a little, and as a friend, assist my passion in this particular.

Arnolph. I really shall use my utmost endeavours.

Horace. My hopes are all in you.

Arnolph. Very well.

Horace. I look upon you as my real father. Tell him that my age—But here he comes; hear the reasons I can furnish you with.

<h3 align="center">SCENE VII.</h3>

HENRIQUES, ORANTES, CHRISALDUS,
HORACE, ARNOLPH.

Horace and Arnolph retire to a corner of the stage,
and whisper.

HENRIQUES to Chrisaldus.

HAD I not been told who you were, I should have known you: I recollected your amiable sister's features, whom the sacred ties of wedlock once united to me; what pleasure should I now have had, in bringing her to fee all our friends, after our numberlefs calamities! but cruel heaven denies me that delight, and has robbed me of her fweet company: Let us therefore endeavour to be contented with the only fruit that remains of our loves. You are very nearly concerned in it, and to difpofe of this pledge without your confent would be very wrong. The choice of Orontes's fon is in itfelf honourable, but you muft be pleafed in the choice as well as me.

Chrifaldus. It is having a bad opinion of my judgment, to doubt my approbation of fo reafonable a choice.

Arnolph afide to Horace.] Ay, I will ferve you in the beft manner.

Horace afide to Arnolph.] But beware of one thing——

Arnolph to Horace.] Be under no concern.

[Arnolph quits Horace to embrace Orontes.

Orontes to Arnolph.] O! how full of tendernefs is this embrace!

Arnolph. What pleafure it gives me to fee you!

Orontes. I am come hither——

Arnolph. I already know it.

Orontes. Have you been informed already?

Arnolph. Yes.

Orontes. So much the better.

Arnolph. Your fon hates this match, and his heart being pre-engaged looks upon it as a misfortune: He even defired me to diffuade you from it; and for my part, all the advice I can give you is to exert the authority of a father, and not let the marriage be deferred. Young people fhould be governed with an high hand, they are frequently fpoiled by being indulgent to them.

Horace aside.] Oh! Traitor!

Chrifaldus. If it is againft his inclination, I think we fhould not force him. My brother, I believe, will be of the fame way of thinking.

Arnolph. What! will he fuffer his fon to govern him? Would you have a father be fo weak as not to know how to make youth obey him? To fee him receiving laws at this time of life from one who ought to receive them from him, would be mighty pretty. No, no, he is my intimate friend, and his honour is mine, his promife is given, and he muft perform it. Let him now fhew his refolution, and force his fon's affections.

Orontes. You fay right, and to what regards this match, I will be anfwerable for my fon's obedience.

Chrifaldus to Arnolph] You furprize me greatly by being fo eager for this match, and I cannot conceive why———

Arnolph. I know what I know, and fpeak what I ought to fpeak.

Orontes. Ay, ay, Mr. Arnolph, he is—

Chrifaldus. He is difpleafed at that name, it is Mr. de la Souche, as you have been told already.

Arnolph. It does not fignify.

Horace aside.] What is this I hear?

Arnolph turning towards Horace.] Ay, there lies the fecret, and you may judge what I ought to do.

Horace aside.] Into what uneafinefs———

S C E N E   VIII.

HENRIQUES, ORONTES, CHRISALDUS,
HORACE, ARNOLPH, GEORGETTA.

GEORGETTA.

AGNES fays fhe will run all hazards to make her efcape, Sir, and will perhaps throw herfelf out at the window, if you do not come and help us to keep her.

Arnolph. Bring her to me, for I intend to take her away from hence immediately. [To Horace.] Do not you be troubled at it, continual good fortune would make a man proud, and every dog has his day, as the proverb fays.

Horace. Never was any body fo unfortunate as I am!

Arnolph to Orontes.] Haften the day of the ceremony? I beg it may be fo, and invite myfelf to it already.

Orontes. That is my real intention.

S C E N E   IX.

AGNES, ORONTES, HENRIQUES, AR-
'NOLPH, HORACE, CHRISALDUS, AL-
LEN, GEORGETTA.

ARNOLPH to Agnes.

COME here, my pretty girl, come here, you who will have your own way, and cannot be managed; here is your fpark, you may make him a fubmiffive courtfy, by way of amends. [To Horace.] Farewel, the affair has not turned out according to our wishes, but lovers are not all lucky.

Agnes. Horace, do you allow me to be forced away in this manner?

Horace. My grief is so great, I am insensible..

Arnolph. Come along, with your chit-chat, come along.

Agnes. I will stay here.

Orontes. Explain this mystery to us; we stare one at another without being able to understand it.

Arnolph. I will tell you at a more convenient time. Your servant.

Orontes. Where do you intend to go to? You do not inform us of what we want to know.

Arnolph. I have advised you to conclude the match in spite of his repining.

Orontes. But in order to conclude it (if you have been told all) did they not tell you that the person who we mean is in your house just now, and is the daughter of the charming Angelica, which she had secretly by Mr. Henriques? What could be the subject of your conversation just now?

Chrisaldus. His behaviour surprized me too.

Arnolph. How?

Chrisaldus. My sister had one daughter by a private marriage, which was unknown to the whole family.

Orontes. And for the sake of keeping it secret, her husband put it out to nurse in the country, under a feigned name.

Chrisaldus. And at that time he was so unfortunate as to be obliged to leave his native country.

Orontes. And in foreign countries to undergo a great many dangers.

Chrisaldus. What he was deprived of at home

by villainy and envy, he has gained abroad by his own induſtry.

Orontes. When he returned to France, his firſt care was to make enquiry after the perſon who had the care of his daughter.

Chriſaldus. He was informed by the countrywoman, that you got her into your poſſeſſion, when ſhe was but four years old.

Orontes. As ſhe was very poor, and you of a charitable diſpoſition, ſhe gave up the child.

Chriſaldus. And he has brought the woman here, to his great joy.

Orontes. In a little time ſhe will be here to clear up the matter.

Chriſaldus to Arnolph.] I have a tolerable good gueſs how you muſt be mortified by this, but fortune is kind to you; and, as to avoid being a cuckold is your very great happineſs, you are ſure to attain it by avoiding matrimony.

Arnolph turning away in a great fury, and unable to ſpeak.

Ah!

SCENE THE LAST.

HENRIQUES, ORONTES, CHRISALDUS, AGNES, HORACE.

ORONTES.

WHAT makes him run away without ſpeaking?

Horace. I will acquaint you with the whole of this odd affair. Father, the ſame thing which your prudence intended for this lovely girl, is come to paſs by accident; the tender ties of mutual love engaged me ſtrictly. She is the very perſon you came in ſearch of, and I thought you would have been diſobliged at my refuſal, on her account.

Henriques. From the firſt minute I ſaw her, I had not the ſmalleſt doubt of it. From that time my heart has yearned after her. Oh, my daughter! I yield to ſuch tender tranſports.

Chriſaldus. With all my heart, I could do ſo, brother, as well as you; but let us go into the houſe to clear up matters, this is not a proper place; let us diſcharge the obligations we owe our friend, and return thanks to heaven, which orders every thing for the beſt.

T H E E N D.

THE

SCHOOL FOR WIVES

CRITICISED.

A

COMEDY.

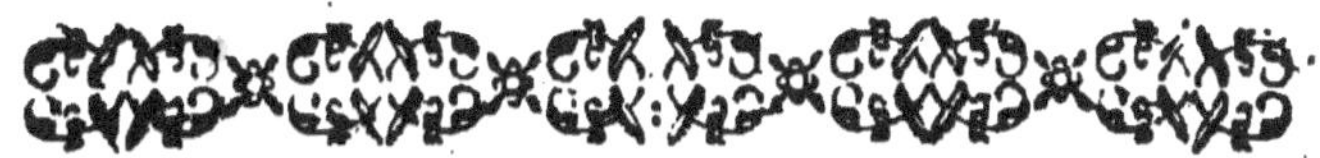

The School *for* Wives Criticised, *a Comedy of One Act, acted at the Theatre of the Palace-Royal the 1st of June* 1663.

THE criticifms upon the comedy of the School for Wives were for a long time no other-wife oppofed by Moliere, than by the continued reprefentations of it, which were always crowded, nor was he at the leaft pains to fupprefs them, in part at leaft, till the month of June, 1663, when he brought out his comedy of the School for Wives Criticised. The fubject feemed only proper for a differtation, and of courfe admitted of neither intrigue nor cataftrophe: But the author always kept in view the object which a comic writer fhould never lofe fight of, in whatever kind of performances he brings on the ftage. He knew, from what had paffed in the polite affemblies of Paris, whilft the School for Wives was talked of, to draw a faithful picture of one part of civil life, by copying the language and character of the common converfations of the people of fafhion. He feems to have had it as much in view, by his choice of ridiculous characters, to fatirize his cenfurers, as to apoligize for his piece: feduced perhaps by the tendency of human fpleen, which makes people think, that by attacking others is the beft way to defend themfelves. Bourfalt played the Counter-Critick, or the Painter's Picture, at the Hotel de Bourgogne, at the fame time, in which he followed Moliere's plan and manner, but went

too far in suppofing a known key to the SCHOOL.
for WIVES, which pointed out the originals copied.
from nature.

A C T O R S.

URANIA.
ELIZA.
CLIMENE.
THE MARQUIS.
DORANTES, or the KNIGHT.
LYSIDAS, a Poet.
GALOPIN, a Footman.

SCENE PARIS, in Urania's houfe.

THE

SCHOOL FOR WIVES

CRITICISED.

SCENE I.

URANIA, ELIZA.

URANIA.

WHAT, is there nobody come to viſit you, couſin?

Eliza. Not a creature.

Urania. Indeed I am amazed that none of us have had company to-day.

Eliza. I am ſurprized too; it is not common, as all the ſaunterers about court generally reſort to your houſe.

Urania. I confeſs the afternoon appears long to me.

Eliza. And very ſhort to me.

Urania. It is common, couſin, for ſolitude to be agreeable to fine wits.

Eliza. Your humble servant; you are senfible I do not affect to be a wit:

Urania. I own, for my part, I love company.

Eliza. Company is agreeable to me too, but only a felect party; the many tirefome vifits one is obliged to endure amongft your other forts makes me admire folitude.

Urania. Your delicacy is too great to be fond of felect company only.

Eliza. I think it is too great complaifance to be equally fond of all company.

Urania. The extravagant divert me, and reafonable people give me pleafure.

Eliza. Really, extravagant people are feldom entertaining after the fecond vifit, their company foon grows tirefome. But let us talk on that head; will you not rid me of your trifling Marquis? Do you fuppofe that I fhall always hold out againft his continual jokes?

Urania. It is a fafhionable language at court, which they make themfelves merry with.

Eliza. It is bad for thofe who do fo, and rack their brains all the day to converfe in this ftupid jargon. A pretty thing to bring into the converfation of the Louvre, your double entendres, raked together from the kennels of Halles and Place Maubert! A fine manner of jefting for courtiers, and of a man's fhewing his wit by coming and faying: Madam, you are at the Place Royal, and all the world fees you three leagues from Paris; for every body fees you with a good eye; becaufe Boneuil is a village at three leagues diftant from hence! Is it not very gallant, and very witty? And have not they who hit upon thefe pretty puns, reafon to be proud of them?

Urania. They do not, at the same time, speak this as a piece of wit, for most of those people who affect this language know that it is ridiculous.

Eliza. It is still worse to study to repeat silly things, and to be sorry jesters on purpose. I think them much less excusable on that account, and I know very well to what I would condemn these joking gentlemen.

Urania. Come, let us have done with this affair, it warms you too much. I think Dorantes is long in coming to sup with us.

Eliza. He may have forgot it probably, and—

S C E N E II.

GALOPIN, URANIA, ELIZA.

GALOPIN.

CLIMENE is come to pay you a visit, Madam.

Urania. Oh! bless me! what a visit is this!

Eliza. In this manner heaven punishes you for your dislike of retirement.

Urania. Haste and tell her that I am from home.

Galopin. She is informed already that you are here.

Urania. Who was so silly as to tell her that?

Galopin. I, madam.

Urania. The devil is in the boy; I shall teach you to give answers before I am acquainted with it.

Galopin. Madam, I will go and contradict it.

Urania. Hold, you little fool, as you have blundered, let her come up stairs.

Galopin. She is still conversing with a man in the street.

Urania. Oh! coufin, how this vifit perplexes me juft now!

Eliza. Really the woman is exceffively trouble-fome: I always hated her, and looked upon her as one of the ftupideft perfons that ever pretended to common fenfe.

Urania. The epithet is rather ftrong.

Elvira. In juftice fhe deferves this and more, I never faw a perfon fo affected.

Urania. Yet fhe would feem quite the reverfe.

Elvira. Indeed fhe would appear otherwife, but fhe is fo formal, that her whole body feems as if it were out of joint; her head, lips and fhoulders appear as if they went by clock-work. She affects a languifhing manner of fpeaking, rolls her eyes to make them appear large, and draws up her mouth to make it look fmall.

Urania. Hufh! what if fhe fhould hear you thus--

Eliza. No, no, fhe is not fo near. Well do I remember the evening that fhe wanted to fee Damon, on account of his reputation, and the things he has publifhed! You are acquainted with the man, and how indolent he is in keeping up a converfation. She gave him an invitation to fup, with half a dozen other people, imagining he would entertain them with his wit; but never did he appear fo fimple; the company expected that he would divert them by his jefts, and that he had fo much wit as to make extemporary repartees upon every thing that was faid, and even not to call for any thing but with a witticifm; but his filence furprifed them, and he gave the lady as little pleafure as fhe gave me.

Urania. Be filent. I will go to the room-door and receive her.

Eliza. Hear one word more. What an admirable union it would be between a she-coxcomb and a jester! I wish she were married to him.

Urania. Here she comes; be silent.

S C E N E III.

CLIMENE, URANIA, ELIZA, GALOPIN.

URANIA.

IT is very late indeed that—

Climene. Order a chair directly, for God's sake.

Urania to Galopin.] Make haste, and bring an armed chair here.

Climene. Oh! Heavens!

Urania. What is the matter then?

Climene. I can support no longer.

Urania. What is the matter with you?

Climene. I faint.

Urania. Are you seized with vapours?

Climene. No.

Urania. Shall I unlace you?

Climene. O no. Oh!

Urania. What is your illness? and when were you seized?

Climene. I came from court three hours ago, and was ill then.

Urania. How?

Climene. I have been punished for my sins, by being present at the performing of that vile rhapsody, the School for Wives. It occasioned me a fainting fit, which I have not yet recovered, nor shall I be well these two weeks.

Eliza. We get illnesses without expecting them.

Urania. My coufin and I muft be of very different conftitutions from you, as we faw the fame piece performed the day before yefterday, and both came home merry and well.

Climene. Have you feen it?

Urania. Yes, and heard it from beginning to end.

Climene. My dear, did it net throw you into fits?

Urania. Thank God I am not fo delicate, and I really think this play fhould rather mend people, than make them fick.

Climene. Blefs me! what do you fay? will a perfon who has the leaft fhare of fenfe, advance this propofition? Can any perfon, with impunity, quarrel with reafon, as you do? And can there really be a mind fo famifhed for drollery, as to tafte the filly things this play is made up of? I really could not find the leaft grain of fenfe in it: children by the ear, had, to my thinking, a deteftable gout: the cream tart turned my ftomach; and I thought I fhould have thrown up all the porridge.

Eliza. Heavens! moft elegantly fpoken! I fhould have thought this piece had been good; but the lady has fo perfuafive an eloquence, fhe turns things in fo agreeable a manner, that one muft be of her opinion in fpite of one's felf.

Urania. For my part, I am not fo complaifant; and to tell you my real thoughts, I look upon this comedy to be one of the moft diverting the author ever wrote.

Climene. Oh! you make me pity you, to talk in this manner; I cannot bear this obfcurity of difcernment. Can one who has the leaft virtue, find any thing agreeable in a piece that keeps one's modesty under a perpetual alarm, and sullies the imagination at every turn?

Eliza. What a pretty manner of speaking is that? How terribly rough you play, madam, in criticism? Moliere is much to be pitied when he has such an enemy as you.

Climene. Believe me, my dear, correct in good earnest your judgment; and for your honour do not let any body know that you were pleased with this comedy.

Urania. Why really I saw nothing in it so shocking to modesty as you say.

Climene. The whole of it is so; and it is impossible for a virtuous woman to see it without confusion, there is so much ordure in it.

Urania. You must have a particular discernment then for ordure; for I saw none in it.

Climene. It is undoubtedly, because you will not see it; for in short, all this ordure is, thank heaven, naked to the eye; it has not the least cover to conceal it, and the nudity of it shocks the boldest eyes.

Eliza. Oh!

Climene. Ha, ha, ha.

Urania. Pray point me out some of this ordure you speak of, if you please.

Climene. Lack-a-day! is it necessary to point it out?

Urania. Yes; I only ask of you one passage that was very shocking to you.

Climene. Needs there any other than the scene wherein Agnes tells what they took from her.

Urania. And is there the least smuttiness in that?

Climene. Ah!

Urania. Pray?

Climene. Fy.

Urania. Nay, but?

Climene. I have nothing to fay to you.

Urania. For my part, I do not fee the leaft harm in it.

Climene. So much the worfe for you.

Urania. Rather fo much the better, I think. I obferve things on the fide that is fhewn me; and do not turn them about, to find what I ought not to fee.

Climene. A lady's modefty—

Urania. Confifts not in grimace. It ill becomes one to be wifer than thofe who are wife: affectation in this affair is worfe than every thing elfe; and nothing appears to me fo foolifh as that delicacy of honour which takes every thing in a wrong light, gives a criminal fenfe to the moft innocent words, and is offended at the fhadow of things. Believe me, they who make fo much ado are not efteemed the moft virtuous women. On the contrary, their myfterious feverity, and affected grimace provoke the cenfure of every body upon the actions of their lives. People are glad to difcover any thing to carp at; and to give you an inftance, there was fome ladies at this play the other day, over againft the box we were in, who by the looks they affected during the whole piece, the turning afide their heads, and the hiding their faces, occafioned feveral filly things being faid on their conduct, all round them, that would never have been faid without this; and even one of the footmen cried out aloud, that they were more chafte in their ears than all the reft of their bodies.

Climene. In fhort, one muft be blind in this piece, and not feem to fee things.

Urania. One ought not to fee in it what is not in it.

Climene. Ah! I maintain it once more, that the fmuttinefs in it puts out one's eyes.

Urania. And I do not think fo.

Climene. What? does not Agnes, in the paf-fage we are fpeaking of, fay what vifibly fhocks modefty?

Urania. No truly: fhe fays not one word but what, of itfelf, is decent enough; and if you will conceive fomething elfe as couched under it, it is you who make the ordure, and not fhe, fince fhe fpeaks of nothing but the ribbon which was taken from her.

Climene. Hoh! Ribbon as long as you pleafe, but that *my* that fhe ftops at is not put there for nothing. Comical thoughts arife upon this *my*. This *my* is furioufly fcandalous; and fay what you can, you can never defend the infolence of it.

Eliza. True, coufin, I am for the lady againft this *my*. *My* is to the laft degree infolent, and you are in the wrong to defend this *my*.

Climene. It has an obfcenity that one cannot bear.

Eliza. How do you call that word, madam?

Climene. Obfcenity, madam.

Eliza. Hoh! good lack-a-day! Obfcenity. I do not underftand this word, but I think it is the pret-tieft I ever heard.

Climene. In fhort, you fee your own relation takes my part.

Urania. O dear! fhe is a tattling girl, who

speaks contrary to what she thinks. You will not much depend upon her if you will believe me.

Eliza. Fy! how cruel you are to make the lady suspect me! consider a little what condition I should be in should she believe what you say. Am I so far unhappy, madam, that you should entertain this thought of me?

Climene. No, no, I regard not her words, I think you more sincere than she says.

Eliza. Oh! you are infinitely in the right, madam; and you do me justice when you believe I think you the most engaging person I ever beheld; that I enter into all your sentiments, and am charmed with every expression you utter.

Climene. Pray speak not so affectedly.

Eliza. One sees it, madam, very plainly, and that every thing is natural in you. Your words, the tone of your voice, your looks, your gait, your action and your dress, have an air of quality in them that inchant people. I study you by my eyes, by my ears; and am so full of you, that I endeavour to imitate you in every thing.

Climene. You are pleased to banter me, madam.

Eliza. Pardon me, madam, who could banter you?

Climene. I am no good model, madam.

Eliza. Oh! yes, madam.

Climene. You flatter me, madam.

Eliza. Indeed, madam, I do not.

Climene. Pray, madam, have a little mercy on me.

Eliza. I have so much mercy on you, that I do not say half of what I think of you.

Climene. Oh heavens! Let us drop it, pray.

You would throw me into a horrible confusion. [To Urania.] You fee in fhort, madam, we are both againft you, and obftinacy fits fo ill upon witty people that———

SCENE IV.

THE MARQUIS, CLIMENE, GALOPIN, URANIA, ELIZA.

GALOPIN at the chamber door.

PRAY ftop, Sir, if you pleafe.

The Marquis. Doft thou know who I am, fellow?

Galopin. I know you very well, but you fhall not go in.

The Marquis. Hey, what a buftle is here, you little fkip-jack.

Galopin. It is not fair to endeavour to get in, in fpite of people's teeth.

The Marquis. I will fee thy miftrefs.

Galopin. She is not within, I tell you.

The Marquis. Why there fhe is in her chamber.

Galopin. That is true, fhe is there; but fhe is not at home for all that.

Urania. What is the meaning of this? what is the matter there?

The Marquis. It is your footman, madam, who is playing the fool.

Galopin. I tell him, madam, you are not at home, and yet he will come in whether I will or no.

Urania. And why did you tell the gentleman that I am not at home?

Galopin. You was very angry with me the other day for telling him you were at home.

Urania. See the infolence of this knave! Pray, Sir, do not believe what he fays; it is a little giddy brained rogue, and he takes you for another perfon.

The Marquis. I faw it plainly, madam, and had it not been in refpect to you, I fhould have taught him to know people of quality.

Eliza. My coufin is much obliged to you for this deference.

Urania to Galopin.] A chair there, fauce-box.

Galopin. Is not there one?

Urania. Bring it hither.

[Galopin pufhes the chair rudely, and goes out.

SCENE V.

THE MARQUIS, CLIMENE, URANIA, ELIZA.

THE MARQUIS.

THAT lacquey of yours, madam, has a contempt for my perfon.

Eliza. He would be much to blame, certainly.

The Marquis. It is perhaps becaufe I pay intereft for my ill looks. [Laughs.] He, he, he!

Eliza. He will know people of quality better when he grows older.

The Marquis. What were you talking about, ladies, when I interrupted you?

Urania. About the play of The School for Wives.

The Marquis. I am but juft come from it.

Climene. Well, Sir, what is your opinion of it?

The Marquis. Why, I think it is very foolish.

Climene. Oh! how glad am I of that!

The Marquis. The most villainous thing in the world. What the duce! I could scarce get a place. I thought I should have been stifled at the door, and never was I so trampled upon. See, pray, what a condition my rollers and ribbons are in.

Eliza. Why really, this cries vengeance against The School for Wives, and you justly condemn it.

The Marquis. I dare say there never was such a wretched performance.

Urania. But here comes Dorantes, whom we expected.

S C E N E VI.

DORANTES, THE MARQUIS, CLIMENE, ELIZA,
URANIA.

DORANTES.

DO not let me disturb you, but pray continue your discourse. The subject you are upon has been the general one through Paris these four days; and never was any thing more diverting than the different judgments that are passed upon it. For the very things which I have heard it esteemed for by some, have been condemned by others.

Urania. Here is the marquis speaks very ill of it.

The Marquis. It is true. I think it detestable, i'gad; detestable to the last degree of detestable; what one may call detestable.

Dorantes. And I, my dear marquis, think the opinion deteftable.

The Marquis. How, knight, do you pretend to vindicate the piece.

Dorantes. Yes, I do pretend to vindicate it.

The Marquis. I'gad, I warrant it deteftable.

Dorantes. That warrant is not city-fecurity. But, marquis, pray, what makes this play deteft-able?

The Marquis. What makes it deteftable?

Dorantes. Yes.

The Marquis. It is deteftable, becaufe it is fo.

Dorantes. There is not a word to fay after this; the caufe is ended. But yet inform us, and tell us what faults it has.

The Marquis. What do I know? I did not fo much as give myfelf the trouble to hear it. But in fhort, I know I never beheld any thing fo villain-ous; and Dorillas, who fat oppofite to me, was of my opinion.

Dorantes. The authority is good, thou art ex-cellently fupported.

The Marquis. One needs only obferve the conti-nual loud laughs fet up in the pit: nothing more is neceffary to prove it is good for nothing.

Dorantes. Then, marquis, you are one of thofe fine gentlemen who reckon the pit even deftitute of common fenfe, and would be grieved to laugh along with that, though it were at the beft thing in the world; I faw the other day one of our friends upon the ftage, who made himfelf ridiculous by this. He heard the whole piece with the moft fullen gra-vity imaginable; and every thing that made others merry made him frown. He fhrugged up his fhoul-ders, when other people laughed, and looked with pity upon the pit; and fometimes again looking down with vexation, he cried out aloud, laugh then, pit, laugh. It was really a fecond comedy to fee our friend fo vexed; he fhewed away like a generous fellow to the whole affembly, and every body allowed no man could play his part better than he did. Learn, marquis, you and others with you, that good fenfe has no determined place at a play; that the difference betwixt half a guinea and half a crown makes nothing at all to a good tafte; and whether ftanding or fitting one may pafs a bad judgment; and that, in fhort, to take it in general, I fhould depend a good deal upon the approbation of the pit, becaufe amongft thofe who compofe it, there are many who are capable of judging of a piece according to rules, and becaufe others judge by a proper method of judging, which is to be guided by things, and not to have any blind prejudice or affected complaifance, nor foolifh delicacy.

The Marquis. So thou art a defender of the pit, knight? I'gad, I am glad of it, and I fhall not fail to acquaint it thou art one of its friends. Ha, ha, ha, ha, he!

Dorantes. Laugh as much as you pleafe, I am for good fenfe, and hate fuch foolifh people as thou art. It vexes me to fee people make fools of themfelves notwithftanding their quality; your folks who are always decifive, and fpeak boldly of every thing without knowing a word of the matter; who fhall clap ye all the bad parts of a play, and not fo much as ftir at thofe that are good; who upon viewing a picture, or hearing a concert of mufic, both blame and praife every thing by rule of contraries; who pick up terms of art wherever.

they can, which they get by heart, and never fail to disjoint them, and difplace them. 'Sdeath, gentlemen, be filent. Since heaven has not bleffed you with the knowledge of one fublunary thing, do not make yourfelves a laughing-flock to thofe who hear you; and confider that by being filent, you may perhaps be thought clever fellows.

The Marquis. I'gad, knight, thou carrieft this matter——

Dorantes. Why, marquis, I do not fpeak to you; it is to a dozen of thofe gentry who difgrace the courtiers by their extravagant manners, and make the people believe we are all alike. For my part, I will do all I can to juftify myfelf from it, and I will fo rally them wherever I meet them, that at laft they fhall grow wife.

The Marquis. Has Lyfander any wit, think you?

Dorantes. Yes, doubtlefs, and a good deal too.

Urania. That is what no body can deny him.

The Marquis. Afk him what he thinks of The School for Wives; you will fee he will tell you it is not to his tafte.

Dorantes. Alas! numbers of people are fpoiled by too much wit, who fee things imperfectly by ftrength of light, and who would even be forry to be of other folks opinion, that they may have the honour of deciding.

Urania. Why really this friend of ours is of that fort: he muft be the firft of his opinion, and have others wait through refpect to his judgment: every one's approbation that gets the ftart of his is an infult upon his underftanding, which he highly revenges by taking the oppofite party: he would have folks confult him in every witty affair; and I am certain had the author fhewn him his play before he reprefented it, he would have thought it the beft piece that poffibly could be written.

The Marquis. And what fay you of the marchionefs Araminta, who publifhes it about town for a dreadful one, and fays fhe could never endure the ordure it is full of?

Dorantes. I fhall fay fhe deferves the character fhe has affumed, and that there are perfons who make themfelves ridiculous for affecting too much honour. Though fhe is witty, fhe has followed the ill example of thofe, who, growing old, want to make amends for what they fee they have loft, and imagine the grimace of a fcrupulous prudery will fupply the defect of youth and beauty. This fame lady carries the affair further than any body; the ingenioufnefs of her fcruples difcovers obfceni ty where it is impoffible for any body elfe to fee it. They tell ye that thefe fcruples proceed fo far as even to disfigure our language, and that there are very few words in it which the feverity of this lady will not retrench either the head or the tail, on account of the immodeft fyllables fhe finds in them.

Urania. You are a perfect wag, knight.

The Marquis. In fhort, knight, you think to defend your play by fatirizing thofe who condemn it.

Dorantes. Not at all; but this lady, in my opinion is unjuftly fcan————

Eliza. Softly, Sir knight; there may be other ladies befides her who may be of the fame fentiments.

Dorantes. I very well know that you are not fo, and that when you faw this performance————

Eliza. It is true, but I am now quite of a different way of thinking, and this lady [pointing to Climene.] supports her opinion by such convincing reasons, that she carried me quite on her side.

Dorantes to Climene.] Oh! madam, I ask pardon: and, if you please, I will unsay, for love of you, all that I have said.

Climene. I will not have it to be for love of me, but for the love of reason; for in a word, that piece, to take it right, is absolutely indefensible; and I do not conceive———

Urania. Hoh! here is the author, Mr. Lysidas; he comes *a propos*, for this affair. Take your chair, Mr. Lysidas, and sit down there.

SCENE VII.

LYSIDAS, CLIMENE, URANIA, ELIZA, DORANTES, THE MARQUIS.

LYSIDAS.

I AM rather late in coming to you, madam; but the lady marchioness I was speaking to you about made me read my piece to her, and the praises given it have detained me longer than I thought of.

Eliza. Praise is a wonderful charm to detain an author.

Urania. Sit down then, Mr. Lysidas, we shall read your piece after supper.

Lysidas. All they who were there are to come the first night, and have promised me to do their duty as they should do.

Urania. I believe it; but pray once more please

to fit down. We are upon an affair here which I should be very glad to go on with.

Lysidas. You will take a box, I hope, madam, for that night.

Urania. We shall fee. Pray let us continue our difcourfe.

Lysidas. Moft part of them are already taken.

Urania. It is mighty well. In fhort, I wanted you when you came, for every body is againft me here.

Eliza to Urania, and pointing to Dorantes.] He was on your fide at firft; but now he knows the lady is at the head of the oppofite party, I fuppofe you have nothing to do but feek out for other af-fiftance.

Climene. No, no. I would not have him ne-glect his court to mifs your coufin, I allow his wit to be on the fide of his heart.

Dorantes. With this permiffion, madam, I fhall prefume to defend myfelf.

Urania. But firft, pray let us know the fenti-ments of Mr. Lyfidas.

Lysidas. Upon what, madam?

Urania. Upon the fubject of The School for Wives.

Lysidas. Ha, ha!

Dorantes. What is your opinion of it?

Lysidas. I have nothing to fay upon that head; and you know that amongft us authors we ought to be vaftly careful how we fpeak of each others performances.

Dorantes. But pray, between us, what do you think of this comedy?

Lysidas. I, Sir?

Urania. Tell us your opinion honeftly.

Lyfidas. I think it an excellent performance.

Dorantes. Really?

Lyfidas. Really; why not? Is it not indeed a very fine one?

Dorantes. Um, um, you are a cruel youth, Mr. Lyfidas; you do not fpeak as you think.

Lyfidas. Pardon me.

Dorantes. Lack-a day, I know you; do not diffemble.

Lyfidas. I, Sir?

Dorantes. I fee plainly that you fpeak well of this piece only out of modefty; and that at the bottom of your heart you are of the opinion of a great many people, who think it bad.

Lyfidas. Ha, ha, ha!

Dorantes. Nay, confefs that this comedy is a foolifh piece.

Lyfidas. Your connoiffeurs do not approve of it.

The Marquis. Faith, knight, thou haft it, thou art paid for thy raillery. Ha, ha, ha, ha, ha!

Dorantes. Laugh on, my dear marquis, laugh on.

The Marquis. You fee we have the learned on our fide.

Dorantes. It is true, Mr. Lyfidas's judgment is fomething confiderable, but he will excufe me if I do not yield for all this; and fince I have prefumed to defend myfelf againft the lady's fentiments, he will not take it amifs if I oppofe his.

Eliza. What, when you fee the lady, my lord marquis, and Mr. Lyfidas againft you, dare you refift ftill? Fie, that's acting with a bad grace.

Climene. For my part, what confounds me is,

that senfible people can take it in their heads to protect the ftupidity of this piece.

The Marquis. Demme, madam, it is a wretched performance.

Dorantes. That is foon faid, marquis, there is nothing more eafy than to cut the matter fhort thus, and I do not fee any thing can withftand thy powerful decifions.

The Marquis. 'Slife, all the other comedians who have feen it fpeak ill of it.

Dorantes. Oh! I fay not a word more, you are very right, marquis, fince all the other comedians fpeak ill of it, we muft certainly believe them. They are all difcerning people, and fpeak without intereft; there is no more to be faid, I yield.

Climene. Yield, or not yield, I know very well you fhall never perfuade me to endure the immodefty of this piece; no more than you fhall the difobliging fatire in it againft the ladies.

Urania. For my part, I fhall take care not to be offended at it, and to take nothing to my own account that is faid in it. This fort of fatire falls directly upon the manners, and hits the perfons only by rebound. Let us not apply to ourfelves the ftrokes of a general cenfure; let us profit by the leffon, if we can, without making as if they fpoke to us. We fhould view all the ridiculous paintings that are drawn upon the ftage, without being uneafy at them. They are public mirrors, where we are never to declare that we behold ourfelves; and it is downright to tax ourfelves with a crime, to be fcandalized at the reproof.

Climene. As to myfelf, I do not fpeak of thefe things in regard to any part I can have in them; and I think I behave myfelf in fuch a manner as not to fear being looked for among the paintings drawn for diforderly women.

Eliza. You, madam, will never be looked for there; your conduct is fufficiently known by every body.

Urania to Climene.] Therefore, madam, I faid nothing that can reach you; and my words, like the fatire in comedy, reft in general pofitions.

Climene. I do not doubt it, madam. But however let us pafs this point over. I do not know what reception you will give the reflections thrown on our fex in a certain part of the piece; I confefs it vexes me to fee this impudent author have the affurance to call us animals.

Urania. Do not you obferve it is a ridiculous character he makes fpeak it?

Dorantes. And then, madam, do not you know that the reproaches of lovers never give fcandal? that it is much the fame with furious as with fondling lovers, and that on fuch occafions the ftrangeft words, and even fomething ftill worfe, are taken very often as marks of kindnefs by the very perfons who receive them.

Eliza. Say what you will I can digeft this no more than the porridge and cream-tart the lady juft now fpoke of.

The Marquis. O! yes, faith, cream-tart; that is what I was obferving a while ago; cream-tart! How am I obliged to you, madam, for having reminded me of cream-tart! Are there apples enough in Normandy for cream-tart? Cream-tart, i'gad, cream-tart!

Dorantes. Well, what mean you with your cream-tart?

The Marquis. 'Slife, cream tart, knight!

Dorantes. But what?

The Marquis. Cream-tart!

Dorantes. Pray let me know your reasons.

The Marquis. Cream-tart!

Urania. But you should explain your meaning, methinks.

The Marquis. Cream-tart, madam!

Urania. What objection can you make to it?

The Marquis. I? Nothing: cream-tart!

Urania. Oh! I give it up.

Eliza. My lord marquis goes the right way to work, and plays ye off finely. But I wish Mr. Lysidas would finish, and give them a little touch or two in his manner.

Lysidas. I am very favourable to other people's performances, and do not chuse to find fault with them. But in short, no offence to the friendship the knight declares for the author, you must own to me these sort of plays are not properly plays, and that there is a great deal of difference between all these trifles, compared with the beauty of serious pieces. Yet all the world gives into it now-a-days; there's no thronging after any thing but this; and you see nothing but a frightful solitude at the grand works, when these silly things shall have all Paris flocking to see them. I own to you my heart sometimes bleeds at it, and it is a scandal to all France.

Climene. It is true, people's taste is strangely corrupted in this point, and the age vulgarizes furiously.

Eliza. That vulgarizes is very pretty; pray did you invent it, madam?

Climene. Ah!

Eliza. I am much in doubt about it.

Dorantes. You think then, Mr. Lyfidas, that all the wit and all the beauty lie in ferious poems? and that comic pieces are trifles which deferve not to be praifed?

Urania. For my part, that is not my fentiment. Tragedy is undoubtedly very fine when it is well touched; but comedy has its charms, and I think one is as difficult as the other.

Dorantes. Certainly, madam; and for the difficulty, fhould you place it more on the fide of comedy, perhaps you would not be in the wrong: for I really think it much eafier to foar upon grand fentiments, to defy fortune in verfe, to accufe the deftinies, and reproach the gods, than to enter properly into the ridicule of men, and to make their faults appear agreeable on the ftage. When you paint heroes, you do what you have amind, thefe are portraits drawn at pleafure, where we feek not for refemblance; you have only to follow the traces of an exalted imagination, which frequently forfakes the true to hit the marvellous. But when you paint men, nature muft be your guide. People expect refemblance in thefe portraits; you have done nothing if you do not difplay the people of the age fo as to make them known. In a word, in ferious pieces it is fufficient to efcape cenfure to fay things that are well written and good fenfe. But this is not fufficient in the others; you muft be merry, and it is a ftrange enterprize to make your better fort of people laugh.

Climene. I reckon myfelf among the better fort of people, and yet I found not a fingle word in it to make any body laugh.

The Marquis. Faith, nor I neither.

Dorantes. As for you, marquis, I am not furprized at it, it is becaufe you found no puns in it.

Lyfidas. Faith, Sir, what we meet with there is not much better, and in my opinion all the raillery that is in it is very infipid.

Dorantes. The court thought not fo——

Lyfidas. Oh! the court, Sir?

Dorantes. Speak out, Mr. Lyfidas. I fee plainly you mean that the court knows very little about thefe matters; and this is the ufual refuge of you gentlemen authors, in the bad fuccefs of your works, to accufe only the injuftice of the age, and the want of difcernment in courtiers. Pleafe to know, Mr. Lyfidas, that courtiers can fee and hear as well as other people; that folks may be ingenious with a Venice point and a feather, as well as with a bob-peruke; that the grand teft of all your play is the court; that you muft ftudy its tafte to find the art of fucceeding; there is no place where the decifions are fo juft; and without bringing into the account all the men of learning there, one forms a manner of genius there only by plain natural good fenfe, and converfation with people of fafhion, who, without comparifon, judge more delicately of things, than all the common-place learning of pedants.

Urania. It is true that if you ftay but ever fo fhort a while there, things enough pafs daily before your eyes to acquire a habit of knowing them; and above all whatever belongs to good or bad raillery.

Dorantes. I own, the court has fome ridiculous people about it, and I am the firft, as you may fee, to banter them. But, faith, there are a great number too amongft the wits by profeffion; and if we ridicule fome marquiffes, I think there are a good

many more authors to ridicule; and what a droll
thing it would be to bring them upon the stage,
with their learned grimaces, and their fantastical
refinements; their vicious custom of affassinating
people in their works; their greediness of praise;
their sparingness of thought; their traffic of reputation; and their lines offensive and defensive! as
also their learned wars and combats in profe and
verfe.

Lyfidas. Moliere, Sir, is very happy in having
fo warm a patron as you are. But however, to
come to the point, the question in debate is, whether his piece be good; and here I engage myfelf
to fhew there are in the whole upwards of a hundred vifible faults.

Urania. It is an odd thing that you authors
fhould always condemn the pieces which every one
runs after, and praife thofe which no body go to.

Dorantes. That is becanfe it is generous to be
on the fide of the afflicted.

Urania. But pray, Mr. Lyfidas, let us fee fome
of thefe faults that I perceived nothing of.

Lyfidas. They who are mafters of Ariftotle and
Horace fee immediately, madam, that this comedy
offends againft all the rules of art.

Urania. I confefs I have no intimacy with thefe
gentlemen, and that I am ignorant of the rules of
art.

Dorantes. One would think, to hear you talk,
that thefe rules of art were the greateft myfteries
in the world; and yet they are nothing but fome
eafy obfervations, which good fenfe has made upon what may take away the pleafure one finds in
thefe fort of poems; and the fame good fenfe which
made thefe obfervations formerly, eafily makes

them at all times, without the affiftance of Horace and Ariftotlo. I would be glad to know whether the univerfal rule is not to pleafe; and whether a piece upon the ftage that has gained its end, did not take a right way? Would you have it, that the whole public is miftaken in thefe matters, and that every one fhould not be a judge of the pleafure he takes in them?

Urania. I have obferved one thing in thefe gentlemen; it is that thofe who talk moft of rules, and know them better than others, make plays which no body thinks good.

Dorantes. And this, madam, is what fhews what little regard ought to be had to their puzzling rules: for in fhort, if pieces which are according to rule do not pleafe, and thofe that pleafe are not according to rule, the rules muft confequently have been made wrong. Let us therefore defpife this chicanery to which they would fubject the public tafte, and never confult any thing in a play but the effect it has on us. Let us heartily follow the things that take our fancy, and never hunt for reafons to prevent our having pleafure.

Urania. For my part, when I fee a play, I only mind whether things touch me; and when I am well diverted by it, I do not enquire whether I was in the wrong, and whether the rules of Ariftotle forbad me to laugh.

Dorantes. It is directly like a man who fhould have found an excellent fauce, and fhould enquire whether it were made by the rules of a French cook.

Urania. Very true; and I admire at the refinements of certain people in matters wherein we ought to follow our own fenfe.

Dorantes. You are right, madam, to think all these myfterious refinements impertinent. For, in fhort, if they take place, we muft ever after difbelieve ourfelves; our own fenfes muft be flaves in every thing; and even in eating and drinking we muft not prefume any longer to think any thing good, without leave from thefe gentlemen adepts.

Lycidas. In fhort, Sir, your whole reafon is, that The School for Wives has pleafed; and you fhould not at all care whether it were done by the rule, provided——

Dorantes. Not fo faft, Mr. Lyfidas, I do not grant you that. I fay plainly the great art is to pleafe, and that this comedy having pleafed thofe it was made for, I think it fufficient for it, and that there is no reafon to mind the reft. But withal, I maintain it does not offend againft any of the rules you fpeak of. I have read them, thank heaven, as well as other people, and I could eafily make it appear that we have not, perhaps, a more regular piece extant.

Eliza. Courage, Mr. Lyfidas, we are undone, if you give way.

Lyfidas. How, Sir, the protafis, the epitafis, and the peripetie——

Dorantes. Nay, Mr. Lyfidas, you knock us down with your hard words; pray do not feem fo learned. Civilize your difcourfe a little, and fpeak fo that people may underftand you. Do you think that a Greek name gives greater force to your reafons? Is it not as pretty to fay the expofition of the fubject, as the protafis; the plot, as the epitafis, and the unravelling as the peripetie?

Lyfidas. Thefe are terms of art, that we are allowed to make ufe of: but fince thefe words offend your ears, I fhall explain myfelf in another man-

ner; and I defire you would anfwer me pofitively
to three or four things I am going to fay: Can one
endure a piece which offends againft the proper
name of theatrical pieces? For after all, the name
of dramatic poem is derived from a Greek word,
which fignifies to act, to fhew that the nature of
the poem confifts in action; and in this comedy
there is no action, but all confifts in recitals made
by Agnes or by Horace.

The Marquis. Hah! hah! Knight!

Climene. Ingenioufly remarked! this is coming
to the niceft point of things.

· Lyfidas. Can any thing be more filly or low,
than fome words in it, which made every body
laugh, and efpecially that of children by the ear?

·Climene. Very well.

Eliza. Oh!

Lyfidas. Is not the fcene of the footman and the
maid within doors very impertinent and tedious?

The Marquis. Indeed it is.

Climene. Certainly.

Eliza. He is in the right.

Lyfidas. Does not Arnolph give Horace his money too freely? And fince it is the ridiculous character of the piece, fhould he have made him do the
action of a worthy man?

The Marquis. Good.   The remark is very juft.

Climene. Admirable!

Eliza. Surprizing.

Lyfidas. Are not the fermon and the maxims very foolifh, and what ftrike at the refpect due to our
religion?

The Marquis. Indeed they are.

Climene. Spoke as it ought be.

Eliza. Nothing can be better.

Lyſidas. And that in ſhort, Mr. La Souche, who is made a man of wit, and who appears ſo ſerious in ſeveral paſſages, does he not deſcend to ſomething too comical, and too extravagant in the fifth act, when he tells Agnes the violence of his love, with that wild rolling of his eyes, with thoſe ridiculous ſighs, and thoſe fooliſh tears, which ſet every one a laughing?

The Marquis. Surprizing, faith!

Climene. Marvellous!

Eliza. Well done, Mr. Lyſidas.

Lyſidas. I paſs over numberleſs other things, for fear of being tedious.

The Marquis. Faith, knight, thou art wel pa id up now.

Dorantes. Stay a little.

The Marquis. Thou haſt met with thy man.

Dorantes. Perhaps ſo.

The Marquis. Anſwer, anſwer, anſwer, anſwer.

Dorantes. Very willingly. It is————

The Marquis. Anſwer then, prithee.

Dorantes. Permit me then. If————

The Marquis. Egad, I defy thee to anſwer.

Dorantes. Yes, if you talk for ever.

Climene. Pray let us hear what he has to ſay.

Dorantes. Firſt of all, it is not true, to ſay that the whole piece conſiſts only of narration: one ſees abundance of action in it, which paſſes upon the ſtage; and the narrations themſelves are of actions according to the conſtitution of the ſubject; inaſmuch as theſe narrations are all innocently related to an intereſted perſon, who by this means is at every turn thrown into a confuſion, which diverts

the fpectators, and takes all the meafures he can upon each information, to ward off the mifchief he
dreads.

Urania. For my part, I think the beauty of the
fubject of The School for Wives confifts in this
continued confidence; and what appears diverting
enough to me, is, that a man who has fenfe, and
who is warned of every thing by an innocent creature who is his miftrefs, and a mar-plot who is his
rival, cannot with all this efcape what happens to
him.

The Marquis. Trifles, trifles.

Climene. A mighty anfwer, indeed!

Eliza. Weak reafons.

Dorantes. As to what regards the children by
the ear, it has no jeft in it but in regard to Arnolph; and the author did not infert it as a jeft of
itfelf, but only for a thing which characterizes the
man, and paints the extravagance fo much the
better, fince he repeats a trivial, filly thing that
Agnes had faid, as the fineft thing in the world,
and what gives him an inexpreffible delight.

The Marquis. Wretchedly anfwered.

Climene. It is not fatisfactory.

Eliza. It is faying nothing.

Dorantes. As to his freedom in giving the money, befides that the letter of his very good friend
is a fufficient fecurity to him, it is not inconfiftent
that a worthy man may be ridiculous in fome
things. And the fcene of Allen and Georgetta
within doors, which has been thought fo infipid
by fome people, is not without proper reafons; and
in the fame manner that Arnolph, by the innocence of his miftrefs, is caught, during his journey,
upon his return he ftands a long time at the door,

by the innocence of his fervants, that he might be thoroughly punifhed by the very things that he expected would make his precautions fure.

The Marquis. Thefe reafons are trifling.

Climene. This is all to no purpofe.

Eliza. It is mean.

Dorantes. The very religious people who heard the moral difcourfe, which you call a fermon, faw nothing that ftruck at what you were fpeaking of; and certainly the extravagance of Arnolph, and the innocence of her he fpeaks to, juftifies thefe words of hell and boiling cauldrons. And in the fifth act, the amorous tranfports, which you think a burlefque, and extravagant, is certainly a fatire upon lovers, and I dare fay the moft ferious people, upon the like occafions, will fay and do things——

The Marquis. Indeed, knight, you had better be filent.

Dorantes. True; but really if we were to be attentive to ourfelves in our amorous moments——

The Marquis. I will not hear you.

Dorantes. Do hear me. Are not we in the violence of the paffion——

The Marquis. Tol, lol, derol.   [Sings.

Dorontes. How——

The Marquis. Fa, lol, fa, lol, fa, lol, derol.

Dorantes. I do not know whether——

The Marquis. Tal, lal, tal, lal, deral.

Urania. I am of opinion——

The Marquis. Fa, lol, fa lol, fa, lol, derol.

Urania. To amend our School for Wives, I think one might make a little comedy out of the merry things that have paffed in our difputes.

Dorantes. Very true.

The Marquis. I think the part you would play, knight, would not be to your advantage at all.

Dorantes. That is true, marquis.

Climene. If they would treat the affair just in the manner that it has passed, I for my part would wish it were done.

Eliza. I would freely give them my character.

Lysidas. And I mine.

Urania. As every body would be pleased, do you, knight, take notes of it, and give it to Moliere, to make it up into a play, as you know he can do it easily.

Climene. It would not be any thing in his praise, so he would set no value upon it.

Urania. No, no, I know him very well; if people crowd to his pieces, he does not value who laughs at them.

Dorantes. But I do not see how we can end this dispute; as there is neither discovery nor marriage, we cannot find an unravelling of the plot.

Urania. We must contrive something for that.

SCENE THE LAST.

CLIMENE, URANIA, ELIZA, DORANTES, THE
MARQUIS, LYSIDAS, GALOPIN.

GALOPIN.

MADAM, supper is ready.

Dorantes. This is the very thing we wanted to clear up our plot; we could think of nothing more natural. There shall be a strong dispute on both sides, no body shall yield; a servant shall acquaint them that supper is upon the table, and they shall all go to it.

Urania. We shall finish here, and the play cannot end better.

THE END.

[illegible]

THE
IMPROMPTU
OF
VERSAILLES.

A

COMEDY.

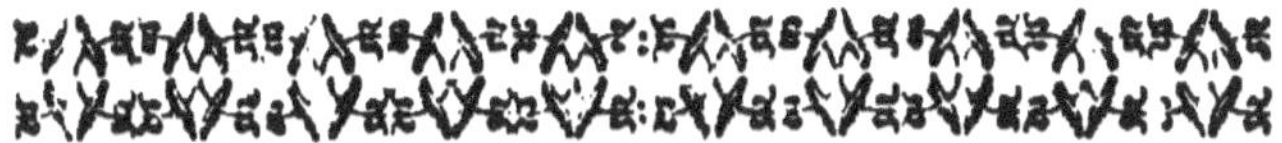

The IMPROMPTU *of* VERSAILLES, *a Comedy of
One Act, acted at Versailles* 14th *of October* 1663,
and at Paris, *at the Theatre-Royal, the* 4th *of
November the same Year.*

MOLIERE, being greatly favoured by the
king, and having juft received fome frefh
marks of his kindnefs, thought that he ought in his
prefence, and before the whole court, to deftroy
the fufpicion of his having drawn the characters of
particular perfons in the SCHOOL for WIVES,
which might have proved difadvantageous to him;
and for this purpofe brought on the IMPROMPTU
of VERSAILLES. He does not fpare Bourfalt in
this piece, and always mentions him with the utmoft contempt: but his talents and genius were only affected by this contempt; he had attacked Moliere in a more fenfible part. We fhould have
thought it a curiofity, had the author's works been
very ancient, to find in this comedy the time of his
marriage with Bejart the comedian's daughter. (See
the IMPROMPTU of VERSAILLES, fcene 1ft.
page 272.)

A C T O R S.

MOLIERE, a ridiculous marquis.
BRECOURT, a man of quality.
LA GRANGE, a ridiculous marquis.
DU CROISY, a poet.
Mrs. DU PARC, a ceremonious marchioneſs.
Mrs. BEJART, a prude.
Mrs. DE BRIE, a ſage coquette.
Mrs. MOLIERE, a ſatirical wit.
Mrs. DU CROISY, a whining gypſey.
Mrs. HERVEY, a conceited chamber-maid.
TORRILLIERE, an impertinent marquis.
BEJART, a buſy-body.
FOUR ATTENDANTS.

SCENE Verſailles, in the king's anti-chamber.

THE

IMPROMPTU

OF

VERSAILLES.

SCENE I.

MOLIERE, BRECOURT, LA GRANGE, DU CROISY, MRS. DU PARC, MRS. BEJART, MRS. DE BRIE, MRS. MOLIERE, MRS. DU CROISY, MRS. HERVEY.

MOLIERE alone, talking to the players, who are behind the scenes.

YOU are not in earneſt ſure, gentle-men and ladies, will you not come hither? Devil take the people! Mr. Brecourt.

Brecourt behind the ſcenes.] What do you want?

Moliere. Mr. La Grange.

La Grange. What is the matter?

Moliere. Mr. Du Croify.

Du Croify. What want you?

Moliere. Mrs. Du Parc?

Mrs. Du Parc. Well?

Moliere. Mrs. Bejart.

Mrs. Bejart. Who is there?

Moliere. Mrs. De Brie.

Mrs. De Brie. What now?

Moliere. Mrs. Du Croify.

Mrs. Du Croify. What is the matter?

Moliere. Mrs. Hervey.

Mrs. Hervey. I am here.

Moliere. I believe thefe people will make me mad! [Enter La Grange, Du Croify, Brecourt] 'Sdeath, gentlemen, I will go diftracted.

Brecourt. What can we do? You diftract us to oblige us to play in this manner, when we have not our parts.

Moliere. Actors are fad animals to manage! [Enter Mefdemoifelles Bejart, Du Parc, De Brie, Moliere, Du Croify, and Hervey.]

Mrs. Bejart. Well, what do you intend to do now when we are all here?

Mrs. Du Parc. What do you mean?

Mrs. De Brie. What fhall we do?

Moliere. As the king is not come yet, nor will thefe two hours, let us ftay here and rehearfe our play, as we are all dreffed, and we will fee how we can play our parts.

La Grange. How can we play what we are ignorant of?

Mrs. Du Parc. I'affure you, I have not one word of my part.

Mrs. De Brie. I am certain that I will have occasion to be prompted from beginning to end.

Mrs. Bejart. And I am ready to take the book
in my hand.

Mrs. Moliere. I am in the same way.

Mrs. Hervey. My part is but trifling.

Mrs. Du Croisy. Mine is but small too, and yet
it is very likely I will be out.

Du Croisy. I would willingly give ten pistoles
to be quit of it.

Brecourt. And I would take twenty good strokes
of a cudgel.

Moliere. What would any of you do if you were
in my place, you are all so distressed with having
a difficult part to play?

Mrs. Bejart. As you wrote the piece, you cannot be afraid of being out, so need not complain.

Moliere. Have not I reason to say, I would give
any thing in the world to have it over? may not
I fear my memory? but this is trifling; may not
an author tremble when a comic performance is
exposed to such an audience as this? to undertake
to divert people who strike us with respect, and only laugh when they please? You cannot think the
anxiousness of success which effects me alone, nothing.

Mrs. Bejart. Then you should not have under-
taken to do in a week what you are now afraid of,
you should be more cautious.

Moliere. When the king commanded me, I was
obliged to do it.

Mrs. Bejart. You might have excused yourself
respectfully, by pleading the impossibility of doing
it in so short a time; any body else would take
care not to expose his reputation. What an ad-

vantage will all your enemies make of it! and what will become of you, if the thing do not fucceed?

' *Mrs. De Brie.* Really you fhould have defired more time; you might have excufed yourfelf from doing it in fo little a time.

Moliere. Madam, nothing is fo agreeable to kings as a ready obedience; obftacles are very difagreeable to them: things do not pleafe but juft at the time defired, and it takes away all the pleafure of their diverfion if they muft wait for it, as chance pleafures are the moft agreeable.　We fhould never confider ourfelves, when they defire any thing of us, but ftudy to pleafe them; and when they defire us to do any thing, it is our part immediately to obey their defires.　We had better perform badly, than refufe to obey them quickly; and if we are not applauded for good performance, we have the credit of being obedient: but let us begin our rehearfal.

Mrs. Bejart. If we do not know our parts, what will you do?

Moliere. Yes you fhall know them, and if you fhould be a little imperfect, as it is profe, and you are acquainted with the fubject, you may fupply any deficiency by your own wit.

Mrs. Bejart. I beg your pardon, but profe is more difficult to fupply than verfe.

Mrs. Moliere. I think you fhould have compofed a comedy which you could have played yourfelf, without any affiftance.

Moliere Hold your tongue, wife, you are a fool.

Mrs. Moliere. I am obliged to you, good hufband.　See what an alteration matrimony makes in people! a year and a half ago fuch words as thefe would never have come from your mouth.

Moliere. Pray hold your peace.

Mrs. Moliere. It is very extraordinary that we fhould be deprived of all our good qualities by a little ceremony, and that the fame perfon fhould appear fo very different in the eyes of a hufband and a gallant.

Moliere. What a prating is here!

Mrs. Moliere. Upon my word, were I to compofe a comedy, it would certainly be on that fubject. I would make the hufbands tremble for the difference there is between their rough manners and the complaifance of a gallant; I would juftify the women in feveral things they are accufed with.

Moliere. Well, be filent at prefent, we have fomething elfe to do than prattle now.

Mrs. Bejart. Why did you not make that comedy of comedians that you have fo long talked of to us, as you were defired to work on the fubject of the criticifm that is made upon you? it was ready invented, and would have come very proper, and fo much the better, as having undertook to paint you, they opened a way for you to do the fame, and it may with more propriety be called their picture, than what they have done can be called yours; to imitate a comedian in a comic part, is not defcribing him, but only defcribing the characters he reprefents, and ufing the fame ftrokes and colours which he is obliged to ufe in the feveral pictures of the ridiculous characters, which he copies after nature. But to imitate a comedian in ferious parts, is defcribing him by faults which are his own, as thofe characters will not bear the ridiculous tone of voice, or the geftures by which he is known again.

Moliere. What you fay is right, but I have reafons for not doing it: between us, I did not think it worth the trouble, and the time it would take to execute that idea. I have not been able to fee them above three or four times fince we came to Paris, as their days of playing are the fame with ours; I fhould like to ftudy them, to make portraits in imitation of them; I got nothing of their manner of acting but what was obvious to the eye.

Mrs. Du Parc. From your defcription of them, I have difcovered fome refemblances of them.

Mrs. De Brie. I never heard this fpoken of.

Moliere. I once thought of it, but have given it up, as an impertinent thing, and a trifle, that would not divert people.

Mrs. De Brie. Tell me a little of it, as you have told it to other people.

Moliere. We have not time now.

Mrs. De Brie. Only in a few words.

Moliere. I once thought of a comedy, in which there fhould be a poet, whom I would have reprefented myfelf, who fhould come to offer a piece to a company of comedians juft come from the country: he fhould have faid, have you actors and actreffes capable of fetting off fuch a piece, for it is an extraordinary one? and the comedian fhould have anfwered, Ah! Sir, we have men and women, who have been looked upon as pretty good performers in all the places we have been in. And who plays the king among you? There is one who fometimes performs it. Is it that fine fhaped young man? You are certainly in banter! You fhould have a man that is very fat, and four-fquare for a king. 'Sdeath a king that's ftuffed as he fhould be. A king of a great fize, that can fill a throne genteelly. A fine-fhaped king indeed! This is one grand fault

already; but let me hear him repeat a dozen verses. Upon which the comedian should have repeated, for example, some verses of the king of
Nicomedia,

> Shall I tell thee, Araspes? He has been too faith-
> ful to me;
> My force encreasing————   .

the most naturally that he possibly could. Then
the poet: What, do you call that repeating? sure
you are not in earnest; you should speak things
emphatically. Hearken to me.

> [Imitating Monfleury, a celebrated actor of the
> Hotel de Bourgogne.
> Shall I tell thee, &c ————

Observe well this posture; There, lay a stress as
you ought on the last verse; that is what gains approbation, and raises a clap. But, Sir, the comedian should have replied, Methinks a king who
is discoursing with the captain of his guards,
speaks a little more humanely, and scarce makes
use of this devilish tone. You do not understand
it. Go and speak as you do, you will see if you
will get the least applause. Ah, let us try a scene
of a lover and his mistress. Upon which an actor
and actress should have played a scene together,
which is that of Camilla and Curiatius,

> Dost go, dear soul, and does this fatal honour
> Please thee at the expence of all our welfare?
> Too well I see, alas! &c.

like the other, and as naturally as he was able.
Then the poet immediately: You jest sure; you
do not repeat it properly, it ought to be thus.

> [Imitating Mrs. Beauchateau, a player of the
> Hotel de Bourgogne.
> Dost go, dear soul, &c.

No, I know thee better, &c.

Observe how paſſionate and natural this is.   Admire this ſmiling countenance which ſhe preſerves in the deepeſt affliction.   In ſhort, this is the deſign; and he ſhould have run over all the players in this manner.

Mrs. De Brie. I think the deſign very humorous, and I knew ſome of them by the very firſt verſes.   Pray continue.

Moliere, imitating Beauchateau, a comedian of the Hotel de Bourgogne, in ſome lines of the Cid.]

Pierced to the bottom of my heart, &c.

And do you know this man in the Pompey of Sertorius?

[Imitating Hauteroche, a comedian of the Hotel de Bourgogne.

The enmity which reigns between both parties
Yields there no honour, &c.

Mrs. De Brie. I believe I am a little acquainted with him.

Moliere. And this?

[Imitating De Villiers, a comedian of the Hotel de Bourgogne.

Lord Polibore is dead, &c.

Mrs. De Brie. Yes, I know who he is; but there are ſome amongſt them, I believe, that you would find it difficult to mimic.

Moliere. O! there is not one of them but what may be caught in ſome place or other, if I had ſtudied them well: but you make us loſe time, which is precious to us.   But pray let us mind our play, and not amuſe ourſelves any more with talking. [To La Grange.] Do you take care to play your part of Marquis well with me.

Mrs. Moliere. Conſtantly marquiſſes.

Moliere. Yes, always marquiffes: What the duce would you have one take for an agreeable character for the ftage? The Marquis now-a-days is the jeft of the comedy; and as in all antient comedies there was always a buffoon fervant that made the audience laugh, fo in all our pieces now there muft be always a ridiculous Marquis to divert the company.

Mrs. Bejart. It it true, that cannot be omitted.

Moliere. For you, madam————

Mrs. Du Parc. You may by affured that I will acquit myfelf very ill of my character, it is too ceremonious for me.

Moliere. Alas! madam, this is what you faid when you had that given you in the School for Wives Criticifed, yet you performed it extremely well, as every one faid who faw you do it. Believe me, this will be the fame, and you will play it better than you imagine.

Mrs. Du Parc. How can that be? for there is not a lefs ceremonious perfon in the world than I am.

Moliere. You really are fo; but by reprefenting a character well fo contrary to your humour fhews your great abilities as an actrefs. Endeavour then, all of you, to take the character of your parts right, and to imagine that you are what you reprefent. [To Du Croify.] Your part is that of a poet, and you ought to fill yourfelf with that character, to mark the pedant air which he preferves even in the converfation of the beau monde; that fententious tone of voice, and that exactnefs of pronunciation which lays a ftrefs on all the fyllables, and does not let one letter efcape of the ftricteft orthography. [To Brecourt.] As for you, you play

a courtier, as you have already done in the School
for Wives Criticifed; that is, you muſt aſſume a
ſedate air, a natural tone of voice, and make very
few geſtures. [To La Grange.] As for you, I
have nothing to ſay to you. [To Mrs. Dejart.]
You repreſent one of thoſe women who, provided
they do not make love, think that every thing elſe
is permitted them; thoſe women who are always
fiercely intrenched in their prudery, look deſpica-
bly upon every body, and think all the good qualities that others poſſeſs are nothing in compariſon
of a wretched honour which every one diſregards.
Have this character always before your eyes, that you
make the grimaces of it right. [To Mrs. De Brie.]
As for you, you play one of thoſe women who i-
magine they are the moſt virtuous perſons in the
world, provided they ſave appearances; thoſe women who think the crime lies only in the ſcandal;
who would carry on the affairs they have quietly
on the foot of an honourable attachment, and call
thoſe friends whom other people call gallants. Enter ſpiritedly into this character. [To Ms. Moliere.] You play the ſame character as in the Criticiſm, I have nothing to ſay to you any more than
to Mrs. Du Parc. [To Mrs. Croiſy.] As for you,
you repreſent one of thoſe perſons who are ſweet-
ly charitable to all the world, thoſe women who
ſpeak contemptibly of all, and would be very ſorry if they ſuffered their neighbour to be praiſed.
I believe you will perform this part very well. [To
Mrs. Hervey.] And for you, you are a conceited
Abigail, who is always thruſting herſelf into converſation, and catching as many of her miſtreſs's
terms as poſſible. I tell you all your characters,
that you may imprint them ſtrongly in your minds.

Let us begin to repeat, and see how it will do.
Oh, here is what we wanted, a curious impertinent.

S C E N E II.

T O R R I L L I E R E, M O L I E R E, B R E C O U R T,
  L A G R A N G E, D U C R O I S Y, M E S D E M O I-
  S E L L E S D U P A R C, B E J A R T, D E B R I E,
  M O L I E R E, D U C R O I S Y, H E R V E Y.

T O R R I L L I E R E.

GOOD-MORROW, Mr. Moliere.
   Moliere. Sir, your servant. [Aside.] The
duce take the fellow!

Torrilliere. How goes it?

Moliere. Very well, at your service. [To the
actresses.] Ladies, do not————

Torrilliere. I come from a place where I have
been saying a vast number of fine things of you.

Moliere. I am obliged to you. [Aside.] Plague
take thee! [To the actors.] Have a little care—

Torrilliere. You play a new piece to-day, do
you?

Moliere. Yes, Sir. [To the actresses.] Do not
forget————

Torrilliere. The king obliges you to do it, hey?

Moliere. Yes, Sir. [To the actors.] Pray remember to————

Torrilliere. What do you call it?

Moliere. Yes, Sir.

Torrilliere. I ask what you call it.

Moliere. Why really I do not know. [To the
actresses.] If you please you must————

Torrilliere. In what manner shall you be dres-
sed?

Moliere. Juft as we are now. [To the actors.]
Pray now———

Torrilliere. When do you begin?

Moliere. When the king comes. [Afide.] Duce
take the queftion-monger!

Torrilliere. When do you think he will come?

Moliere. Indeed, Sir, I do not know.

Torrilliere. Do not you know————

Moliere. Look you, Sir, I am the moft ignorant man in the world, I know nothing of whatever
you may afk me I proteft to you. [Afide.] I am
mad, this troublefome fop comes with an air of
tranquillity afking one queftions, and never confi-
ders that one has other things in one's head.

Torrilliere. Ladies, your fervant.

Moliere. Good. Now he is got on the other
fide.

Torrilliere to Mrs Croify.] You are as lovely
as a little angel.   Do you play, both of you, to-
day?

                              [Looking on Mrs. Hervey.
Mrs. Croify. Yes, Sir.

Torrilliere. The comedy would be very little
worth if you had not a part in it.

Moliere whifpering the actreffes.] Will not you
fend that man there a-going?

Mrs. De Brie to Torrilliere.] Sir, we have fomething to repeat together.

Torrilliere. Pray do not be hindered by me. You
having to do but go on.

Mrs. De Brie, But————

Torrilliere. No, no, I fhould be very forry to
difturb any body; do freely what you have to do.

Mrs. De Brie. Yes, but————

Torrilliere. I am a man of no ceremony, I tell you, and you may repeat any thing you chuse.

Moliere. Sir, these ladies are unwilling to tell you, that they could wish no body were here, during this rehearsal.

Torrilliere. Why? there is no danger as to me.

Moliere. Sir, it is a custom which they observe, and you will be more delighted when things surprize you.

Torrilliere. I will go let them know then that you are ready.

Moliere. Pray do not be in such a hurry, Sir.

SCENE III.

MOLIERE, BRECOURT, LA GRANGE, DU CROISY, MESDEMOISELLES DU PARC, BEJART, DE BRIE, MOLIERE, DU CROISY, HERVEY.

MOLIERE.

WHAT a vast number of impertinents there are in the world! Well, come, let us begin. First then imagine that the scene is in the king's anti-chamber, for that is a place where witty things enough daily pass. It is easy to bring there all the persons we have a mind to, and we may even find reasons to warrant the coming in of the women which I introduce. The comedy begins with two marquisses meeting each other. [To La Grange.] Remember you to come as I told, you, there, with that air which is called the Bel Air, combing your peruke, and humming a tune between your teeth. Fal lal de rol lol lol. Do you range yourselves then, for the two marquisses

muſt have room, they are not people to be con-
tained in a little bounds. [To La Grange.] Come,
ſpeak.

La Grange. " Good-morrow, marquis."

Moliere. Alas! marquiſſes do not ſpeak in that
tone; you muſt take it a little higher, the moſt
part of theſe gentlemen affect a particular manner
of ſpeaking, to diſtinguiſh themſelves from the vulgar. *Good-morrow, Marquis.* Begin again.

La Grange. " Good-morrow, Marquis.

Moliere. " Hah! Marquis, your ſervant."

La Grange. " What doſt thou do here?"

Moliere. " 'Sdeath! you ſee I wait till all theſe
" gentlemen have unſtopped the door to ſhew my
" face there."

La Grange. " What a prodigious croud there
" is! I do not care to thruſt my noſe in amongſt
" them, and had much rather be laſt in going in."

Moliere. " There are twenty people who are
" certain they will not get in, and yet will not
" forbear crouding and taking up all the avenues
" of the gate."

La Grange. " Let us bawl out both our names
" to the porter, that he may call us in."

Moliere. " That is well enough for thee, but for
" my part I will not be played by Moliere."

La Grange. " However, marquis, I think it
" was you he played in his Criticiſm."

Moliere. " I! you are very much miſtaken, it
" was yourſelf."

La Grange. " Hah! faith you are good enough
" to apply your own character to me."

Moliere. " I'gad, you are a pleaſant mortal, to
" give to me what belongs to yourſelf."

La Grange laughing.] " Ha, ha, ha! that is
" drole."

Moliere laughing.] " Ha, ha, ha! that is comi-
" cal."

La Grange. " What! you will maintain that it
" is not you that is played in the character of the
" marquis in the School for Wives Criticifed."

Moliere. " It is true; it is I. *Deteflable, 'fdeath!*
" *deteflable, cream-tart.* It is I, it is I, it is cer-
" tainly no one elfe."

La Grange. " Yes, i'gad, it is you, you have no
" need to rally; and if you will, we will lay a wa-
" ger, and fee which of us is in the wrong."

. Moliere. " And what will you lay?"

La Grange. " I will lay an hundred piftoles that
" it is you."

Moliere. " And I, an hundred piftoles that it
" is you."

La Grange. " A hundred piftoles down."

Moliere. " Down. Ninety piftoles upon A-
" myntas, and ten piftoles down."

La Grange. " I will."

Moliere. " It is done."

La Grange. " Your money runs a great rifque."

Moliere. " Your's is well ventured."

La Grange. " Who fhall determine it?"

Moliere to Brecourt.] " Here is a man that
" fhall judge us. Chevalier."

Brecourt. " What?"

Moliere. So, there is another takes the tone of
a marquis. Did not I tell you that you played a
part wherein you fhould fpeak naturally?

Brecourt. True.

Moliere. Come then. " Chevalier?"

Brecourt. " What?"

Moliere. " Judge between us on a wager we
" have laid."

Brecourt. " And what is it?"

Moliere. " We difpute who is the marquis of"
Moliere's Criticifm; " he lays it is me, and I lay
" it is him."

Brecourt. " And I judge that it is neither
" of you; you are both fools to apply fuch things
" to yourfelves; and this is what I heard Mo-
" liere complain of the other day, fpeaking to
" perfons who charged him with the fame thing
" that you do. He faid that nothing difpleafed
" him fo much as being accufed of having an eye
" to fome particular perfons in the pictures he draws:
" that his defign is to paint the manners, without
" touching the perfon; and that all the characters
" he reprefents are airy characters, and properly
" phantoms, which he dreffes according to his fan-
" cy to pleafe the fpectators: that he fhould be
" very forry if he had marked any body in them;
" and that if any thing was capable of difgufting
" him againft writing comedies, it was the refem-
" blances which people will always find in them,
" and the notion which his enemies malicioufly
" endeavour to keep up, to do him ill offices with
" fome people whom he never thought of. And
" indeed I find he is in the right; for why pray
" fhould people apply all his geftures and all his
" words, and endeavour to bring him into quar-
" rels by faying openly, he plays fuch a one, when
" they are things which may fit a hundred perfons?
" As the main defign of comedy is to reprefent in
" general all the imperfections of men, and prin-
" cipally of the men of our age, it is impoffible
" for Moliere to write any character which will
" not hit fome one or other; and if he muft be ac-

" cufed of having aimed at all the perfons in whom
" the faults he defcribes are to be found, he muft
" certainly give over writing comedies."

Moliere. " Faith, Chevalier, you have a mind
" to juftify" Moliere, " and fpare our friend there."

La Grange. " Not at all; it is you he fpares,
" and we will get other judges."

Moliere. "Be it fo. But, Chevalier, do not you
" think, that your Moliere is exhaufted now, and
" that he will find no more matter for——

Brecourt. " More matter? Ah dear marquis, we
" fhall always furnifh him with enough, and we
" do not take the way to grow wifer for all that
" he does, and all that he fays."

Moliere. Stay. You muft mark all this paffage
more. Here me fpeak it——" And that he will
" find no more matter for——more matter? Ah!
" dear Marquis, we fhall always furnifh him with
" enough; and every thing that he does and fays
" never makes us wifer. Do you think he has
" exhaufted in his comedies all the ridicule of man-
" kind? And, without going from court, has he
" not ftill twenty charaçters of people he has not
" yet touched upon? Has he not for example
" thofe who profefs the greateft friendfhip in the
" world, and who, as foon as their backs are turn-
" ed, efteem it a piece of gallantry to tear one ano-
" ther in pieces? Has he not thofe egregious fyco-
" phants, thofe infipid flatterers, who do not fea-
" fon with the leaft falt the praifes they beftow,
" and all whofe flatteries have a fulfomenefs which
" makes thofe that hear them fick at heart? Has he
" not thofe bafe occafional courtiers, thofe perfi-
" dious adorers of fortune, who praife you in pro-
" fperity and run you down in adverfity? Has he

" not thofe who are always difcontent with the
" court, thofe ufelefs attendants, thofe trouble-
" fome affiduous creatures, thofe people I fay who
" can only reckon their importunities for fervices,
" and who expect a reward for having befieged the
" king ten years running? Has he not thofe who
" equally carefs every body, who hand round their
" civilities from right to left, and run to all they
" fee with the fame embraces, and the fame pro-
" teftations of friendfhip? Sir, your moft obedient
" humble fervant; Sir, I am entirely devoted to
" you. Reckon me amongft yours, my dear."
" Efteem me, Sir, as the warmeft of your friends.
" Sir, I am delighted to fee you. Do me the fa-
" vour to employ me, be perfuaded that I am en-
" tirely yours. You are the man of all the world
" I efteem the moft; there is nobody I honour e-
" qual to you; I befeech you to believe it; I con-
" jure you not to doubt it; your fervant, moft
" humble flave. Go, go, marquis, Moliere will
" always have more fubjects than he defires, and
" every thing that he has touched upon hitherto
" is but a trifle in comparifon of what remains."
This fhould be played in this manner.

Brecourt. Enough.

Moliere. Continue.

Brecourt. " Here is Climene and Eliza."

Moliere to Mrs. Du Parc and Mrs. Moliere.]
Upon which you two are to come. [To Mrs. Du
Parc.] Do you take care to make grimaces as you
ought, and to be very ceremonious. This will be
a little conftraint upon you, but we muft fometimes
do fo.

Mrs. Moliere. "Certainly, madam, I knew you

"a great way off, and faw plainly by your air that
" it could be nobody but you.

Mrs. Du Parc. " I am come to wait here, do
" you fee, till a man comes out with whom I have
" fome bufinefs."

Mrs. Moliere. " And fo am I."

Moliere. " Ladies, thefe trunks will ferve you
" for elbow chairs."

Mrs. Du Parc. Come, madam, pray take
" your place."

Mrs. Moliere. " After you, madam."

Moliere. Very well. After thefe little dumb
ceremonies, let every one take their place and fpeak
fitting, except the marquiffes, who muft fometimes
fit and fometimes ftand, according to their mutual reftleffnefs. " 'Sdeath, Chevalier, you ought
" to give your rowlers phyfic."

Brecourt. " How?"

Moliere. " They are very bad."

Brecourt. " Your punfter's fervant."

Mrs. Moliere. " Lard! madam, I think your
" complexion is of a dazling whitenefs, and your
" lips of an amazing flame-colour.

Mrs. Du Parc. " Ah! What do you fay, ma-
" dam? Do not look at me, I am very ugly to-day.

Mrs. Moliere. " Lift up your hood a little, ma-
" dam, if you pleafe.

Mrs. Du Parc. " Fie! I am quite fhocking, I
" tell you, and quite frighten myfelf."

Mrs. Moliere. " You are fo beautiful!"

Mrs. Du Parc. " No, no."

Mrs. Moliere. " Shew yourfelf."

Mrs. Du Parc. " Oh! pray do not."

Mrs. Moliere. " Pray now."

Mrs. Du Parc. " Lard! no."

Mrs. Moliere. " Yes, do."

Mrs. Du Parc. " You vex me."

Mrs. Moliere. " One moment."

Mrs. Du Parc. " Ah!"

Mrs Moliere. " Pofitively you fhall fhew your-
" felf, we cannot bear not to fee you."

Mrs. Du Parc. " Lard! What a ftrange perfon
" you are! you are furioufly fet upon what you have
" a mind to."

Mrs. Moliere. " Ah! madam, I will fwear you
" have no difadvantage in appearing in full light.
" How cruel people are, who fay that you lay on
" fomething! Truly, I fhall now be able to difprove
" them."

Mrs. Du Parc. " Alas! I do not fo much as know
" what they call laying on fomething. But where
" are thefe ladies going?"

Mrs. De Brie. " Allow us, ladies, to tell you,
" by the bye, the moft agreeable news in the
" world.   There is Mr. Lyfidas come to let us
" know, that there is a play made againft Mo-
" liere, which is to be performed by the grand
" comedians."

Moliere. " It is true, they would have read it
" to me, and it is one called Br—Brou—Brouf-
" faut that made it."

Du Croify. " Sir, it is pofted up under the
" name of Bourfalt; but to tell you the fecret,
" feveral people have fet their hand to this work,
" and a pretty high expectation ought to be con-
" ceived of it.   As all the authors and all the co-
" medians look on Moliere as their greateft ene-
" my, we are all united to do him a differvice;
" every one of us has given a ftroke of the pencil
" to his picture, but we take care not to put our

"names to it: It would have been too glorious
"for him to sink in the eyes of the world, under
"the efforts of all Parnassus; and to render his de-
"feat more ignominious, we have chosen an author
"without reputation on purpose."

Mrs. Du Parc. "For my part, I own to you,
"that it gives me great delight."

Moliere. "I am glad at it too. I'gad the jest-
"er shall be jested on, he shall be under the claw
"i'faith."

Mrs. Du Parc. "That will teach him to sati-
"rize every body. What? would the impertinent
"fellow have us women to be destitute of wit?
"does he condemn all our elevated expressions,
", and pretend that we should never talk in any
"but a low style?"

Mrs. De Brie. "Language is nothing; but he
"censures all our attachments, however innocent
"they may be, and according to his way of talk-
"ing, it is being criminal to have merit."

Mrs. Du Croisy. "That is insupportable; there
"is no woman can do any thing for the future.
"What business has he to disturb our husbands,
"and, by opening their eyes, make them perceive
"things they never thought of?"

Mrs. Bejart. "All that is not worth minding,
"but he even satirizes virtuous women, and this
"wicked buffoon calls them virtuous she-devils."

Mrs. Moliere. "It is an impertinent mortal, he
"ought to have his pennyworth of it."

Du Croisy. "The representation of this come-
"dy, madam, will have need of being supported,
"and the comedians of the hotel"————

Mrs. Du Parc. "They need not be in the least

" fear about their piece, I will venture my life on
" the fuccefs of it.

_ Mrs. Moliere. You are in the right, madam,
" too many people arc concerned to think it good.
" I will leave you to imagine if all thofe who think
" themfelves fatirized by Moliere will. not take
" the opportunity to be revenged on him by ap-
" plauding this comedy."

Brecourt ironically.] " Certainly, and for my
" part I can anfwer for twelve marquiffes, fix ro-
" mantic ladies, twenty coquettes, and thirty cuck-
" olds, who will not fail to clap it."

Mrs. Moliere. Really. What is the reafon that
" he offends all thefe perfons, and particularly
" cuckolds, who are the beft people in the world ?"

Moliere. " By the ftars, I am told that they will
" pay off both him and all his comedies in a hand-
" fome manner, and that all his comedians and
" authors, from the cedar to the hyffop, are devil-
" ifbly animated againft him."

Mrs. Moliere. " It will fit him but right. Why
" does he write odious pieces which all Paris go
" to fee, and wherein he defcribes people fo well
" that every body knows themfelves in them? Why
" does not he compofe comedies like thofe of Mr.
" Lyfidas? he would have nobody againft him,
" and all the authors would fpeak well of it.   It
" is true that fuch plays have not that great con-
" courfe of people; but in return they are always
" well written, nobody writes againft them, and
" all thofe that fee them are extremely defirous to
" think them good."

Du Croify. " It is true, I have the advantage of
" not making myfelf enemies, and of having all
" my works approved of by the learned."

Mrs. Moliere. " You do well to be satisfied
" with yourself. That is worth more than all the
" applauses of the public, and than all the money
" which may be got by Moliere's pieces. What
" matter is it to you whether people come to
" your plays, provided they are approved of by
" the gentlemen your brethren?"

La Grange. " But when do they perform the
" Painter's Picture?"

Du Croify. " I do not know, but I shall be in
" the utmost readiness to appear in the first row
" to clap it."

Moliere. " And so shall I."

La Grange. " And I likewise, as I hope to be
" saved."

Mrs. Du Parc. " For my part, I will shew my-
" self a woman there as I ought, and answer for
" a bravery of approbation, which shall rout all
" the adverse judges; it is really the least thing
" we ought to do, to support with our praises the
" revenger of our interests."

. Mrs. Moliere. " It is well said."

Mrs. De Brie. " And what we all must do."

Mrs. Bejart. " Certainly."

Mrs. Du Croify. " Undoubtedly."

Mrs. Hervey. " No quarter to this mimicker of
" people."

Moliere. " I'faith, friend Chevalier, your Mo-
" liere must conceal himself."

Brecourt. " Who, he? I promise you, marquis,
" he intends to go upon the stage to laugh with
" all the others at the picture they have drawn of
" him."

Moliere. " I'gad, it will be on the wrong side
" of his face that he will laugh then."

Brecourt. Come, come, perhaps he will find " more caufe to laugh than you imagine : I was. " fhewed the piece, and as every thing that is a- " greeable in it are actually the thoughts that were " taken from Moliere, the joy which that may. " give will undoubtedly have no reafon to dif- " pleafe him: for as to the part where they en- " deavour to blacken him, I am the moft decei- " ved in the world if any one approve of it. And " as to all the people whom they have ftrove to " animate againft him, becaufe he makes too " great refemblances they fay in his pieces, befides " that it has an ill look, I never faw any thing " more foolifh, or worfe taken, and I never yet " thought that a comedian ought to be blamed for " defcribing men too juftly."

La Grange. " The comedians told me they ex- " pected an anfwer from him, and that————"

Brecourt. " An anfwer! faith I fhould think " him a great fool if he took the pains to anfwer " their invectives. Every body very well knows " from what motive they proceed, and the beft an- " fwer he can make them is a comedy that may " fucceed like all his others. That is the true " way of being revenged on them as he ought; " and of the humour I know them to be, I am " well affured that a new piece, which may take " away people from theirs, would vex them more " than all the fatires that can be made on their " perfons."

Moliere. " But, Chevalier————"

Mrs. Bejart. Let me interrupt the rehearfal a little. [To Moliere.] Allow me to tell you, if I had been in your place I would have carried things otherwife. Every one expects a vigorous anfwer from you, and after the manner they tell me that you are treated in this comedy, you ought in juftice to fay every thing againft the comedians, and not to fpare one of them.

Moliere. Your talking thus provokes me, and this is the madnefs peculiar to you women; you would have me take fire at once againft them, and after their example go and break out immediately into invectives and abufes. A vaft deal of honour I fhould get by it, and a great deal of vexation I fhould give them! Are not they readily prepared for fuch fort of things, and when they are delibe-rating if they fhould play the Painter's Picture for fear of an anfwer, did not fome amongft them an-fwer, let him abufe us as much as he will, provided we can get money? Is not that the mark of a foul very fenfible of fhame, and fhall not I be well re-venged of them by giving them what they are wil-ling to receive.

Mrs. De Brie. Yet they complained much of three or four words which you faid of them in your Criticifm, and Romantic Ladies.

Moliere. It is true, thofe three or four words are very offenfive, and they have great reafon to quote them. Go, go, it is not that; I have done them no prejudice, only I was fo fortunate as to pleafe more than they wifhed I fhould. They ri-dicule my pieces, which I am glad they do; I would not wifh to write one to pleafe them, it would not be for my benefit; the whole of their proceedings fince we came to Paris, fhews plainly what affects them; but they may do their worft, it fhall give me no uneafinefs.

Mrs. De Brie. However, there certainly can be no pleafure in feeing our writings taken to pieces.

Moliere. As I have got all I wifhed by my comedy, it is of no confequence to me; as I have had the happinefs of pleafing their majefties, whom I make it my ftudy to pleafe, I may be content with its fortune; all other reflections are of no confequence to me. Now, it is attacking the judgment of perfons who approved my piece, rather than the writer of it.

Mrs. De Brie. Upon my word, I would play off the little Monfieur Author, who attacks people that do not trouble themfelves about him.

Moliere. What a fool you are! Mr. Bourfault would have been a fine fubject to divert the court indeed! I would like to know how they would fit him out to make him amufe them; and were he to be criticifed upon the ftage, he would be fo happy as to make people laugh. To be played before an auguft affembly would be doing him too much honour, and that is all he could wifh for: he attacks me chearfully, on purpofe that people may know him. As he can lofe nothing, he is fet up againft me by the comedians with an intention to engage me in a filly quarrel, and to divert my time from my other writings, by that foolifh artifice, and you are filly enough to be caught by their fnare; but I am determined to declare publickly upon this point, to all their criticifms, that I will make no reply; let them take my writings to pieces as much as they pleafe, I fhall not differ with them for that; they may new-make them after us, if they chufe it, and bring them upon their ftage, and if they will be fatisfied with what I can conveniently fpare them, I will gladly contribute to their fupport, by their ufing my pieces. But there fhould be bounds fet to civility; fome things will not create a laugh either to the person of whom they are spoken, or the spectators. I freely give to them my works, figure, gesture, tone of voice, and manner of reciting, to say and do what they please with; if they are of any benefit to them, I will chearfully allow all this, and will be pleased if it be serviceable to them. But when I am so civil as to give up so much, they should favour me with the rest, and not attack me in such things as I am told they do. This is all I request of the good gentleman who writes for them, and they will get no other answer from me.

Mrs. Bejart. But really——

Moliere. Really you would make a fool of me. We divert ourselves with talking, instead of rehearsing our play; let us therefore talk no more, but go on. I have forgot whereabouts we were.

Mrs. De Brie. You were at the passage just now——

Moliere. Bless me! the king is certainly come, for I hear a noise, and now we have not time to go through it. You see how foolish it is to trifle away time! You must even do as well as you can for the rest.

Mrs. Bejart. But upon my word, I am afraid, and cannot play till I have rehearsed it all.

Moliere. How! Cannot you play your part?

Mrs Bejart. No.

Mrs. Du Parc. Nor I mine.

Mrs. de Brie. Nor I neither.

Mrs. Moliere. Nor I.

Mrs Hervey. Nor can I.

Mrs. Du Croisy. Nor I.

Moliere. Do you all make a jest of me? What do you intend to do?

SCENE IV.

BEJART, MOLIERE, LA GRANGE, DU
CROISY, MESDEMOISELLES DU PARC,
BEJART, DE BRIE, MOLIERE, DU
CROISY, HERVEY.

BEJART.

GENTLEMEN, I am come to acquaint you, that the king is come, and waits for you to begin the play.

Moliere. Oh! Sir, I am diftracted juft now, the women are afraid they cannot play, and tell me they muft rehearfe it before they begin. The king is good, he muft favour us with a moment longer, he is fenfible it was done in a hurry.

SCENE V.

MOLIERE, and the fame actors, except Bejart.

MOLIERE.

PRAY do endeavour to recover yourfelves; I beg you will take courage.

Mrs. Du Parc. You fhould go and excufe your-felf.

Moliere. How can I excufe myfelf?

SCENE VI.

MOLIERE, and the same actors, A BUSY-BODY.

A BUSY-BODY.

GENTLEMEN, begin.
    Moliere. In a little, Sir. I believe I shall
go mad in this business, and——

SCENE VII.

MOLIERE, and the same actors, A SECOND
BUSY-BODY:

A SECOND BUSY-BODY.

GENTLEMEN, begin.
    Moliere. This minute, Sir. [To his com-
panions.] Can I have the assurance————

SCENE VIII.

MOLIERE, and the same actors, A THIRD
BUSY-BODY.

A THIRD BUSY-BODY.

GENTLEMEN, begin.
    Moliere. Sir we are just going to begin.
How busy these people are to come and desire us
to begin, when the king did not send them to do it!

SCENE IX.

MOLIERE, and the same actors, A FOURTH
BUSY-BODY.

A FOURTH BUSY-BODY.

GENTLEMEN, begin.

Moliere. Yes, Sir. What then! shall I
have the confusion————

SCENE THE LAST.

BEJART, MOLIERE, and the same actors.

MOLIERE.

SIR, you are come to desire us to begin, but—

Bejart. No, gentlemen, I come to inform
you that the king has been told of the confusion
you are in, and will, in his goodness, take any comedy now, and have the new one afterwards, when
they are all more perfect.

Moliere. Sir, you transport me with joy; the
king has done us an exceeding great favour, by giving us time, and we will go and return him
thanks for his goodness.

END OF VOLUME SECOND.